Prai
Anderson
and the Craig
Virtual Destru

"The A & B Team strikes again! A taut SF mystery set inside one of the country's most sensitive installations."
—Allen Steele, author of *The Tranquillity Alternative*

"Blends hard SF and detective fiction to preview the dazzling next step in virtual reality . . . the VR gimmickry is fascinating." —*Booklist*

"I like hard SF, and I love a good mystery. This one has the best of both worlds. There's a sequence in this book I will never forget!"
—Jack McDevitt, author of *Engines of God*

"A killer of a mystery."
—*Newsline*, Lawrence Livermore National Laboratory

"A fast-paced, fascinating techno-thriller that takes the reader down one potential future path."
—*Paperback Forum*

"The lollipops for many hard-SF fans will be the speculative VR system which is the immediate scene of the crime, and the actual Lawrence Livermore National Laboratory which is the community that provides the setting, victim, and most of the suspects." —*Locus*

"Anderson and Beason are true 'insiders' in the world of government research laboratories."
—*Livermore Independent*

"The authors have a fine grasp of character and a slick writing style." —*Science Fiction Review*

LETHAL EXPOSURE

KEVIN J. ANDERSON
and
DOUG BEASON

ACE BOOKS, NEW YORK

This book is an Ace original edition,
and has never been previously published.

LETHAL EXPOSURE

An Ace Book / published by arrangement with
the authors

PRINTING HISTORY
Ace edition / July 1998

All rights reserved.
Copyright © 1998 by Kevin J. Anderson and Doug Beason.
Cover art by Danilo Ducak.
This book may not be reproduced in whole or in part,
by mimeograph or any other means, without permission.
For information address: The Berkley Publishing Group,
a member of Penguin Putnam Inc.,
200 Madison Avenue, New York, NY 10016.

The Penguin Putnam Inc. World Wide Web site address is
http://www.penguinputnam.com

Check out the Ace science fiction/fantasy newsletter, and much more, at
Club PPI!

ISBN: 0-441-00536-5

ACE®
Ace Books are published by The Berkley Publishing Group,
a member of Penguin Putnam Inc.,
200 Madison Avenue, New York, NY 10016.
ACE and the "A" design are trademarks
belonging to Charter Communications, Inc.

PRINTED IN THE UNITED STATES OF AMERICA

10 9 8 7 6 5 4 3 2 1

To Kathy Dyer and Leslie Lauderdale, who have spent many hours reading our draft manuscripts and offering their suggestions as test readers to make the books as good as they can be.

—KJA

To the men and women of the FBI—with special thanks to Tom and Bob, for taking the time to help us get this right.

—DB

We'd like to thank all those who have helped to make this book possible by offering their expertise, suggestions, and enthusiasm: Dr. Henry G. Stratmann, Dr. Steve Howe, Kevin Mengelt, Bill Higgins, Darren Crawford, Todd Johnson, Tom Stutler, Ginjer Buchanan, Catherine Ulatowski, Lillie E. Mitchell, Angela Kato . . . and of course, Rebecca Moesta Anderson and Cindy Beason.

Any mistakes, though, remain our own.

For more information on the works of Kevin J. Anderson and Doug Beason, try their web site at http://www.wordfire.com

"Big science projects—in particular, these immense particle accelerators that involve hundreds of scientists and hundreds of millions of dollars to field an experiment to detect
one elusive particle—are the nation's last payback to the
[Manhattan Project] physicists for winning World War
Two."

Off-the-record interview, 1993
White House Science Office

"Using one of the world's most powerful research tools,
scientists at Fermilab have made yet another major contribution to human understanding of the fundamentals of the
universe."

—Secretary of Energy Hazel O'Leary,
March 1995,
on the discovery of the top quark

"We have much to learn . . . and more of nature's best-kept
secrets to explore. We look forward to beginning a new era
of research with the Tevatron, making the best use of the
world's highest-energy collider."

Fermilab Director John Peoples
March 1995

LETHAL
EXPOSURE

Sunday, 8:23 P.M.

Fermi National Accelerator Laboratory
Batavia, Illinois

A whirlwind of high-energy particles coursed underground along the four-mile circular path. With each pass through the booster, superconducting magnets pumped the particles to higher and higher energies until they collided with a counter-rotating beam at nearly the speed of light, a quarter million of them each second.

The impact sparked microscopic fireworks far grander than anything Dr. Georg Dumenco had seen these Americans display on their Fourth of July celebrations.

The Ukrainian émigré devoted his time to worrying about physics instead of politics. His days of research for political expediency were long over, now that he had fled to America and made his home alone, near Chicago, where he could work at Fermilab's magnificent Tevatron, the world's largest particle accelerator— or, as the local newspaper called it, an "atom smasher."

Even here after hours, twenty feet underground, the buried racetrack of the Main Ring and the parallel Tevatron hummed continuously. When the Fermilab teams had "good beam," they liked to keep the accelerator running without interruption.

Dumenco worked down in one of the experimental target chambers, a dead-end bull's-eye at the termination of a shunt path a quarter mile long. There, the main beam could be deflected like a high-energy bullet into a small target of metal foil. The crash of the beam into the foil was enough to shatter nuclei and pound protons into constituent elementary particles with a resulting shower of radiation.

With the Tevatron operating in its continuous loop, Dumenco could tinker with his own apparatus in the distant target chamber. He wasn't supposed to be in this room when the beam was actually running, but the confusion of Fermilab's new Main Injector Ring under construction allowed him to circumvent a few interlocks. Even with all the chaos of construction, sufficient checks and controls still operated to protect any personnel in hazardous locations. He felt safe.

Relatively safe.

Unlike back in the Ukraine, he did not waste time with paranoia. Not any more. Now, six years after the nail-biting time of his defection, and his dire worries about the safety of his family members, Dumenco knew he had made the right choice to flee, despite all the heartache.

At Fermilab he didn't have to inflate his results, cope with incompetent technicians or shoddy apparatus, watch the administrators for bureaucratic bumbling, or protect himself from the suspicious eyes and narrow minds of the political police.

One of his coworkers had called Fermilab a "Willie Wonka's Chocolate Factory for high-energy physicists," referring to a children's film Dumenco had never seen. But he understood the reference—the Tevatron and the high-energy experiments provided a virtual playground for physicists like himself.

Dumenco walked down the low tunnel. Inside protective cages, the bright lights flickered with a barely perceptible rhythm, the pulse of the accelerator. Overhead, a heavy dirt berm shielded the beam tube itself, while a thick concrete housing surrounded the test area like a munitions bunker.

Munitions, weapons, high-energy power sources. It felt so rewarding to be working on pure science instead, fundamental studies, the creation of antimatter particles, increased production of antiprotons from the existing beam and collisions with targets in experimental chambers. . . .

In the six years since he had left the Ukraine—after Chernobyl, after the fall of the Soviet Union—Dumenco had re-created his life's work from scratch. He pushed to reconfirm his ground-breaking theories, his fantastic results about the nature of antimatter. He had sworn to keep that old research secret—to protect his family, if not himself—but he had already re-created the groundwork from first principles. The march of science swept on like a swollen river out of control.

Surrounded by motivated graduate students—some more motivated than others—Fermilab's support staff, and a generous grant from the National Science Foundation, Dumenco had accomplished so much so quickly, in part because he had already made the time-consuming initial mistakes where no one in the West could see them. This year he was already under serious consideration for the Nobel Prize in Physics. And winning the Nobel would justify all that "other work."

But right now, nothing seemed to be going right.

Growling, he took his tools and his diagram to inspect the antimatter flow, the diagnostics, the p-bar traps. If he hadn't already secretly known the results to expect from his classified work years ago, he would never have suspected anything was wrong.

But his experimental runs weren't producing nearly the amount of antimatter particles he expected.

Breathing heavily, tasting the sour leftovers of coffee in his mouth, Dumenco crawled into the beam-tube alcove. For the fifth time in an hour, he traced a complicated logic-flow diagram with a thin finger. The diagram outlined the complex interconnections, the feedback mechanisms, and the fault-tree circuitry of his experiment.

And he couldn't find what was wrong.

Nicholas Bretti, his graduate student assistant, always grumbled that Dumenco did too much of the "grunt work" himself, but the truth was Dumenco didn't have a terribly high opinion of Bretti's competence, or his scientific intuition, or his imagination for solving unexpected problems.

Fermilab had few holdout scientists who tried to do everything by themselves. In the era of Big Science, breakthrough technical papers were more likely to carry dozens and dozens of coauthors. In March 1995, when international teams of experimenters at Fermilab had announced the long-awaited discovery of the top quark, each technical paper cited 450 names! Probably everyone down to the custodians and cafeteria workers, Dumenco snorted. *Physics by lemmings!*

He preferred working alone; that way he knew he could trust everyone around him.

He wheeled a metal tool cart into position and unfolded a sturdy stepstool beneath the beam tube. Dumenco used a hand tool to remove an access port in front of the foil target. Detectors stood dull and dormant, waiting for an experiment to begin. A portable radiation detector sat in place on the cart, occasionally sounding a click from the natural background level.

The painted white walls and sealed concrete floor gave the experimental target chamber a cold, sterile feel—like a newly constructed sewer. Rugged instruments protruded from ports in the beam itself, shielded from the radiation that scattered during a high-energy impact. Superconducting magnets and capacitors covered portions of the beam pipe.

Inside the beam line itself, Dumenco's antimatter "sieve" stood ready to measure the flux of antiprotons in the stream, recording each blip on computers in the main control room, which was located behind gates, fences, and safety interlocks.

But the detectors simply weren't encountering as many antimatter particles as he expected. It was all so straightforward, and it had worked years before— so what was wrong now? The nuclear resonances excited by the gamma-ray laser should generate orders of magnitude more p-bars than any other production method, but he had measured only a few million antiparticles. He should have found billions upon billions more. Even that amount would be measured in tenths of milligrams, but it was more antimatter than had ever been produced in the free world.

His diagnostics had to be malfunctioning.

He tried to concentrate on the intricate diagram, but he had difficulty blocking out the background chugging of vacuum pumps, the hum of electronics, the stealth of shadows.

As he stood precariously on his stepstool, Dumenco looked behind him, but the long, empty tunnel responded only with an oppressive silence. He hated the constant uneasiness of feeling like someone was watching him. He had been free for years, and his family was safe, but still the fear hadn't gone away.

Putting the logic-flow diagram aside, Dumenco rubbed his eyes. Numerous steaming cups of coffee had been unsuccessful in masking his tiredness. In times like these he longed for Luba and the children. He had been alone so long.

Alone with his work. When he was deepest in thought, trying to unravel the most intricate details of a physics problem, the memories of his family came the strongest.

He stretched higher, grunting and wedging himself into the crawlspace where he shined a small flashlight into the beam tube. He decided to take another look at the crystalline wafers that made up part of the detector. Dumenco shuffled around on the stepstool and peered toward the experimental cavity. Small discs were arranged at various angles to the incoming beam, some with shiny surfaces, some with a wafered texture. Braids of thin fiberoptic wires lay in twisted bundles, carrying data to diagnostic units throughout the shunting area before forwarding impulses to a gigantic farm of supercomputers that analyzed the millions upon millions of particle collisions. Here in the target area, the staff placed their ''oh shitski'' tests—high-risk, little-understood experiments used only when the particle beam was diverted from the racetrack and dumped into the shunt area.

As Dumenco traced the connections, he heard a loud *click* from somewhere in the shunting bay. The lights flickered. The distant, low-frequency drone of the accelerator changed—and before Dumenco could react, he heard a muffled explosion off in the distance, down the tunnel and outside the bay.

The lights in the tunnel blinked; the air-conditioning sighed to a stop. Magenta emergency lights flared on simultaneous with automatic alarms triggered by Continuous Air Monitors.

Startled, not yet terrified, Dumenco scrambled out of the beam tube as the air crackled indistinctly around him. He lost his footing on the stepstool, stumbled, then dropped from above, falling to his knees on the concrete floor. A siren wailed, running up and down the scale.

Then he heard ominous, frenzied clicks from the radiation monitor, like popcorn.

Dumenco crouched on the floor, his knees bent and his hands spread out on the cold concrete. *What had happened?* He tried to think, but his attention was fixed on the rotating light.

Within seconds, the radiation detector relaxed to a much quieter series of clicks. The rotating alarm light bathed the shunting bay with a magenta strobe, which then switched to amber. *Use caution. Okay to enter.*

With sweat prickling at the back of his neck, Dumenco looked up at the experimental cavity. He had been standing inside only moments earlier.

Magenta: *Extreme danger. Radiation hazard.*

He had heard an explosion. If an accident in the Main Ring had caused a beam dump, the stream of high-energy particles would have crashed into the experimental target area. Right here, where he was.

"Don't panic," Dumenco whispered to himself, proud to note that he had not slipped back into his native Ukrainian. "Keep calm and try to reconstruct the events."

Shaky, getting back to his feet, he stumbled down the concrete tunnel, toward the locked gates and the exit to the cold October night. He still clutched his logic-flow diagram, and the rotating amber light splashed blotches of yellow across the pages.

He had been bombarded with an immense amount of radiation. He had a pen in his pocket—he could calculate the dosage in seconds if he could just collect his thoughts. He had dropped from the cavity quickly, but even sub-microseconds would have been much, much too long. It had all happened in an instant.

With shaking hands he jotted down the formulas: Bragg deposition, rad to rem conversion, Q quality factors . . .

How could this have happened? A mere accident, right when he was about to make a breakthrough on the dangerous Soviet work he had sworn never to repeat? A mere accident, right when he was likely to be nominated for the Nobel Prize? When his grad student Bretti was gone on vacation, when Dumenco himself was conveniently working late and alone in the experimental target area?

The accelerator had too many interlocking safety features, even with the Main Injector construction. He himself had checked the integrity of the protection mechanisms, even with the temporary bypasses.

It couldn't have been an accident.

Dumenco continued to scribble calculations, literally on the back of an envelope, and arrived at a range of possible exposures. It felt as if his heart had crawled into his throat. He tried to swallow but couldn't.

Even best case, the calculated exposure fell high on the lethality curve.

After receiving that much radiation, Georg Dumenco would die within a week.

If he was lucky.

•
•
•
•
•
•
•

Monday, 2:04 P.M.

**FBI Regional Headquarters
Oakland, California**

"Sorry to disturb you, Craig," Randall Jackson said. "The SSA wants you in her office in five minutes."

Craig Kreident turned to see the tall, lean form of his junior partner, who stood dressed in a dark suit and tie, his skin dark as polished wood, his black hair neatly trimmed. Jackson had high cheekbones, deep brown eyes, and a serious demeanor that proved to be a perfect counterpoint to the good humor of his other partner, Ben Goldfarb—a pairing that June Atwood, the Supervisory Special Agent for Squad 22, recognized as being the best in the Oakland office.

"What, June can't use the intercom?" Craig flipped his *Science* magazine shut. The desk was strewn with several months' worth of *Scientific American*, *Science News*, *Nature* and other popular technical publications. He kept back issues of his magazines in a credenza behind his desk, cross-referenced so he could look things up.

It was his job to remain savvy on new developments, considering his specialization in technology-based crimes. Technology, inventions, and gadgets fascinated him, especially how the latest innovation could be replaced by a new design in such a short time.

Jackson shrugged, letting his lips curve upward with a trace of a smile. "Why should she use an intercom when she can use a personal messenger? Goldfarb is better at that sort of thing, but he's still in Washington, so I got tapped to track you down.''

Craig sketched a comb through his chestnut brown hair. ''I hope she's got a new case for me.''

''I wouldn't want to spoil the suspense for you.''

''Thanks, Randall,'' Craig said dryly, standing.

''You got it.'' He turned to leave. ''And by the way, no matter what Goldfarb says, that Russian certificate looks great on your wall. Gotta run.'' Grinning, he disappeared, leaving Craig looking back at his trophy wall.

Craig's other citations came from several political entities, Bureau headquarters, even the Lieutenant Governor of California. But this newest award had been issued by the Russian Foreign Ministry, and it had already been the cause of some good-natured ribbing from his fellow field agents.

General Gregori Ursov, current commander of the Russian Strategic Rocket Forces, had applied considerable diplomatic pressure for the award—enough to convince Craig that the former nuclear inspector was far more important than his dossier implied. In overblown prose, the citation thanked Craig for his efforts at the Nevada Nuclear Test Site, and acknowledged him for ''displaying remarkable foresight and cooperation in assisting General Ursov and his team.''

Craig had to snort at that, considering the stormy relationship he'd had with the Russian general, especially since Ursov had demanded to be included in every step of Craig's murder investigation at the NTS.

Most curious of all was the personal letter Ursov had written along with the official transfer of the diplomatic document. The general cheerfully claimed that he had finished his final round of treatment for the radiation exposure he'd received at the Test Site, and while he would be required to maintain a careful watch for cancer signs, he was back on active duty again.

At the bottom of the letter Ursov had scrawled a perplexing postscript, "Our mutual friend says hello!" Craig wondered if he referred to their Department of Energy escort Paige Mitchell, other members of the disarmament team, someone from the Nevada Test Site, or even a fellow FBI agent.

Or perhaps Ursov had just written the note to baffle him. If so, it had worked.

Craig noted how the framed certificates covered most of the meager wall space. If he got too many more citations, June Atwood would have to move him to a bigger office. *Right*, he snorted. As if she even paid attention to details like that. He slipped on his jacket and turned down his small radio just as the headlines announced one of the year's Nobel prizes, then walked down the hall to his supervisor's office.

June Atwood sat at her desk waiting for him. She was a petite woman with well-manicured hands and a carefully molded brush of black hair just turning gray at the temples, which gave her a distinguished "elder statesman" look. She always claimed, with apparent seriousness, that her agents' aversion to following the rulebook had given her the gray hair years before her time, though she was loath to admit her actual age.

Before he had a chance to knock, she looked up and nodded to him. "Inside, Craig." She glanced back down at some papers on her desk, then flicked her eyes upward again. "And close the door behind you."

That was Craig's first indication of a bad sign. But once the door had clicked shut and he stepped forward to stand next to June's desk, she gave him a broad, warm smile.

"Sit down, Craig. I just wanted a bit of privacy so no one would see me revert to my Old Softy persona." Smiling mischievously, she pushed a folder toward him and leaned over the desk to shake his hand. "Congratulations. I want to give you a heads up that the Bureau will be awarding you the Shield of Bravery for the job you did in Nevada. The Director will be flying out next month to personally present the award. So at the risk of giving you a swollen head, you've truly become the Oakland office's top asset.''

Craig shuffled his feet, feeling his cheeks flush. He looked down at the paper without seeing the words on them. *The Shield of Bravery!* The names of those who had won the prestigious award were engraved on metallic plaques back in the Hoover Building.

June continued to talk, and he missed part of what she was saying. ''. . . your knowledge and expertise in technology-based violations has made you indispensable.'' Then she amended quickly, ''To a certain extent.''

He gave an uncomfortable cough. ''June, you always yell at me for the way I handle things in the middle of a case, and then you pat me on the back for doing such a good job after it's over.''

''Can't argue with success, Craig,'' she admitted, ''but it's also my job to correct you when you don't follow procedures.'' She picked up a sheet and slid it over to him. She seemed incredibly amused by his discomfort.

She steepled her fingers. ''And speaking of following procedures, the newest list of approved weapons just came out. The Director is concerned that some field agents are carrying unapproved handguns—and we all know what that means. Could you make sure your partners are briefed on this?''

Craig glanced over the sheet, then folded it and stuffed it in his shirt pocket. June knew very well he didn't care for any of the handguns on the official list. And as expected, the Beretta he carried was not listed, so he made a mental note to exchange the small caliber weapon with one of the larger Sig-Sauers as soon as he could. ''I understand,'' he said, trying not to sound annoyed.

''I thought you would,'' she said with an even tone. ''Getting this Shield of Bravery will put you in a fish-bowl, make you even more visible than being an ordinary relief supervisor for your squad. So watch it.''

Craig nodded. Somedays he imagined that June pictured herself as a reincarnated army drill sergeant who had missed her true calling in life.

''Now finish catching up on your paperwork before I assign you to something less interesting . . . say investigating unauthorized uses of the Smokey Bear symbol.''

Craig blinked, not knowing if she was joking or not. *But either way she's right*, thought Craig. *It's in the statutes.* ''I'm on my way, ma'am.'' He quickly left the office, closing the door behind him again.

At his own office he saw one of the squad rotors looking for him. He waved. ''I'm down here, Shelly.''

She looked up. ''You've got a call—long distance from Fermilab, some woman says it's important. Insisted on speaking to you, in person.''

Craig took a deep breath. ''Thanks.'' He grabbed for the phone before Shelly could leave. He punched the blinking line after pausing just a moment to gather his thoughts, calming himself and also slightly befuddled by how his pulse had quickened.

Fermilab—a woman. He knew instinctively that it must be Paige Mitchell, who had transferred out to the accelerator laboratory after the Nevada militia incident. He hadn't talked to her in some time, but she had his home number. Why would she be calling him at work? He kept his voice even, businesslike. ''This is Special Agent Kreident. How may I help you?''

''Hello, Craig—this is a voice from your past.''

It wasn't Paige. Instead, the rich, husky voice spoke of dark hair and flashing, sepia eyes. It reminded him of a compact figure with gentle movements that held more than their share of class, creamy skin that would never have been sullied by too much time out in the sun, and of white teeth evenly spaced, except for a thin, enticing gap that made her all the more attractive. . . .

Craig swallowed hard. ''Trish? Is that you?''

''It's been quite a while.'' As he remembered that she

preferred to be called Patrice now, her voice became serious on the phone. "I'd love to catch up, but I wouldn't be calling you if it wasn't urgent. I need your help here. I'm calling from a hospital near Chicago—Aurora, Illinois, actually, near a research facility called Fermilab."

"I'm . . . I'm at a loss for words."

She sighed with a breath that might have been a still-born laugh. "You always were, Craig, but let's try to have a good conversation now. I'm in the middle of a murder case, and you're the only person I know who might be able to help me. From what I remember, you've been handling investigations that fall right under this umbrella."

"What murder case?" he said, concerned now. He sat up straight in his chair, feeling sweat prickle beneath the armor of his suit. "How are you involved in it? Are you in trouble, uh, Patrice?"

"No Craig, not me—but the victim is. There's been a terrible accident, and everything's very confused. We don't have much time."

"The victim's in trouble? What are you talking about?" Craig's brows knitted. "You said it was a murder case."

He hadn't heard from Trish LeCroix since they had gone their separate ways two years before. They had been together for two and a half years in a comfortable if slow-burning relationship. They each had their own interests and they each had careful walls between them, never completely opening up.

In retrospect, after the pain had dulled, Craig realized they had both fooled themselves for a long time, but still he hadn't been the one to make the break, and that hurt him all the more. Trish had finally chosen a path that would force them apart, take her to the other side of the country as she pursued her medical career at Johns Hopkins, specializing in nuclear medicine and radiation treatment.

They had parted amicably, promised themselves they would always be good friends, kissed each other good-bye . . . and had somehow managed not to speak to each other since.

"Craig, I need your help," she said, and the tone in her voice alarmed him. Trish had always been relatively emotionless, intellectual, focused on her thoughts instead of her heart—much like he himself was. The plea in her words seemed out of character. "I'm calling in every favor I still have. The FBI is already at Fermilab, but they're more interested in the explosion than in the murder. They think it's just an accident—the murder, I mean. But believe me, this is a homicide case unlike anything you have ever seen before. I want you here. I trust you."

Craig shook his head, growing more confused with Trish's conversation. "I've seen plenty of unusual murder cases," he said, dancing around the subject. He leaned back in his chair. The suit jacket had become uncomfortable, his shirt sweaty. He shuffled his feet beneath the desk as if he might somehow kick up appropriate words from beneath the floor.

"I'll bet you dinner," she answered, "a *nice* dinner, mind you—that this one is different. You have to come out to Chicago. I'll meet you here."

Craig knew he couldn't say no to her. He pulled out a scrap sheet of paper, cradling the phone between his shoulder and his ear. "I'll see what I can do, Trish. I've got some vacation time built up."

He scrawled down her contact information and then hung up, realizing that his hand was shaking. He pressed his fingers down hard on the desktop to get himself under control again. He had longed for an excuse to go out to Fermilab, and now he had one—but before, the motivation had been to visit Paige Mitchell.

After his first case out at the Lawrence Livermore National Laboratory, when he had investigated the bizarre death of controversial scientist Hal Michelson, he had spent an increasing amount of time with Paige, a DOE protocol representative. She had been his escort through the Livermore Lab and had again helped him out while trying to crack the militia infiltration of the Nevada Nuclear Test Site.

But after the distressing events in Nevada, Paige had changed jobs, using her DOE connections to get her a similar job out at Fermilab near Chicago—a national laboratory that did no weapons work, concentrating instead on high-energy physics with the nation's largest particle accelerator.

Now, the thought of spending time with his former girlfriend made him uneasy . . . *No*, he thought, *be honest with yourself—it makes you downright nervous.*

Some things were better left alone.

Tuesday, 5:15 A.M.

O'Hare International Airport
Chicago, Illinois

Craig was convinced that whoever had designed the red-eye flight from San Francisco to Chicago should be shot. The plane had departed at 11:20 P.M. and would arrive into O'Hare at 5:30 in the morning.

Even so, the flight was packed full of weary passengers who had either been willing to put their bodies through this ordeal to save a few bucks, or had been too pressed for time to come in the day before. For Craig, this was his only option to meet Trish at the Fox River Medical Center the following morning.

June Atwood had been happy to give him a few days leave, *personal* leave, since this case wasn't under his jurisdiction. Also, according to Trish—*Patrice*, he reminded himself—an FBI team was already investigating an unrelated case, some sort of explosion near the particle accelerator, and he didn't want to step on any toes. Some agents got touchy over their turf, so he had made a quick call to let them know he was coming.

Ben Goldfarb, Craig's partner and designated alternate for his caseload, was set to return from Washington today, but Craig had arranged for him to stop off at O'Hare on the way. Though Goldfarb hadn't seen his wife Julene and the girls for two weeks, he agreed to an extra day or two in Chicago, his old stomping grounds. Craig expected he and Goldfarb could meet with Trish and take care of her questions in a minimal amount of time.

"Trish LeCroix's involved in a murder case, and you're going out to help?" Goldfarb had sounded astonished. "Why would you want to do that?"

Defensively, Craig said, "It's not like she's the wicked ex-wife or anything. We're still really good friends."

"Oh sure, that's why you talk about her all the time and write her letters every week," Goldfarb said. "But if you need me, I'll be there." The truth was, though the short, curly-haired agent was a top-notch investigator, Craig also wanted him there for moral support.

After getting an armed boarding pass at the airline's counter, Craig had boarded the flight well before the First Class passengers, took his new Sig-Sauer out of his holster and had placed it in his bag stowed under his feet. Now the flight played a film, one of the summer's popular children's features; Craig could not fathom why the airline would play a *children's* movie from one o'clock to three o'clock in the morning, when any self-respecting parent would have made sure a child was deeply asleep.

Craig dozed off and on, cramped in his seat with an airline blanket wrapped around him. He had stored his suit jacket in the overhead bin to keep from looking disheveled in the morning. He tried to read a few of his science magazines on the way, but had trouble concentrating.

Craig chased dreams and memories that had been lurking beneath his subconscious, visions of a saucy, dark-haired Trish as they went to movies together, or walked up the steep streets in San Francisco's Chinatown looking at bizarre trinkets. Trish never liked to buy, but she had a voracious appetite for window shopping. When she did want to purchase something, she went only to the best of stores, never to a street vendor.

Overlaid on those dreams came other memories.

Memories of Paige Mitchell, who was laughing and easy to talk to, always ready with conversation. Dreams tumbled together as they went swimming in the cold Livermore Lab pool, as they met at King Arthur's Buffet at the Excalibur Casino in Las Vegas, and as they discussed cases over microbrewed beers.

Craig struggled back to full wakefulness as the airplane began to descend. Paige and Trish both in the same place—Fermilab was going to be interesting all right. . . .

Barely awake at the crack of dawn, he fought his way along the jetway, trying not to bump too many bleary-eyed passengers. Carrying his briefcase in one hand and his garment bag in the other, Craig spotted Goldfarb immediately.

The shorter agent grinned, his curly hair tousled as it always was. "Welcome to the Windy City, Craig," Goldfarb said. "City of the Big Shoulders, and all those tourist clichés." He cradled a full cup of Starbucks coffee in his hand as he tossed an empty one into a trash can. Craig wondered how many the other agent had already gulped while waiting. He seemed unconscionably full of energy for such an early hour.

Goldfarb took Craig's garment bag with his free hand as he extended the full coffee cup. "Here you go—a grande double espresso. I thought you'd need it."

Craig took the cup gratefully. The first rich sip burned his tongue, but the second warmed his chest like a shot of smooth, single-malt scotch. "Thank you," he said. "Sorry you had to get here so early."

"Anything to meet a friend," Goldfarb said. "Besides, I got to watch the Concord come in about an hour ago. Very slick. It's a promotional event from British Airways this month, O'Hare direct to New Delhi, India. They say it decelerates over Lake Michigan so the sonic boom doesn't knock out any windows." He gestured down the long concourse. "The little bird is still parked at the gate. You can go see it if you want."

The supersonic jet aircraft was indeed something Craig would like to see as part of his interest in high-tech gadgetry, but he just wanted to get the day started, freshen up in the rest room where he could shave and prepare himself to meet Trish. He took another swallow of his coffee, a big one. "I'll catch it on the way out."

Goldfarb led the way from the gate. "I checked with the Chicago SSA about the explosion at Fermilab, let him know we'd be in town. Some kind of substation or blockhouse blew up near the accelerator. The case agent is a guy named Schultz—lots of Germans around here—and he's just starting the investigation, looking into various kinds of explosives, terrorist connections. Doesn't have many leads yet, though."

"What about the murder victim?" Craig asked, then sipped more coffee.

Goldfarb shrugged. "That's the funny part. Some scientist got a radiation overdose, but he wasn't close to any of the blockhouses—and he certainly wasn't murdered. The explosion at the blockhouse happened after hours, and the place was deserted. They're just toolsheds for diagnostic equipment. No record of any person nearby getting killed, or even injured." He paused. "I think Trish's just yanking your chain. Crying wolf because she knows you'll come running out here."

Craig scowled. "We'll find out as soon as we get there. I've arranged to meet her at the Fox River Medical Center in Aurora, Illinois. It should be about an hour drive."

"I already rented the car," Goldfarb said. "The best I could get us was a Ford Taurus, gold. Hope that doesn't shatter Trish's image of you."

Craig brushed the comment aside. "She goes by Patrice now. And I'm not concerned about my image with her. Just here to help out, that's all."

"Whatever you say, boss," Goldfarb said. He was quiet for a moment, as if there was something else on his mind. He scratched the back of his head. "Say, didn't Paige Mitchell get assigned here too?" He raised his eyebrows in an impish expression.

Craig nodded brusquely and headed off to the rental-car pickup with Goldfarb close beside him, surrounded by airport crowds.

Goldfarb pulled their rental car up to the Fox River Medical Center, a brick-walled hospital built sometime in the late 1960s, surrounded by grass and tall oak trees. The medical center butted up against the languid Fox River, which meandered across the flatlands of Illinois, through the old city of Aurora. Tree-lined walkways sliced across the hospital grounds, interrupted by scattered benches and a few drinking fountains. The trees were spotted with yellow, red, and gold leaves, showing the first signs of the coming winter.

Inside, Craig paced the lobby, glancing up too quickly every time the elevators dinged and the doors opened. He caught Goldfarb watching his reactions in bemused silence. "What?" demanded Craig.

Goldfarb spread his hands. "Nothing."

When Trish finally emerged from the elevators, she wore a neat, white uniform, moving with confident grace. Craig froze. He suddenly forgot all of the clever opening phrases he had intended to say.

Trish spotted him instantly and came right over, tossing her short, dark hair. She always moved in a straight-line path, never deviating along the way.

"Craig!" she said. "So good to see you again. Thanks for coming." She gave him a quick formal hug, which he returned stiffly. They backed apart, perhaps more quickly than was necessary, and she looked at him through subtle, wire-framed glasses that showcased her sepia eyes.

"Good to see you again, too. Your call was quite a surprise." He fumbled for words. "Um, I've brought Ben Goldfarb with me. You might remember him."

"Of course I remember Agent Goldfarb." She reached out a slender hand to grasp his.

"If you're going to call me Agent Goldfarb, do I have to call you 'Doctor LeCroix,' or can I just go back to calling you Trish, and you call me Ben?" He grinned at her.

Trish laughed. "All right, first names then," she said, "but you may as well call me Patrice. Trish was from a long time ago. A kid's name."

Goldfarb glanced at Craig and shrugged. "Whatever you say, ma'am."

Trish turned all business. "I'm sorry we had to get together again like this. It's been a very difficult few days for me, Craig, as you'll see in a minute. You'll need to get moving before it's too late."

"Too late for what?" Craig asked. "And why were you here in Chicago? I thought you were at Johns Hopkins—"

Trish was already marching toward the elevators. "Come on, I want you to meet the victim."

"Great way to start out my day," Goldfarb said as he trailed along.

Visiting hours had not yet begun, but the three had to contend with orderlies and nurses on the early morning shift. They found a spot in the next elevator, but instead of going down to the morgue as Craig had expected, Trish took them to the third floor and down a corridor through doors marked "Intensive Care."

"I'm here because of my work in the PR-Cubed, Craig," she said. "You know I'm very active in the Physicians for Responsible Radiation Research."

Craig nodded, stifling his distasteful expression. PR-Cubed was *all* she had talked about for months, but to him they seemed to be a bunch of blowhard Chicken Littles screaming that the sky was falling.

"We were here for a conference and seminar, and we met with the Director of Fermilab. He's very anxious to make a good impression on us."

"Did you know the victim?" Goldfarb asked.

"Yes, I know him. I met him in the Ukraine when I went over there to do my Chernobyl follow-up. That's why I called you, Craig. I need to cut through the telephone-tag games and get somebody on this right away. He doesn't have much time."

She led the way to a room where the lights were on. A patient lay on the bed, a man with shaggy salt-and-pepper hair, long sideburns, and a sharp aquiline nose. A telemetry monitor, hung from a bracket in the ceiling, was connected to him. Four round, sticky patches on his chest held small clips to wires that led to a single cable plugged into the monitor. The man received oxygen through nose prongs, and an IV line snaked from a plastic bag marked 0.9% NaCl.

The man was half dressed, scribbling equations on a piece of scratch paper. In frustration he crumpled the paper, struggled to a sitting position, and tossed the wad toward the wastebasket. He looked up, startled to see them at the door.

"Georg, you're supposed to be lying down!" Trish scolded. "You're only making things worse."

"Worse?" he said in a rough, scratchy voice. "I am wasting time—and *that* makes things worse."

Trish sighed and introduced them. "Georg, these are two FBI agents, Craig Kreident and Ben Goldfarb. They're here to look into your case. This is Dr. Georg Dumenco, one of the most prestigious scientists at Fermilab. He's on the short list for this year's Nobel Prize in physics."

Craig frowned, then lowered his voice. "I thought you said we were going to see the murder victim. Are you playing games with me?"

"*He's* your murder victim," Trish said, crossing her arms over her chest in challenge. "At the same time as the explosion at the accelerator, Georg was working in one of the experimental target areas. Something triggered an emergency beam dump, and Dr. Dumenco received a massive radiation exposure, more than fifteen hundred rads. Definitely lethal."

"Ah, the scientist who received the radiation dose," said Goldfarb, nodding. "But the Chicago office said he wasn't anywhere near the blockhouse explosion. And . . . aren't murder victims usually dead?"

Dumenco listened, unaffected, but Trish's flat statement of the facts made Craig uncomfortable. He knew that bedside manner had never been one of her strong points.

"The explosion is irrelevant, Craig. This is about a lethal exposure. Georg has only a few days left to live—even less time than that before he degenerates so badly he won't be any help at all."

"Any help at all?" Craig raised an eyebrow at Trish.

"To find out who murdered him. Dumenco's convinced his exposure was no accident. And I believe him. Someone did this to him intentionally, and he's going to die for it."

"Whoa!" Goldfarb said.

"Why didn't you report this to the Chicago FBI office?" Craig said. "They've already got a team here investigating the explosion."

Trish shook her head. Her short hair swung from side to side, catching the fluorescent lights. "I did. But their official position is the same as Fermilab's—Dr. Dumenco's exposure was an unfortunate accident, pending further investigation. He was in the wrong place at the wrong time. They're putting together a review board to study the matter, but it'll take *weeks* to go over all the details, and Georg will be long dead by then. That's why I need you to get on the case right away."

Craig looked at Dumenco. The man's skin had a ruddy appearance, as if he had been severely sunburned. The eyes were bright and intelligent, but shadowed with worry.

"Please do it, Craig—for me?" Trish said, reaching out to touch his arm. If anything, the gesture had the opposite effect, and Craig resented the fact that she played on his emotions.

But then Goldfarb spoke up. "Come on, Craig. Think of it as a challenge. It's not often we have the murder victim himself still around to help us solve our case."

Tuesday, 10:11 A.M.

**Fermi National Accelerator
Laboratory
Batavia, Illinois**

Fermilab lay only a dozen miles from the Fox River Medical Center in Aurora. Craig sat back in the passenger seat of the rental car as he watched the farmland and the suburbs roll by. Overhead, the October sky had become a leaden gray that threatened no storm, just sunlessness.

Goldfarb insisted he knew the way just by "Chicago instinct." He had the radio set on a local station, and aside from hearing the latest news about the Nobel Prize in medicine, Craig tuned out the early morning chatter, instead spending his time pondering Trish's unusual request. He wanted to get more background on Dumenco's accident and the substation explosion, wanted a second opinion on the case. . . .

He wanted to talk to Paige.

He still knew very little about the actual crime, or accident, or whatever had happened Sunday night. Apparently, Dumenco had been working in a small alcove in the experimental target area, which was like a "runaway truck ramp" to dampen a rush of energetic particles. When the Tevatron became unstable, an emergency shutdown dumped the beam into the target chamber where the scientist had been standing, instantly showering him with a lethal dose of high-energy particles.

At the same time, one of the dozen concrete substations along the mounded perimeter of the accelerator circle had exploded. But the blockhouses contained no explosive materials, no volatile chemicals, nothing that should have caused such a blast.

An FBI team had gone to Fermilab the previous day to begin their official investigation, since the explosion had taken place on Federal property. But they had quickly dismissed Dumenco's "murder" as an unfortunate accident. Trish and Dumenco thought otherwise.

Before he could even begin to form an opinion, he needed to see the place with his own eyes. Craig yanked out his cellular phone and found Paige Mitchell's work number in his pocket notebook. "I want to double check the arrangements before we get there."

Goldfarb raised his dark eyebrows. "You have some kind of pull with Fermilab just because you know somebody in the Public Affairs Office?"

"Just drive, Ben," Craig answered.

As the phone rang, Craig glanced at his watch. He hadn't slept well on the plane and they had gone directly over to the hospital. His body felt achy, his eyes dry and sore, giving him the illusion that he had been working all day, though it was barely midmorning. He hoped Paige was in.

She answered the phone, cheerful and professional as usual. Her voice made Craig's heart skip a beat. "Office of Public Affairs, this is Paige Mitchell."

"Hi, it's Craig. Want some company this morning?" he said, smiling. He enjoyed being able to take her off guard for once. He turned his face away from Goldfarb.

"Craig?" She recovered much more quickly than he had expected. "As in Special Agent Craig Kreident of the Federal Bureau of Investigation?"

"That's me," he said.

She finally laughed. "What do you mean, do I want company? Are you here in Chicago? Did you come to investigate the explosion? We've had your FBI Evidence

Response Teams crawling all over here since Monday morning, not to mention our own people from the Department of Energy.''

"It's a . . . a related case. Maybe. One of your scientists received a lethal radiation exposure Sunday night. Ben Goldfarb and I are heading out to Fermilab right now, from Aurora. We'll be there in a few minutes.''

"Dr. Dumenco? But that was just an accident. The DOE made that call right away, otherwise the whole lab would have been shut down.'' Her voice became stern. "That's not just a PR line, Craig. As far as I know, it's the total truth.''

"I'd rather not talk about it on an unsecured channel,'' Craig said. "Just give me directions on how to find you, and we'll discuss it at the site.''

Before she hung up, Paige said, "It'll be good to see you again, Craig.''

"Same here,'' he answered, then ended the call. He smiled to himself. Glancing over, he saw Goldfarb staring at him with a broad grin on his face.

Craig snapped, "What are you looking at?''

The main entrance to the giant accelerator laboratory lay on Kirk Road and Pine Street, where the landscape opened up to a broad, flat expanse of grasses more than waist-high, dead and brown with the snap of autumn. A few surrealistic, modern-architecture buildings seemed to spring up out of the prairie.

The Fermilab site looked more like a college campus than a government research facility. It reminded him of the Lawrence Livermore National Lab, where he had first met Paige—but without the ever-present security.

As Goldfarb drove to the main entrance, they passed under a bizarre metal sculpture, a three-span arch that straddled the road. Craig stared out the window, noting how the blue-painted arches looked extremely off-balance but perfectly symmetrical when viewed from directly beneath.

"Modern art," muttered Goldfarb.

"It was 'modern' in the sixties," Craig answered. "Now I think you're supposed to call it 'high-tech nostalgic.' "

Passing the white-lettered blue sign—UNITED STATES DEPARTMENT OF ENERGY, FERMILAB, OPERATED BY UNIVERSITIES RESEARCH ASSOCIATION, INC.—Goldfarb headed toward the main sixteen-story administrative building, Wilson Hall, which stood like a monolith on the flat terrain.

"At least we won't have to go through security procedures to reach the scene of the crime," Goldfarb observed as he approached the single tall building. A ring of colorful flags fluttered from poles, as if they had been transplanted from the United Nations building.

"We haven't proven it's a crime," Craig replied. "And technically, we don't even have a murder. "

"Yet," said Goldfarb.

In front of the cathedral-inspired architecture of Wilson Hall, a stainless-steel obelisk rose thirty feet out of a reflecting pond, sleek and streamlined with mathematical precision, like the gnomon of a gigantic sundial. The admin building itself was composed of two gently sloping concrete towers that curved toward each other as if they were snuggling up. The center gap was framed in glass.

"Looks like we've stepped onto a movie set built a few decades ago," Goldfarb said, craning his head to look through the windshield.

Craig looked around and saw that all of Fermilab's buildings, experimental structures, and lab complexes carried a militantly modern feel of someone too-consciously trying to make the place look futuristic: all concrete and metal and precise curves.

Goldfarb pulled up in the guest parking area, and they both stepped out of the Taurus. Craig adjusted his sunglasses, straightened his jacket, and combed his hair. He gave Goldfarb a quick warning look before the curly-haired agent could tease him about being meticulous. His attention to personal detail had nothing whatsoever to do with seeing Paige again.

"Her office is on the first floor," he said, "on the west side." They trotted upstairs to a concrete courtyard, then through glass doors. The Office of Public Affairs was just off the lobby.

Before they could head to her office, Paige hurried down the corridor toward them. "Hi, Craig!"

In a single, intent glance Craig took in the details of her appearance like a dry sponge doused with water. She wore a tight-fitting raspberry chenille pullover, a trim black skirt, and dark panty hose. Her blond hair had been done up in a French braid.

He waved to her, and she stepped forward to shake hands with Goldfarb before she also greeted Craig formally. Her smile was warm, and her eyes flashed in the bright lights of the lobby as she gently took Craig's hand. She lingered, and Craig didn't want her to let go.

Goldfarb cleared his throat; releasing Craig's hand, Paige became all business again. "In light of your investigation, I made a quick phone call and set up a meeting with Dr. Nels Piter. He's the Director for High-Energy Physics—the same department Georg Dumenco worked for. He can answer questions about the scientist's work and show us where the radiation exposure occurred. In the meantime I'll take you on a quick tour over to the Tevatron."

"Can we see where the explosion happened, too?" Craig asked. "I really should check in with the agent in charge."

"Right on the way," she agreed. She snagged the keys for a government car and led them out to the rear parking lot. A fountain splashed around a rotating, welded metal sculpture of a Moebius strip, flashing the cloud-dimmed sunlight. Small, curved buildings stood spaced symmetrically behind the towering admin building, like giant stereo speakers. Signs on the structures labeled them as Antimatter Storage Rings.

Paige pointed to the sweeping, grass-strewn prairie. Craig saw power lines, trees and farm buildings in the distance, and the thin line of the highway. ''From here, you can see a few Fermilab structures around the four-mile ring—the Collider Detector, the Dee-Zero detector, the Feynman Computing Center, as well as some of the concrete blockhouses and beam-sampling substations.'' She climbed into the car and adjusted the seat and mirrors as she continued her canned speech.

Nearby, connected to the main underground ring, a large construction site was like a scab on the prairie, earth cleared, big machinery rolling about in the dirt, excavating, moving huge concrete tubes. Craig had read about the adjacent accelerator under construction, the Main Injector, a new loop that would increase the energy of particle collisions. Seeing all the heavy machinery and earth-moving trucks, Craig wondered how such a huge and disruptive project could be compatible with delicate diagnostics and subatomic particle tracings.

''Seems weird to have such a high-tech island in the middle of farm country,'' Goldfarb said.

''For the most part, the accelerator is low-impact, environmentally. We're very conscious around here about taking care of nature. In fact, on our Web Page, the article about Fermilab's buffalo herd and the tallgrass prairie restoration is longer than any piece about high-energy physics.''

''Buffalo?'' Goldfarb said, buckling his seat belt as she pulled out of the parking lot. ''You mean so they can stampede and help some of those particle collisions take place?''

''That's a lame joke, even for you, Ben,'' Craig said.

''The buffalo live in fenced areas on Fermilab property. Recently, some of them have been left to graze in the middle of the circle, right over the accelerator ring—and they don't even know the difference,'' Paige said. She pointed to plastic-wrapped photocopied signs tacked up on temporary wooden stakes. *Prairie Harvest—next Saturday!*

"There's a great deal of work going on to restore the tallgrass prairie, the original ecosystem that covered Illinois before the settlers came. See the brown grass?" She gestured off into the distance. "In order to keep it natural, volunteer groups burn the grass every year—and we're about ready for another torching before winter. Before that, groups of people spend the weekends trudging through the open areas, plucking seeds and filling barrels, so we can plant a broader area next spring."

Paige drove along the narrow, patched service road past other strangely shaped facilities and unique designs. Craig asked, "Ben and I noticed all this unusual architecture. What's with all the odd buildings?"

Paige laughed. "Indulgence, I suppose. Robert Wilson, the first director of the laboratory, was an aspiring architect. Very much influenced by Frank Lloyd Wright. Wilson designed a lot of the buildings himself. It was his opinion that a research laboratory should be an attractive cultural center in the community and the nation. He actually won a few architectural awards for the uniqueness of our design."

"As long as it's functional," Craig said.

"And beautiful," Paige added. "The buildings here serve both purposes. Though you might get a little tired of blue and orange after a while. It seems everything here is either one color or the other, down to the linoleum on the lab floors."

She turned from the main road to a narrower access lane that followed the ring of the particle accelerator. "I'll show you where the substation exploded. The FBI team is already running plenty of tests. That should kill enough time before our meeting with Dr. Piter underground at the Collider Detector."

Craig stared out the window, adjusting his sunglasses. "Can you think of any connection between the explosion out here and Dumenco's exposure in the experimental target area?''

Paige shook her head. "Not as far as anyone can tell. The accelerator experienced an uncharacteristic fluctuation, which caused an emergency shutdown to take place. But since the explosion occurred a few seconds *after* the emergency shutdown, it couldn't have caused Dumenco's accident.''

"No clue back in the substation?" Goldfarb asked.

She turned around in her seat. "Ben, there isn't even any substation left.''

She slowed the car as they approached a sloppily erected drift fence wound with yellow police tape. The barricade blocked a large area from curiosity seekers. "This is the spot," Paige said. "I've only been out here once, and it's still incomprehensible to me. Reminds me of Sedan Crater out in Nevada, only on a smaller scale.''

Two other workers adjusted the fence, while a safety crew and some sort of administrator walked on the far side of the blast area, all wearing hardhats. An inspector holding a radiation detector crouched over a section of dirt. Craig recognized evidence technicians, FBI inspectors, and one man in a suit similar to his own.

Craig got out of the car. An FBI agent came toward him, his face round and sunburned, his pale hair blowing around his head. "This is a restricted area, gentlemen, with an investigation pending.''

Craig removed his ID wallet and badge. "Special Agent Craig Kreident, sir. This is my partner Ben Goldfarb. I checked in with your SSA.''

Ben shook his hand. "And I spoke to you yesterday on the phone.''

"That's right. I'm John Schultz.'' He studied Craig's ID. "You're from the Oakland office? How can I help you guys?''

"It's in an unofficial capacity," Craig said. "Checking into a radiation exposure, supposedly a fatal one. The victim is . . . a friend of a friend.''

Paige looked at him curiously.

"The Ukrainian guy, right?" Schultz asked. "His accident occurred the same night as this explosion, but the two were widely separated in distance. One event could not have influenced the other."

"Still seems an awfully big coincidence," Craig said. "Could we see the site of the explosion?"

Schultz snorted. "You can see the *crater*, but that's about all. It didn't leave very much else for us to sweep up for analysis. There's some residual radiation around, so be careful."

Craig looked up sharply. "A nuclear explosion?"

"No way. The spectrum is off, and nothing was activated by neutron radiation. We've shipped a sample back to the Hoover building for crime lab analysis."

Craig walked up to the sagging drift fence and peered over, sucking in a deep breath of astonishment. The crater was like a glassy bowl vaporized from the dirt, as if someone from high above had stubbed out a giant cigar butt, annihilating the entire substation. The earth had been fused in the flash, the blockhouse itself totally obliterated.

"Wow—I've never seen anything like that," Goldfarb said.

Agent Schultz said, "The detonation was equivalent to a few hundred pounds of high explosive—extremely high energy, with a small amount of residual radiation. It's almost like a massive electrical explosion happened, since the power was knocked out—but the techs find no indication of a short. We can't figure it out."

Craig wiped his sunglasses clean as his stomach clenched with awe. He couldn't imagine what could cause specific, incredible destruction like this.

Trish had been right to call him after all. This case was getting stranger and stranger by the moment.

Tuesday, 11:23 A.M.

Collider Detector at Fermilab

Once Craig followed Paige and Goldfarb into the experimental area, he felt as if he had entered another world, one detached from the prairie above them, away from the buffalo and tall, waving grass. This was the business end of the laboratory, the reason why Fermilab existed in the first place. Craig couldn't tell how thick the concrete walls were, but they sprawled up in massive blocks, as if formed from an enormous mold.

"Feels like we entered the bowels of a power plant," Goldfarb said.

The low ceilings were strung with piping and electrical conduits. The air smelled of cement, grease, and metal. An oppressive background of white noise droned around them.

Craig tried to reach a chain-link gate before Paige, so he could hold it open for her, but she beat him to it. After she telephoned in for access to the next section of tunnel, they walked briskly along the sealed concrete floor toward the Collider Detector. Racks of machinery and diagnostics stood next to a large cylindrical apparatus that resembled an iron lung.

"Nels!" Paige called, raising her voice to be heard over the background drone echoing in the confined tunnel. She moved to meet a dapper-looking, thin man who wore a lab coat like a costume over his brown suit. He stood behind the apparatus, glancing over the shoulders of the technicians actually running the diagnostics. His face and hands were tanned, his thinning sandy hair neatly combed. The man didn't seem to belong down here at all with the intent technicians in their casual flannel shirts and old jeans.

His face brightened upon seeing her. Craig fought off his instinctive and immediate reaction to dislike the man.

"Craig, this is Dr. Nels Piter, one of our most respected scientists at Fermilab." Paige reached out to brush her fingers against the scientist's sleeve. "At CERN he made quite a name for himself with his crystal-lattice trap storage device."

Nels Piter reached out to shake Craig's hand with a soft, cursory grip. Craig spotted a gold Rolex watch on the man's wrist. "That was just my early work. I've moved on to other things now."

Craig fished his FBI ID from his jacket. "Thank you for taking time from your schedule to see us, Dr. Piter."

Piter waved the FBI credentials away. "Any friend of Paige's is certainly a friend of mine." He slipped into a pleasant, chatty demeanor as he tried to establish rapport with the two FBI agents.

Craig encouraged the man to talk—it always amazed him how much people would reveal about themselves without being prodded. He quickly discovered that Piter, a native Belgian, had worked for years at the European Laboratory for Particle Physics, known as CERN, in Geneva, Switzerland. His early research there had gained him attention from this year's Nobel committee.

"So, do you actually do much science anymore, Dr. Piter?" Craig asked. "Or are you primarily involved in managerial functions?"

The Belgian smiled tightly. "Ah, Agent Kreident, a scientist is a scientist is a scientist, no matter what the surroundings. Perhaps I am more concerned now with details of an administrative nature, but we do what it takes to get the job done, even if that entails tedious paperwork." When Piter smiled, he had amazingly white teeth. His pale blue eyes kept flicking back to the technicians, to the work.

Piter adjusted his lab coat, trying to make it neat over his jacket. On closer inspection, Craig saw that the brown suit was tailored of a tightly woven wool fabric, and the suit's cut and hang were impeccable. He wore polished brown shoes with little tassels; the other technicians wore workboots or tennis shoes.

Piter cleared his throat, getting down to business. "Paige tells me you're operating under certain time constraints, and so am I. Experimental deadlines are approaching, and I'm expediting things so one of our research groups can get a final paper submitted to *Physical Review Letters* before the end of the week. I think it's best we get started right away."

"Sounds good to me," Goldfarb said.

The technicians suddenly chattered among themselves, rising half out of their chairs. They scrambled with controls, watching oscilloscope traces on their monitors overlaid on computer-generated statistics.

"What is it, Chang?" Piter turned, concerned and flustered. He spoke to one of the technicians. "More beam variation?"

A young man with long hair neatly tied in a ponytail, called over his shoulder. "We've got it under control."

Piter turned apologetically to Paige and the two FBI agents. "The Tevatron has been touchy for the last day or so. The heavy construction is causing all sorts of problems, and our only consolation is that when the Main Injector is finished we'll have even higher energies at our disposal."

"You've trained your technicians well," said Craig, watching the long-haired man quickly check over a bank of diagnostics.

"Graduate students," corrected Piter curtly. "Mr. Chang and the others are working on their Ph.D. thesis topics. Their degrees ride on the success of this experiment."

"Did the explosion at the substation cause any problems?" Craig asked. "We saw the crater."

Piter sighed, maintaining his sidelong glance toward the grad students' station. "Luckily, with more than three meters of dirt berm and the concrete shielding of the buried tunnels, neither the Main Ring nor the Tevatron suffered significant distress. My technical crew checked the bending magnets to insure that the vacuum pipes are sealed down to correct operating pressure. We've verified that the data ports, computer links, and optical diagnostics are all up and running. So far, the beam seems clean and consistent."

"Can't have a dirty beam," Goldfarb muttered.

As if to bely Piter's optimism, the grad students scrambled over each other to correct alignments and alter power outputs and sensitivities in probes within the flow.

Piter continued, "The FBI team out at the crater, however, wanted us to shut down the accelerator, the colliders, everything, while they investigate." He chuckled scornfully. "Obviously, that is impossible. Every airport in the country doesn't shut down because of one plane crash. Hundreds of people here and around the world depend on the results from these test runs. No technical flaw could have caused the explosion, and so there's no reason to put our work on hold."

The graduate students settled down, and Piter relaxed visibly. "My office is fielding phone calls from irate researchers, to crackpot groups that claim we're leaking radiation into the environment, to the Physicians for Responsible Radiation Research—we were unfortunate to experience an accident while their annual gathering was taking place in Chicago."

Craig kept his face expressionless, knowing that Trish LeCroix had come here for the PR-Cubed conference, and that she had stumbled into Dumenco's case.

Paige took charge. "Nels, it would be very helpful if you could show us where Dr. Dumenco had his accident.

Is the area safe, or are you running fixed-target experiments?''

"Those areas aren't online yet." He touched Craig's elbow, guiding him down the claustrophobic tunnel. "Right this way, Agent Kreident. We'll need a car. I'd like to be outside and away from all this noise and clutter."

They parked outside another low building like a Quonset hut with curving channels on its roof and brilliant orange exterior walls framed with deep blue: Fermilab colors. An offshoot beam pipe from the Tevatron deflected high-energy particles away from the main stream and shot them a quarter mile down to the experimental target area.

Inside the locked building and underground again, Craig squinted down the long, garishly lit tunnel. Access doors, chain-link gates, and interlock codes prevented Piter from letting them inside until he had bypassed numerous safety procedures. "It seems kind of deserted around here for all the repair activity," Craig observed. "Where is everybody?"

Piter's eyebrows shot up. He had removed his out-of-place lab coat and now wore only his well-fitted suit jacket. "I suppose it does look deserted to a nontechnical person, but you must remember the sheer size of our facilities."

Craig bristled with irritation—Piter had no idea that he had completed extensive scientific training.

"We have teams out in the diagnostic alcoves, a few in the beam-sampling substations around the Main Ring, but most of us just get our results and work in our offices. We're interested in the data, not the . . . the *hardware*." He said it like a dirty word. "Most of the people you'll see here are contract workers for the Main Injector construction. Normally, this is a fairly quiet place."

"Unlike some other labs," Paige said. Craig caught her smiling as he noted the reference to their previous work at the Lawrence Livermore Lab and the Nevada Test Site.

As they walked down the long tunnel, their footsteps echoed in the enclosed space. Given an active imagination, night shadows, and a sickening fear after receiving a radiation exposure, Craig could imagine how Dumenco could have become suspicious, even paranoid. The place was so *empty*.

"Was this Dr. Dumenco's experimental area?" Craig asked. "Did he work with any of the technical people directly?"

Piter swelled with pride. "Many of the graduate students and faculty members are continuing the work I started at CERN. Georg preferred to work alone, or with a very small crew. One of his graduate students, Nicholas Bretti, has been here for many years."

Craig turned to Goldfarb. "Make a note for us to talk to Bretti."

Paige interrupted. "I already checked, after you called this morning. He's on vacation and not expected back for a week or two."

Piter frowned, his lips pale with distaste. "Other than that, I can't say that Georg has made many professional relationships. He's the type who wants all the credit for himself, if you'll pardon my being so blunt."

Goldfarb flipped open a small notebook and looked at the Belgian scientist. "Why do other researchers have so many people working for them, Dr. Piter? Are their experiments more important than Dumenco's?"

Piter paused in his tracks and brushed a hand down his suit jacket. "It's not a matter of importance. As Director of High-Energy Research, I allocate people and money to projects. If successful, the experiments continuing my own work could have profound scientific consequences. It is just that their work is much more manpower intensive than Dumenco's—they need the entire Tevatron."

They reached a thick conduit that ran out of the concrete wall and splayed into several smaller pipes leading in different directions down branched tunnels. Piter pointed out a jumble of equipment. "When the Tevatron is running in fixed-target mode, the beam can be diverted to this location. The particles strike various targets with sufficient energy to create a shower of subatomic particles. We trace the collisions, looking for the secrets of the universe."

"Unless some guy happens to be standing in the way," Goldfarb said.

Nels Piter bridled. "Dr. Dumenco risked a great deal by working in here when the accelerator itself was running. Our safety interlocks are normally impossible to circumvent, but many of them have been kludged together so we could keep the Tevatron running during the Main Injector construction. Dumenco himself subverted the mechanisms designed to protect him, and unfortunately he is paying the price for his foolishness."

Craig noted the man's indignation with interest. "You don't think the substation explosion was *meant* to cause Dr. Dumenco's exposure?"

"Absolutely not!" Piter said, lifting his chin. "The two incidents are totally unrelated."

Goldfarb dutifully scrawled a few comments on his notepad; Craig knew, though, that nobody would ever be able to read the words. "So if Dr. Dumenco was working on something different from the other experiments, what was he doing, exactly?"

"Well, it's very technical," Piter said evasively. "Dumenco was attempting to radically increase the number of p-bars present in our beam—"

"You're going to have to define 'peebars,' please," Goldfarb said. Craig suppressed a satisfied smile to see his partner playing the dummy and drawing the Belgian out. Paige seemed to know exactly what they were doing, but Nels Piter didn't catch on at all.

"Antiprotons," Piter said with a dismissive wave. "The antimatter analog to protons."

"Like the antimatter in *Star Trek*," said Goldfarb.

Piter said coldly, "Yes, I suppose so." He turned back to Craig. "For years, Dumenco's been publishing highly theoretical papers on how to pump up antimatter production by using a gamma-ray laser to excite certain resonances in the target nuclei. His results—which have not been verified—indicate that this should greatly increase the production of p-bars. Since obtaining a gamma-ray laser from Los Alamos, he has been involved in quite a number of experiments to verify the increase."

"Any luck?" said Craig.

Piter shook his head. "This is frontier physics, pushing the envelope. After Fermilab discovered the top quark, some of the teams wanted to concentrate on the Higgs boson—although at these energy levels, I'd be surprised if they were successful. My own work in p-bar phenomena followed a much more traditional, and less risky, path. It's the right way to go."

"Well, I guess we can let the Nobel Committee decide," Paige Mitchell said in her best peacemaker voice, then brushed a strand of hair from her eyes. "Nels is being seriously considered for the Physics Prize this year, as is Dr. Dumenco. We're very fortunate to have so many world-class scientists working at Fermilab."

Craig's interest clicked as Piter nodded. *Was there more than professional jealousy between Dumenco and Piter?*

Piter placed his hands on the railing in front of him, a ruler looking out over his kingdom. He came up to Craig's chin, and his blond hair looked wild from the quick walk down the tunnel. Unconsciously, he combed it with his fingers.

"You never told us exactly what you worked on at CERN, Dr. Piter," Craig said.

"Storage of p-bars, Mr. Kreident. Not just tens of thousands of antiparticles at a time, but a new way to hold them in a portable container. Until recently, people have been able to store only minuscule amounts of antimatter in magnetic bottles—Penning traps, they call them. The antimatter is cooled and injected into a long cylinder with specially designed magnets on either end. The particles bounce back and forth between the magnets, but they tend to leak out.''

Paige interrupted. ''At CERN Dr. Piter demonstrated a more efficient storage device, the Howe crystal-lattice trap. Unfortunately, we've never had access to large enough amounts of antimatter to test the actual limits of his device.''

Piter's face twisted, as though annoyed Paige had interrupted. ''Yes, my design was based on an idea first suggested by a Los Alamos scientist, Larry Campbell. It was then popularized by another Los Alamos scientist, Steve Howe, who thought it might be possible to trap antimatter particles inside the molecular lattices of crystals—simple salt crystals.'' He drew himself up. ''But it was *I* who took the idea beyond theory, and actually made it work.

''Years ago, the initial experimental team that detected the first particles of antimatter won the Nobel Prize in Physics. My work is just as significant. My crystal-lattice trap stores its p-bars at crystal lattice sites, reinforced through resonances in crossed laser beams. In theory, enormous amounts of p-bars may be stored this way.''

''How much is an 'enormous amount'?'' Goldfarb asked with a faint mischievous grin. ''Or would it be too technical for me?''

''The million million p-bars in a Penning trap amounts to mere picograms—my crystal-lattice trap could hold up to tens of *milli*grams, more than has ever been produced in the world.''

''Enough to power the Starship *Enterprise*.''

Piter ignored Goldfarb's observation.

Craig looked out at Dumenco's experimental area. Several small ladders gave access to the main beam pipe above the floor. Three carts of diagnostic equipment were spaced along the tunnel, each loaded with bundles of wire connected to laptop computers.

Craig watched Piter carefully as he mused, "I don't suppose you and Dr. Dumenco had any rivalry going? A race for the Nobel Prize."

Piter blinked in astonishment, as if Craig had somehow blasphemed the prestigious award. "One doesn't *compete* for the Nobel, Mr. Kreident. The Prize goes to those who are worthy. It is an arduous process, and the Nobel committee ensures the best person is chosen for the best work. It is certainly not a race." He hesitated, then stared coolly at Craig. "Surely you're not implying that I would somehow engineer Dr. Dumenco's accident for a physics award? I've won enough prizes to be beyond that."

"Just asking, Dr. Piter. I have to probe all possibilities." Craig was uncomfortable, though, at how the Belgian scientist's gaze had lighted on Paige when he mentioned his *prizes*. "I think we've seen enough here. Ben, if you're willing to check out one of the intact beam-sampling substations, I'd like to stop by Dr. Dumenco's office now."

Tuesday, 1:47 P.M.

Fermilab,
Beam-Sampling Substation

Working alone now, fully charged with a fresh cup of coffee from the Fermilab cafeteria, Ben Goldfarb went searching for scraps of evidence. He preferred being a field agent, investigating the scene of the crime, trying to uncover something the evidence technicians had missed. Maybe even something Craig Kreident hadn't noticed.

Since Fermilab was a nonsecured facility, unlike Lawrence Livermore or the Nevada Test Site, Goldfarb could walk around by himself. Having another person looking over his shoulder as he snooped put a crimp in his style. He went around the service road by the huge Tevatron, glancing at the other small concrete substations identical to the one that had been vaporized.

Special Agent Schultz, in charge of investigating the crater, told Goldfarb he was welcome to take a second look, but Schultz assured him that they had already been through each one of the substations with bomb-sniffing dogs and nitrogen detectors. They had found no evidence of explosives, no sabotage—only incomprehensible diagnostics and technical equipment. The blockhouses didn't look as if they were used too often, and they had little strategic importance, as far as Schultz could see.

All that was well and good, Goldfarb thought, but he

wanted to make up his own mind. The glassy crater itself offered no evidence for him, no leads, but he made his way to one of the other beam-sampling substations to see if there might be an overlooked connection with Dr. Dumenco's accident. Schultz wasn't even thinking about the deadly radiation exposure.

The unobtrusive concrete structures stood at regular intervals around the raised dirt berm above the Main Particle Accelerator Ring. Tall brown grass filled the middle of the giant circle, dotted by occasional ponds and the dark forms of distant buffalo grazing within the high-tech enclosure.

Goldfarb trudged along the service road, pushing his hands into his jacket pocket; despite the watery sun poking through the clouds, the air retained the chill of late fall. He supposed the substations would be locked, since they contained delicate diagnostics and complex sampling systems. Later, he could always arrange to get a key from Paige Mitchell. For now, he just wanted the look and feel of one of the places, to get into the mindset of someone working inside . . . or hiding inside, plotting some sort of sabotage.

Since Fermilab paid little attention to security or accountability, they had no records of employee whereabouts during the times of interest. No one had been scheduled in that substation at the time of the blast, but since the energy burst had vaporized everything, they wouldn't find even a bone fragment if a saboteur had been inside. But no personnel had been reported missing, either.

Too bad the explosion of an empty blockhouse gained all the attention instead of a man dying at the hospital. Perhaps that was for the best, though—the media would go all weak-kneed at the story of Dumenco's lethal radiation overdose. Even Trish LeCroix's hardliner group, Physicians Against Radiation, or whatever it was called, would make a circus out of the tragedy. But at least

Craig's former girlfriend was keeping the situation quiet, and he respected her for that.

As he approached the nearest substation, Goldfarb made a mental note to stop in at the gift shop to pick up souvenirs for his two daughters. The only way they forgave him for being gone on FBI business so often was that he brought them tiny keepsakes. The one time he'd forgotten, Megan and Gwendolyn had heaped him with massive guilt unsurpassed even by the efforts of his own Jewish mother. Goldfarb had vowed never to forget again.

Since it was Chicago, he thought he might get something nice for Julene, too. His wife always worried about him when he was on a case, paranoid that he'd get hurt in the line of duty. Last year, during an investigation of a Nevada militia group, he'd been caught in an explosion and suffered a broken pinkie—but Julene had fretted so much that it seemed as if he had become a lifetime paraplegic. Goldfarb worried about getting hurt more for *her* sake than for his own.

Standing outside a locked and nondescript concrete building didn't seem terribly hazardous. The squarish pillbox appearance of the beam-sampling substation made it look like a bunker for decommissioned military ordnance. Conduits ran from the substation at strategic points to sample the energetic flow, diagnostic probes dipping into the uniformity of the currents. The sampling stations were simple enough, just data-recording devices in austere equipment racks, with pipes that ran across to the huge ring of the accelerator buried under the flat Illinois prairie.

Goldfarb pondered the whirlwind of high-energy particles, trillions of electron volts sweeping clockwise underneath the bucolic landscape. When the counter-rotating beams collided, physicists like Georg Dumenco and Nels Piter studied the shrapnel of subatomic particles.

But one of the blockhouses had vanished in a flash of

light on the very night Dumenco had received his lethal exposure. There *must* be some connection. He just had to figure out what it was.

Goldfarb walked around the concrete blockhouse, crunching across the uneven gravel, but he found nothing interesting, only signs announcing NO TRESPASSING and DANGER—HIGH VOLTAGE.

When he rounded the last corner of the blockhouse, he saw that the heavy metal blast door hung ajar, its padlock dangling on the hasp. Goldfarb stopped, cocking his eyebrows. This substation should have been sealed, like the others. Perhaps Schultz and his bomb-sniffing dogs had been careless. Maybe a technician or a custodian had opened up the place for routine maintenance. He was in luck. This way he'd have a chance to look inside.

He held the badge and ID wallet in his left hand as he pulled the door wide enough for him to enter. It was heavy and squeaked on its hinges, an iron plate that might have come from an old battleship hull. He grunted with the effort.

Inside, he saw two naked bulbs burning inside wire cages. The unfinished ceiling was strung with pipes, wires, and cable-trays leading down to a bank of old computer monitors, oscilloscopes, and strip-chart recorders. He smelled tobacco smoke, as if someone had just snuffed out a cigarette. As he stepped into the shadows, the sudden difference in light was enough to blind him. He blinked, holding up his badge wallet.

"This is the FBI," he called. "Identify yourself."

He heard a rapid movement, a sucked intake of breath, and a gasped "Oh, shit!" A metal swivel chair slid aside, rattling its casters.

Goldfarb instantly became alert. "Wait a minute," he said. His eyesight was still too murky for him to make out many details, but he did see a figure, a man with dark hair and a goatee wearing a lab technician's smock. The figure staggered backward from some kind of apparatus hooked up below the oscilloscopes and computer monitors.

"Federal agent," Goldfarb said, "I just want to ask you a few questions about—"

But the other man wasn't in the mood for conversation. He lunged toward Goldfarb, brandishing something heavy and metal in his hand. He uttered no outcry, no roar of challenge: he simply attacked.

"Whoa, wait a minute!" Goldfarb shouted, but the man hurled the object—a wrench he had been using on the diagnostics. The wrench flew with the precision of a circus knife thrower and struck Goldfarb high on the chest near his right shoulder. His arm instantly felt an explosion of pain, then went numb. He heard a crack of his collar bone, then the ball joint in his shoulder erupted in white internal fire from his nerve endings.

Goldfarb ducked aside while reaching behind him with his left hand. He dropped his badge wallet and ID, fumbling awkwardly for his weapon in the pancake holster beneath his belt. His right hand was useless, so he'd have to do the best he could, shoot left-handed.

The suspect's eyes carried a feral glint of terror and desperation, like a cornered rat. The man wasn't thinking about his actions, merely acting on keyed-up instinct. Goldfarb had stumbled upon something—and this man didn't seem ready to surrender; he wasn't even cowed by the presence of the FBI.

The man charged forward, head down. Goldfarb got his hand on the butt of his pistol and started to tug it free, though that sent another wave of pain through his broken shoulder. He clenched his teeth, working his finger around the trigger guard.

"Stop!" he commanded.

With a fleeting thought, a tiny scolding voice in his head told him how remarkable it was that he always managed to get himself into these situations.

The man rammed into Goldfarb like a linebacker smashing into an opposing quarterback. Goldfarb slammed backward into the computers and oscilloscopes, fighting for balance. Papers and desk paraphernalia scattered on the floor. The wind whooshed out of him.

He managed to wrench his pistol around, pointing it at his opponent. But the man did not hesitate to grab Goldfarb's wrist and jerk the pistol away from the aim point. The first, instinctive gunshot went wild, ricocheting off the concrete wall and embedding itself in the ceiling of the substation.

"You asshole," the man said, yanking Goldfarb's arm. The pain in his broken collar bone made him want to vomit.

Instead, using the momentum in his turning body, Goldfarb swung one of the desk chairs around. It was heavy and metal like surplus from an old army base. It struck the other man in the hip, knocking him sideways. Then Goldfarb jabbed upward with his knee, hoping to catch the outraged man in the groin—but instead he only brushed the side of his leg.

Viciously, the man swung a fist down, smashing Goldfarb's collar bone where the wrench had hit. The pain made a black thunderstorm in his head, and Goldfarb's knees turned to water.

Seizing his chance, the man grabbed the agent's handgun. Goldfarb struggled to remain conscious against the waves of nausea, but the other man twisted the pistol around. Goldfarb lurched away from the computer terminals against which he had been pressed, gave one last burst of strength—but the man countered him, clawing at the pistol.

Again, the gun went off.

The shot sounded like a hand grenade exploding, and Goldfarb felt the bullet plow into his ribs with all the force of a pickup truck. The impact threw him into the wall of computers and oscilloscopes again. He heard shattering glass, sparks.

Unable to stand any longer, he slid down to the concrete floor, barely able to focus his eyesight against the competing avalanches of pain. His enemy wrenched the pistol out of his limp hand and stepped back, aiming the weapon toward Goldfarb. The FBI agent had a last, unsettlingly clear glimpse of a man with dark disheveled hair and a matted goatee, his face tightened into a knot of anger and panic.

Goldfarb hadn't even had a chance to cry out.

Then the man stepped back, pointed the pistol again, and shot Goldfarb once more in the chest for good measure.

He fell the rest of the way to the hard, cold floor in a rapidly widening pool of his own blood.

Tuesday, 2:07 P.M.

**Wilson Hall
Fermi National Accelerator
Laboratory**

In the open-air lobby of Wilson Hall, Paige led Craig past a Foucault pendulum on display, dangling from the rafters and sweeping through its delicate arc as the Earth rotated. Late lunch dishes clattered in the cafeteria; most of the tables were empty except for a few groups of scientists engaged in low discussions, seeking an area free of secretaries and telephones. She pushed the button for the elevator, and they both waited.

The fourth floor had an open, spacious feel, with cubicle-divided work areas for grad students and temporary hires. As they walked down the carpeted hall, Craig saw homey touches on each cubicle, plastic action figures of monsters and cartoon characters, yellowed comic-strip clippings; one wall was completely covered with outrageous tabloid headlines.

Paige flicked her blue eyes from name plate to number, trying to find her way. Clearly, she hadn't had occasion to visit Georg Dumenco before.

When they reached his office, though, the Ukrainian scientist was there in person, despite his radiation exposure. Dumenco looked up, startled, as he sifted through a whirlwind of papers and printouts on his desk. File drawers were opened and ransacked, and his bloodshot eyes looked wild.

"Dr. Dumenco, what are you doing here?" Craig asked.

"This is my office," Dumenco answered indignantly. He swallowed hard, then held onto the edge of his desk for support.

"You're supposed to be in the hospital," Paige said.

"I need my work, the results from my last test run. My graduate student Bretti isn't here. He's supposed to be on vacation, but I can't reach him . . . he's on a fishing trip somewhere, out of touch—and I don't know how he files his records." With an angry gesture, Dumenco slapped a pile of old memos and unopened mail on the floor.

Craig went forward to grasp his arm. "You drove here by yourself? I need to take you back to Trish—uh, I mean, Dr. LeCroix." Paige's eyes widened as she made the connection, but she didn't say anything.

Dumenco shook off Craig's grip and unsteadily drew himself up. "I am dying from radiation exposure, sir. My body is falling apart rapidly, and very soon I won't be able to stand. I must use every moment of clarity left to me. Once I get back into that hospital bed, I know I'll never leave." He drew a thick breath. "This may be the last time I'll set foot in my office—and I need my papers so I can keep . . . occupied."

Craig gripped the decidedly unsteady scientist, and Paige helped usher Dumenco out of his office. "I'll get you everything you need," she said. "We'll go through your files and find the printouts from your last test run."

"I'm driving you back to the hospital," Craig said, tolerating no argument. Dumenco seemed ready to resist until Craig added, "I need you to stay alive long enough to help me solve this case."

On the drive from Fermilab toward the Fox River Medical Center, Craig watched Dumenco brood in the car. The dying scientist longingly stared at the lab buildings, the low ring that marked the underground particle accelerator, the small, restless herd of buffalo behind their rickety fences.

Craig used their private time to discuss the case. The Ukrainian looked at him with watery, glassy eyes that were bleary and pinkish from thousands of tiny hemorrhages. Inside his body, the damage had already been done—cells were dying in droves, his internal organs were failing; soon his thought processes would also suffer, making him delusional or incoherent.

The worst part was that the great scientist *knew* it was happening.

"Now then, sir, let us discuss this case," Dumenco said. He tried to smile through cracked lips. "You put me in a difficult position. I have very little time left to complete my work, or to help you solve my murder. Which do you believe is more important—progress or revenge?"

"I'd call it *justice*, rather than revenge."

Dumenco was silent for a moment. "In the grand scheme I think you've found the difference. My life is more than just a drop in a tiny pond in a vast universe. Justice is what I really want."

Craig followed a cement mixer and a dump truck leaving the Main Injector construction site. "And that's what I'm here for. Let's solve this case quickly so you can use any remaining time on your physics."

"A good plan, kind sir."

"All right," Craig answered. "This morning we went to the site of your accident and also viewed the crater left by the blockhouse explosion. Dr. Piter walked us through the details. My partner, Agent Goldfarb, is right now looking at one of the intact substations to see if he can pick up any clues."

"I know nothing of the explosion," Dumenco said, stifling a cough. "I know only that someone intentionally caused the beam dump, and that I am paying the price for it."

Craig wished he had been able to take out his notepad.

"So why would someone want to kill you?"

"I have done many things in my career, Agent Kreident." Dumenco's voice was strong but carried a hint of hoarseness from phlegm building up in his throat and lungs. "I left the Ukraine during the downfall of the Soviet Union. I abandoned my career and all my research, and I came here to work as a high-energy physicist. Your American government has been very kind, but I have paid a high price."

Craig made a mental note. "And were you welcome here, or did some of the other physicists resent your background?"

"On the contrary, I was most heartily welcomed. Fermilab is accustomed to international collaborations. After the Soviet collapse, your government was most eager for me to use my talents for your benefit, rather than some less desirable country. They allowed me to work here . . . without hassle, and without the usual paperwork that comes with being a foreign national. The United States values scientific talent."

Dumenco cleared his throat, then delicately spat into a wadded handkerchief he withdrew from his pocket. Craig could see flecks of blood in the spittle before the scientist quickly tucked the cloth away.

"The Russians were quite . . . upset after I had fled. My recent work has apparently made some people very nervous. I received veiled threats, but I was promised protection by your State Department. However, it seems someone has managed to kill me anyway, here on the eve of my Nobel nomination."

The Ukrainian closed his reddened eyes and took a deep breath. "Did you know the Committee is not allowed to give a Nobel Prize to a dead man? I hope I don't miss my chance."

Craig stopped at a traffic signal, watched the trucks and cars bustling through the center of Aurora. Tall brick buildings lined the narrow main street, coffee shops and greasy-spoon cafes at street level; several blocks away from the downtown area, old suburban houses sat on broad, grassy lots.

"What about your graduate student, Mr. Bretti?" Craig asked, focusing on the case again. "Was he aware of these threats on your life? Did he feel himself in any danger for assisting you?"

Dumenco gave a wan smile. "No, Bretti would never have been a target. He is a big talker, and often indignant, but the truth is he has not managed to complete his thesis during the seven years he has assisted me, and I doubt he ever will." He snorted. "I hope he is a better fisherman than a scientist, otherwise he will have a very disappointing vacation."

Inside the Medical Center, Trish LeCroix met them like a mother hen, scolding Dumenco for leaving her. She helped Craig whisk him off to his hospital room. The old physicist endured her ministrations as she took his blood pressure, temperature, heart and respiratory rate, and prodded him into changing back into his hospital gown. She made a point of taking his street clothes, his keys, and his wallet, so she could put them in a hospital locker.

Dumenco seemed penitent. "Dr. LeCroix is a bossy woman, Agent Kreident. She seemed so nice when I knew her in the Ukraine."

Craig smiled. "Trish doesn't like to deal with anything unexpected."

She made an indignant noise. "Listen, Georg—I'm here to help you, and I'm the best radiation-exposure physician you're going to get. If you'd like, I can just let you back into the hands of a general practitioner."

Dumenco actually chuckled as she herded him into the bed. He pulled the sheet up, but Trish kept his bare arm available. "You're dehydrated. I'm hooking you up to a saline drip." She looked at the physicist, then at Craig, placing her hands on her hips. "All right, I'll leave you two to keep talking—but no more sightseeing!'' Moving like a true professional, Trish hurried out of the room to fetch IV supplies and a bag of normal saline.

The Ukrainian rolled closer to the tray table that separated him from Craig. Someone had set out a small plastic chess set with magnetized pieces, all the chess men lined up in perfect ranks.

''Let's have a game while we continue our conversation, kind sir,'' Dumenco suggested. Craig noticed that the skin on his forehead was white and scaly. ''Do you play?''

Craig looked down at the pieces as his thoughts spun. *The man's dying, and he wants to play chess?* ''Not with any skill,'' he said. ''I used to goof around with my dad, but don't expect any championship strategy.''

Dumenco waved a swollen hand. ''I just want to occupy my mind. It will take all of my concentration to keep my thoughts sharp and focused . . . until the very end.''

The scientist chose white and moved first, picking up the little plastic piece and sliding it across the squares. ''For a game like this it seems we should be using a fine onyx and jade set, don't you think?'' Dumenco raised his eyebrows. ''After all, I must savor the niceties of life, while I can.''

Craig moved a pawn. ''I don't suppose the hospital's game chest has anything like that.''

Years ago, he had played with his father, more as an excuse to spend time together than through any passion for the game. Craig had never been terribly good at small talk, and the two had needed a catalyst for conversation—especially since Robert Kreident's life revolved around the football, baseball, and hockey teams in the Bay Area. Craig's interests in science and technology had diverged from his father's interest in sports, but they could chat about chess moves and occasionally other things as they played.

Now, though, Craig focused his attention on the

Ukrainian's rambling speech, moving only defensively to counter Dumenco's pieces.

"What kind of strategy do you call this?" the physicist said, watching Craig move a bishop to a seemingly pointless position.

"I told you I didn't play often," he answered. He looked at the chess pieces, then at his notes. "Explain to me why you were running experiments on a Sunday, and after dark."

Dumenco glanced at the large round clock on the wall. "The hour of day makes no difference underground," he said. "During an experimental run, the accelerator operates round the clock. Computers record the collisions, sample the daughter particles, and sort out anything worthwhile." He shook his head. "Maybe I can reach some valuable conclusions before time grows too short . . . if Ms. Mitchell ever gets here with my results."

"But you're dying," Craig said bluntly; Dumenco didn't seem to mind. "Do you want to be looking at technical readouts during your last days?"

"I must!" He said with such vehemence that his reddened hand clenched into a fist. He winced at the pain, then lowered his voice. "My results, my theories are what I leave behind. My family is . . ." he paused uncomfortably, ". . . not with me, so my work is my legacy. I have cracked open the door to God's mysteries, and I must make sense of my results to prop open that door, prepare it for the next person. If I die with my work unresolved, the door will slam shut again. All my thoughts—all my life—will be worthless."

Craig tried to be soothing. "If you're already up for the Nobel Prize, you've done plenty in your life. Your work will be carried on by others."

"Consider it this way, sir," Dumenco said. "If you were to leave this case, another agent could pick up the clues and perhaps solve my murder. Forgive my arrogance, but if *I* die now it will be many years before someone grasps this esoteric subset of particle physics to synthesize what I have done and take it to the next step.''

He moved his rook into position and scanned the board. Craig moved another piece, and Dumenco countered rapidly. ''Check,'' he said simply.

With sudden embarrassed alarm, Craig studied the board. He moved to counter the Ukrainian's ploy.

''Are you a scientist, Agent Kreident?'' Dumenco said.

''I have some training,'' Craig said. It had been a long time since putting himself through Stanford, working for Elliot Lang's PI agency. . . . ''I've got a physics undergraduate degree, and I went into patent law after law school—I thought that was where the money was, but it was boring.''

Dumenco moved his queen, calmly said, ''Checkmate,'' then leaned back into his pillow as if exhausted. He closed his eyes as Craig scrutinized the little magnetic chess pieces, trying to understand what the Ukrainian had done. He could find no last-ditch way out.

''Have you heard of the mathematician Fermat?'' Dumenco asked.

Craig frowned. ''Of course.''

The old man's lips were swollen, and he spoke in a quiet whisper. ''After his death, someone discovered a handwritten notation in one of his texts—Fermat claimed to have found an 'elegant proof' for one of the great mathematical mysteries. But he didn't write down that proof, and mathematicians wracked their brains for centuries to rediscover it. Until just recently, Fermat's Last Theorem remained unproven.'' Dumenco finally opened his eyes again to look at Craig. ''I don't want to be the high-energy physics equivalent of Fermat.''

Craig swallowed a lump in his throat.

''Maybe this will help.'' They both turned to see Paige Mitchell standing at the door to the intensive care room, a folder full of papers in her hand. But Trish LeCroix bustled up to block the way.

"You can't go in there." Trish looked sourly down at the sheaf of printouts. "Dr. Dumenco needs to rest and gather his energy. If you give him those papers, he won't sleep a minute."

Paige held the folder so tightly her knuckles whitened. "He was quite insistent about having them. Let me guess—you must be Trish?"

"It's Patrice." The room temperature seemed to drop twenty degrees.

Craig interrupted. "This is Paige Mitchell, from Fermilab, on Dr. Dumenco's request. It was the only way he would agree to go back to his hospital room." He looked intently at Trish's sepia eyes behind her delicate eyeglasses. "Let him have the papers," he said, lowering his voice. "Those experimental results mean more to Dumenco than anything right now. Maybe he loses a little sleep, but he'll die a lot happier."

Trish's eyes flashed, but she backed away, gesturing Paige inside.

Dumenco sat up in his hospital bed with an expression of such extreme delight that Craig knew he had made the right decision. The scientist swept the chessboard off the small table, knocking magnetic pieces in all directions. "Bring them here—thank you, thank you. You're very kind."

"It's the least I could do," she said. "Dr. Piter also asked me to pass along that he is at your disposal if you require anything else."

Dumenco rolled his eyes. "That man has been a thorn in my side for years, just because some of my work contradicts his old CERN papers. I'm glad he is at least pretending to have a change of heart."

As the scientist pawed through the papers, Craig knew he would have to look elsewhere for clues. Georg Dumenco was otherwise occupied.

Maybe Goldfarb had found something.

Tuesday, 2:37 P.M.

Fermilab,
Beam-Sampling Substation

Breathing hard, Nicholas Bretti paused to take a closer look at the man he had just shot, even as he tried to scramble out of the isolated blockhouse.

Everything had happened so fast, so unexpectedly. He hadn't meant to do it. But, shit—*the FBI!* You take one quick little step down that slippery slope, and it sucks you down to hell like grease-covered glare ice!

The federal agent looked like a dark-suited Pillsbury doughboy on the floor. He didn't move, didn't appear to breathe. Dark liquid oozed from the wounds in his chest.

Bretti looked to the heavy door, the harsh glare of sunlight outside. No one ran into the blockhouse to see what was the matter, no one raced to investigate the gunshots. Should he call for help? Get an ambulance?

Or was there a chance he might be able to get away? Nobody knew he was here—he was supposed to be gone, days' deep into his annual fishing trip in the wilds of West Virginia.

Bretti slapped his hands together, stepped toward the shot FBI agent, then turned toward the door. *I must look like an idiot,* he thought, confused, panicked.

Keep cool, he reminded himself. Get the apparatus. Pack it in the car, and drive to the embassy. Just like the plan. They had gotten him into this, and they could

help him out. No problem, no sweat, no heartburn . . .
no fucking way!

Bretti had never hurt anyone before, certainly never
killed anyone—hell, he'd never broken the law, never
cheated on a college exam . . . though if he had, maybe
it wouldn't have taken him seven years as a grad student
and still no hope of seeing a Ph.D. anytime soon. This
should have been his ticket to a better life. Antimatter.
A simple, invisible embezzlement of atomic particles,
bled off from the main beam.

No one should have noticed, except maybe that
damned Dumenco. But then, nothing in Bretti's life had
ever turned out the way it should. Though it sure seemed
possible when that Indian, Chandrawalia, had first approached him, showed up at his apartment. No wonder
he had tracked Bretti down—the world's oldest grad student.

He swallowed hard, close to hyperventilating, took a
half step toward the man on the floor, then ignored him
entirely. No turning back now. He had to deliver the old
Penning trap with whatever load it had managed to store
in two days. Maybe that would be enough. It would *have*
to be enough, since the main p-bar supply had been annihilated.

The FBI man's handgun burned a hole in his pocket.
He wanted to get rid of it, but he couldn't leave it there.
Fingerprints, evidence . . . he didn't know what sort of
magic the crime lab could do these days.

How could things go so wrong so fast? First the emergency beam dump on Sunday, which caused a power
outage, blowing the hell out of his demo stash. And now
some FBI suit came snooping around when he was trans-
ferring the last day's run of p-bars.

Why couldn't the bastard have waited another ten
minutes? Bretti would have completed his task, and no
one would have suspected. Nobody was supposed to see
him at Fermilab. During his week of vacation, he should
have had plenty of time to slip off to India, make his

delivery, take his payment, and get back to Illinois to pretend that nothing had happened. Nobody would have noticed, or cared, except maybe Dumenco and his unexpected results.

Well, after the curmudgeonly Ukrainian's radiation exposure, Dumenco wouldn't be chasing lost antiprotons for long. He certainly hadn't spent much time being a good advisor, helping Bretti make it through the academic hoops, taking the grad student under his wing, using a bit of professional pull to get him through the hard parts.

Crap, the old fart only cared about his own theories and the damned Nobel Prize. Now, maybe Bretti would have to accept it for his dear-departed mentor.

Nicholas Bretti took a deep breath. The fading rush of adrenaline had left him with a case of the shakes. He had to move fast before anyone found the man he'd shot. He had to take his equipment and get out of there.

Over at his work station, Bretti carefully disconnected the transfer mechanism from the Penning trap. Working quickly, he attached the much smaller, but much more efficient crystal-lattice trap and accelerometer to a port upstream from the main detector, where the substation tapped into the Tevatron flow. The crystal trap was the real key, a treasure chest for storing antimatter—but it needed nearly a week to collect enough p-bars to make it worthwhile.

Similar to the hundreds of other diagnostics attached to the beam channel, his small device had never drawn attention. Many teams of technicians had their own equipment in these substations, and nobody ever messed with someone else's diagnostics. It just wasn't done.

Instead of passively imaging the intense, rotating beam of p-bars, Bretti's lattice trap would bleed off antimatter particles after they had been laser cooled and slowed by the accelerometer.

Glancing at an oval clock that one of the grad students had wired to run counterclockwise, Bretti saw that it hadn't been more than three minutes since he had fired the shots. Still, much too long. He had to get out of there.

Grunting, Bretti lifted the disconnected Penning trap. Its case was lined with high-efficiency lithium-ion batteries, making up the majority of the weight. Two insulating Dewars, one inside the other, held the Penning trap itself—three strips of room-temperature superconducting magnets that created a precise magnetic field shaped like a bottle, bouncing the p-bars back and forth along the axis. Over time, the bottle would leak, but the lithium-ion batteries would keep the magnetic field alive long enough for him to get to India, while he filled the more efficient crystal-lattice trap that could literally hold nine orders of magnitude more antimatter.

He walked carefully away from the isolated substation as if carrying a suitcase full of bricks. He locked the door to the blockhouse—with any luck, and with many of the temporary hires on break, the agent's body wouldn't be found until Bretti was safely out of the country.

Making his way to his car, Bretti realized he didn't even have time to drive back to his apartment and pick up his bags. He had a plane to catch.

This early on Tuesday afternoon, Bretti didn't have to worry about rush hour traffic heading into downtown Chicago. Still, with his battered nerves, he didn't want to push his luck finding a parking spot for his small red Saturn—leased, but still a good bargain on his grad-student salary. He couldn't walk for blocks lugging the bulky Penning trap. Every bag lady and cab driver would spot him and wonder. He tossed a cigarette out the window and started for the embassy.

But first he pulled off to the side, stopping by a jetty on the shore of huge, gray Lake Michigan. The old concrete jetty was just remote enough that no one questioned people who stopped to gawk. Gold and red leaves from a cluster of trees hid him from others along the shoreline. A place for early-morning joggers; not many in the midafternoon.

The traffic was sparse, and he waited scant seconds before he fumbled in his pocket for the stolen FBI handgun. The gun was slick and still seemed hot—hot from firing the bullets that had torn into the agent's flesh. Bretti thought he could still feel the heat on the barrel, the unexpected *kick* from the recoil as he reacted without thinking.

Standing on the jetty, he tossed the handgun underhand into the chilly depths where waves churned with the brisk October breeze. The heavy gun made a soft splash like a gulp, and was swallowed up by the gray surface.

Much farther down the shore, a kid threw stones into the water, then ducked back as a wave splashed against the rocks. He waved at Bretti, who was too terrified not to wave back. Bretti was back in his car and jockeying into the fast lane in less than a minute.

"Not enough time as it is," he muttered while clutching the steering wheel. *And I've just shot a man over a difference of ten minutes. The embassy can damned well treat me like a VIP for once. And the man was FBI yet! They'll be crawling all over my ass.*

Racing down embassy row near Lakeshore Drive, Bretti passed stately buildings hidden behind ten foot wrought-iron and brick fences. Immaculate guard shacks nestled beside every gate, partially obscured by thick shrubbery. Some embassies were protected with bullet-proof glass windows; others were more inviting, giving an impression of openness—friendly nations, proud and colorful flags. The whole area oozed high society—the kind of life Bretti deserved, not some apartment hole in the burbs.

Bretti pulled up to the guard gate of the Indian embassy. Inside the shack, a guard took notice and motioned for him to stop. He hadn't thought what he would say, but he rolled down his window anyway.

The faint smell of flowers and spice drifted into the car. A curving cobblestoned driveway wound around immaculately kept gardens. Not much like the boring homes around Batavia and Aurora—he would sure as hell be glad to get away from that. But first he had to get through the gate.

The embassy itself stood behind a fortress of aesthetically pleasing protective buffers—beige flower planters each the size of a small car, thick stone columns, ornate wrought-iron fencing. Unseen among the splendor, Bretti knew sophisticated microwave sensors stood watch over the compound.

A dark man wearing a white coat and turban, maroon pants, and a long ceremonial sword emerged from the guard shack. The man smiled through a black beard and mustache, but his eyes never lingered on Bretti. Instead, they swept back and forth along the red car for unforeseen threats.

Bretti recognized him. This was the same guard who had been present the two previous times he had visited the Indian Embassy.

Placing his hand on the silver hilt of his curved sword, the guard smiled tightly. "Welcome to the Indian Embassy, sir. What may I do for you here today?"

"I'm Nicholas Bretti," he snapped, irritated that the man didn't recognize him. "I have an appointment with Mr. Chandrawalia."

"Very good, sir." The guard reached into the shack, pulling out a clipboard. He ran his white-gloved fingers down a list. "Ah, yes, Mr. Bretti. You are somewhat late. Would you please park your car outside and enter through this gate?"

"I have an important . . . *delivery* for Mr. Chandrawalia. It's in the trunk."

The guard lifted an eyebrow. "You may unload the item here if you please while you park your car outside."

"It's quite bulky and—look," said Bretti in exasperation, "this is extremely important, and Mr. Chandrawalia is expecting this right away. I'm late as it is, and I'm sure you don't want to upset anyone else." *Especially me.* He felt sweat prickling along his clothes.

He wondered if the FBI agent's body had been found yet. His stomach lurched with nausea. My God, he had killed a man, shot him—how many times? Bretti didn't even know.

"Why don't you pick up the *phone* and *call* Mr. Chandrawalia. I'm sure he'll authorize you to let me in with my car."

"I will do what I can, but we usually do not go to such lengths to accommodate a guest." Turning briskly, the guard's white coat flapped in the air. His eyes continued to scan the street as he spoke to Bretti, as if a horde of terrorists might suddenly appear to storm the embassy. *And in Chicago, for God's sake*, Bretti thought. *Can you believe the security?*

Rapidly tapping his fingers on the steering wheel, Bretti felt confined. What if someone had seen him leaving Fermilab? He had to get to cover somehow, and the Indians were his only hope.

A bearded face thrust into the car window. "Mr. Bretti? You are quite correct. Mr. Chandrawalia is indeed anxious to see you. A driver will be out shortly to bring your car to the front. Please walk into the complex to meet him." The guard opened the car door and waited for Bretti to get out.

Cursing under his breath, Bretti scooted out from the seat and left the keys dangling in the ignition. He nervously ran a hand through his black hair, then popped the trunk. The guard towered over him, emotionless as he carefully closed Bretti's car door. Turning a key in a control box, the guard swung open the gate. "We will take good care of your car, sir."

Bretti walked around to the trunk and lifted the unwieldy suitcase out of the car. No fuckin' way he was going to let these towelheads get hold of his Penning trap. It was only Phase One of the down payment he owed the Indians, but he wasn't going to let this get out of his sight. Swinging the bulky case by his side, he made for the embassy house.

Inside the fence a short man in a white tunic ran from the main building, taking no notice of him. Bretti passed bumblebees drifting lazily around the garden. The flowers made the air thick, sweet, and nauseating. He entered the embassy, glad to be behind the protective walls.

Bretti had never been able to figure out Chandrawalia's exact title and position in the Embassy. But it had to be high up in the food chain, judging from everything he had promised Bretti. The man smiled graciously as he sat behind a polished wooden desk, gesturing him into the private office.

Paintings of Hindi women dressed in colorful garb were positioned across the wall next to photographs of elaborate Mughal-era temples, photos of vast cities taken from the air, and the standard picture of the Taj Mahal. Green marble elephants stood two feet tall on either side of the desk.

"Welcome, Dr. Bretti. I am honored to listen, though my time is somewhat at a premium this afternoon." Chandrawalia's dark face contrasted with his impossibly white teeth. He had deep wrinkles, and a white beard shot with strands of iron gray.

"This is important enough to be worth your time."

"Very well, Dr. Bretti. Would you care for some tea?"

Tea? How could Bretti think of tea at a time like this? His whole life, his future had just disintegrated around him—like an antimatter explosion. He wondered if he should confess to Chandrawalia, explain about the FBI agent, his flight, all because the Indian government wanted a secret stash of p-bars. Would Chandrawalia help him out of this mess?

Bretti knew it would be a mistake to think of this man as his friend.

"No. No tea." Bretti shifted in his chair, setting the heavy suitcase of p-bars on the floor beside him. He plugged an extension cord from the wall to the suitcase, recharging the lithium batteries. "Things have changed at the Lab. I need to get out of here today like we planned, but I won't have as much of the . . . uh, product as I had promised. I have a more efficient trap collecting particles of antimatter right now. In less than a week—after the excitement cools down—it'll have a full supply. When I return, I can make good on the final delivery."

Chandrawalia's facial expression remained frozen in a perpetual smile. "I am sorry to hear that. Will this affect our agreement, Dr. Bretti?"

"*Mr.* Bretti. Call me mister." Bretti screwed up his face. The man knew damned well he was still a grad student. "I've got some antimatter, enough for your people to start their medical isotope project. And that's the important thing. Now get me out of here."

"We've inspected your holding apparatus," said Chandrawalia smoothly. "Your device is making our security people nervous. They think it could be some sort of sophisticated bomb."

"Just don't x-ray the container. That would increase the antiproton diffusion rate out of the magnetic bottle." To Chandrawalia's blank stare, Bretti growled, "You'll make it *leak* faster. It's tough enough keeping the p-bars contained in this type of trap without agitating them."

Did they really think he was stupid enough to bring a bomb into this place? And what on earth for? Of course, enough antimatter particles could be as deadly as a bomb—as the vaporized substation proved—but this Penning trap didn't hold nearly enough p-bars to cause any damage. Later in the week, when he returned for the crystal-lattice trap, then he would have enough antimatter to make someone worry.

"I see." Chandrawalia reached into a drawer, withdrew a folder and slid it across the polished desktop. "Here are tickets for today's flight to New Delhi. Your passport is in there as well, stamped with our visa. You leave at five P.M. We are putting your storage device in a diplomatic pouch—a container that can be hooked up to the plane's electrical system during the trip to India. It will not be inspected by your customs officials."

Bretti scooped up the ticket. "You've got me flying out on the Concord. Cool." The Indians really wanted those p-bars. Their stake in major new medical research and opening the process to lucrative markets supposedly depended on it.

"The program in Bangalore is anxiously waiting for your material. One of my associates will meet you there." Chandrawalia held up a finger and frowned for the first time in the conversation. The expression sent a chill through Bretti. "Please remember the need for discretion, Mr. Bretti. This, ah, *project* is hardly well publicized, or even endorsed by my government. Few people in this embassy are aware of what we are doing. If it proves to be a success"—he shrugged—"then things may change and everyone will want to take credit. But for now, the fewer people who know about this, the better."

"That's the tack I've been taking," said Bretti sourly. The less said the better, and the less chance any sort of investigation would finger him. He wasn't even supposed to be in Illinois this week.

"Good." Chandrawalia stood, clearly ending the meeting. Placing his hands on the desk, he bowed slightly. "Please instruct my people as to the care and operation of your storage device. We will then escort you to O'Hare and past customs as my official guest to our country."

"What about my car?" Things were moving too fast. He didn't even have a suitcase with him, no clothes, not even a toothbrush. But if Chandrawalia came through with the money they had promised, Bretti could buy all he wanted when he got to India.

"It will remain in our garage until you return."

For the first time since things had taken a nosedive at the substation, Bretti actually felt calm and somewhat hopeful again. He allowed a small smile on his face as he shook hands with Chandrawalia. He just might pull this off after all. . . .

But the official's grip was cold and his expression hard. "Do not forget that your device will be in the passenger hold. If anything goes wrong, both you and your plane will meet the same fate. Have a nice flight . . . and enjoy India."

Tuesday, 3:49 P.M.

Fermilab

The dogs strained on their leashes, intent on their job—professionals, just like everything else the FBI used. But Special Agent Schultz didn't expect them to find anything. He had already been over the various substations, searching for some hint as to the cause of the massive explosion that had vaporized one of the blockhouses.

The handler from the county sheriff's office followed the two dogs to the next substation. They barked and sniffed, making a beeline toward the heavy metal door. Schultz had a key to each of the padlocks, and this one looked just as secure as the others had. It would probably be a dud too.

He and his team had been on the scene for two days already, but still had found no clues. His evidence technicians and crime-scene chemists had narrowed the list of possibilities until nothing remained.

Normal bombs left telltale trace compounds, chemical residue, nitrates, by-products—but the fused crater showed nothing at all. The explosion had been clean, with intense heat, and of extremely short duration; electrical power from miles around had been disrupted. At first, the investigators had detected a small increase in the background radiation, but the crater was the wrong shape for even a miniature atomic weapon. Schultz could not begin to imagine what could cause such destruction.

The dogs scratched against the metal door of the blockhouse, anxious and whimpering. "Something's got them excited," the handler said.

Schultz came forward, sorting through a string of keys the Fermilab Director's Office had provided him. "One of the techs probably left a box of takeout chicken inside."

He didn't like being in charge of such a high-profile investigation with nothing to show for it. FBI headquarters didn't look at that too kindly. The other two California agents were working on their own, looking into the radiation exposure case, but they didn't have any assistance, no backup, no facilities at their disposal. Given those stumbling blocks, he certainly didn't expect them to uncover anything he and his people had missed.

He twisted a key in the padlock, then pulled the heavy door open. The two dogs impatiently pushed their way into the small substation. One even let out a yip, and Schultz frowned at their poor training. The sheriff's dogs should behave better than that.

But then he noticed that the lights were on. The last person in there must have left everything on, everything running. The walls were covered with diagnostics racks, oscilloscopes, computers, TV monitors, like props from an old TV show. One of the chairs had tipped over, and notepads and debris had fallen from the shelves.

Sprawled on the floor lay a man in a pool of blood.

Schultz froze, falling into his role as crime scene investigator. He recognized the dark suit, curly hair, pudgy physique. "It's that FBI agent from Oakland," he said, "Goldfarb." He hurried forward, dropping to his knee as the handler tried to keep his dogs under control.

"Get out your phone," Schultz snapped. "Call for emergency medical assistance. And get me the Chicago office. Code Red—an agent is down."

In the Fox River Medical Center, Craig found a bank of pay phones and tried Goldfarb's cell phone again. He had already been scolded twice by the nurses that he wasn't allowed to use his own cell phone inside the hospital itself, because it might interfere with pacemakers or medical diagnostics—not that he got good reception inside the heavily shielded building anyway.

Along the same lines, with Goldfarb snooping around the accelerator, the tunnels and metal reinforcements might also mess up his signal. He hung up the phone and returned to Dumenco's room.

Light spilled through a single window, where three more baskets of flowers had joined the potted plant on the sill—one from Trish, another from Dr. Piter's division, and the third from the Fermilab Director's office. Dumenco's friends were indeed limited.

Wearing a white lab coat and tennis shoes, Trish studied a history of radiation accidents she had gotten from her contacts at the PR-Cubed. The medical organization had been happy to provide all the details they could find. Some members of the Board of Directors wanted to make a news event out of Dumenco's radiation exposure, but Trish had so far held her ground. She flipped through the faxed summary documents with her back to Craig.

Stretched out on his bed and propped up on pillows, the old scientist frowned at his sheaf of papers. Craig had looked at some of the less technical articles, but they were more indecipherable than the nuclear data sheets he had perused during his case at the Nevada Test Site. At least in Nevada, accounting procedures and engineering diagrams helped explain the technical language; here, Craig found so many references to *annihilation operators, production cross sections, nuclear resonances, scattering matrices*, and *Feynman diagrams* that he was totally lost.

He prided himself on being one of the more technical special agents, but when thrown in the middle of cutting-edge high-energy physics, he was at a loss. He'd have to rely on Dumenco to help him out on this one.

But the Ukrainian was torn between his goals of solving his murder and unraveling his last great physics problem.

Craig's cell phone in his jacket pocket rang; he flipped it open. "Hello—Ben, is that you?"

"Craig, this is Paige." She hesitated. "Where are you?"

"At the medical center." He could hear the stress in her voice. "What's wrong?"

"I just got a call from the Director's office. Ben Goldfarb's been shot. He's being rushed to the hospital right now."

Craig stood, knocking his chair backward. "What happened? Is he all right?" Trish turned and looked up sharply. Dumenco put down his papers on the bed and raised an eyebrow.

"He was found by the FBI team in one of the beam-sampling substations. He's alive—that's all I know. Meet them at the emergency room. Sorry I can't tell you more."

Trish took a step toward Craig, questioning, but he flipped the phone shut and headed for the door. "Dr. Dumenco, your suspicions just became a whole lot more likely."

For once in his career, Craig's FBI badge did not magically open doors for him. The emergency room nurse stood her ground, refusing to give Craig access to his partner, and his friend.

"We'll update you as soon as we can, Agent Kreident," she said. "Right now, the doctors are more concerned with saving his life than answering your questions."

A dozen people sat miserably in waiting-room chairs against the wall. They watched Craig take on the petite, redheaded nurse, but even an FBI agent could not make her budge. An old Zenith TV on a platform attached to the ceiling displayed a local talk show host interviewing

a member of the PR-Cubed, who had come to Chicago
for their annual conference. Anyone spouting the hazards of radiation—especially a respected doctor—made
for good news coverage. Craig wondered if the PR-
Cubed spokesman would be talking about Dumenco's
"tragic accident."

Craig lowered his voice and stepped closer to the
nurse. "We're in the middle of a murder investigation,
and I need to be present in case my partner says anything, especially . . . especially if he doesn't make it. He
might provide the only break we have."

The nurse remained unmoved. "Mr. Kreident, from
the looks of your partner, I wouldn't count on him saying anything in there. It's a miracle he's even still alive.
So please, leave him alone—the doctors need all the
help they can get, but not from someone like you."

Two orderlies pushed past Craig into the emergency
room. Maybe he could get Trish to help him out. Or
maybe he should just wait and trust the medical professionals. Like everyone else in the room was doing.

Craig turned and, spotting the bank of pay phones
against the wall, dug out his contact list. He had a lot
of people to contact, but first he'd make the hardest
phone call of all—to Goldfarb's wife Jlene and their
girls.

The voice of June Atwood, Craig's Supervisory Special Agent, exploded over the phone as if she wanted to
reach across the fifteen hundred miles and grab him by
the collar.

"Craig, I can't begin to tell you how many Bureau
regulations and policies you've broken by starting this
investigation on your own time! We can't have our
agents working freelance, putting themselves—and others, dammit—in danger, on their free time! There's already an FBI team at Fermilab! Why couldn't you just
leave it to them?"

"Because they were investigating the wrong crime, June—"

"That's not the impression I got from Agent Schultz. This leaks out, and the press will have a field day."

Craig kept his mouth clamped, his emotions boiling inside. June remained quiet for a moment, as if she were going through several options in her head. Craig huddled closer to the pay phone against the activity around him— people crying while waiting for loved ones, nurses and doctors rushing to their next patient. An orderly wheeled an old man in a green surgical gown, IV lines dangling from plastic bags on a metal rack.

June's voice came back, this time calm. "Okay, now the damage is done, but we've got to get on top of this, and right now. You are there to investigate the lethal radiation exposure of Mr. Dumenco, under my authorization. You will cooperate in every way possible with Agent Schultz and the Chicago team already in place. With your technical background, however, you may well be the best person to head up this investigation. I'll have our SAC call their SAC, see what I can do."

"Agent Schultz hasn't been having much luck so far," Craig said. "He may want to leave the case."

"You let me decide that!" June replied, and Craig held the phone away from his ear. She fell silent for a moment, then became businesslike again. "Now, is there anything else you need while we're on the phone?"

"I've already spoken to Goldfarb's wife," said Craig. "She and the girls are booked on the next flight to Chicago. They're on their way to the airport now, Code Red. But I think it would be good to have Randall Jackson accompany her out here."

"Done," said June, her voice still simmering with anger. "You find the sleazeball who shot Ben. You'll pay the bar bill later, when you get back to Oakland."

Tuesday, 7:49 P.M.

Fox River Medical Center

Despite his insistence, Trish refused to let Dumenco go outside for a walk. "You have to take care of yourself. Rest, conserve your strength."

"Take care of myself!" he said, partly amused, partly outraged. "I am dying—I am already dead. What does it matter? I wish to go outside and breathe the air, see the trees, listen to the river."

Finally, she agreed to take him in a wheelchair. Grabbing their coats, she wheeled him out onto the sidewalks where he could watch the stars.

The hospital was surrounded by ancient oak trees that had shed brown and yellow leaves on the cropped grass and across the pavement. Acorns and dry twigs crunched as she pushed the wheelchair. Dumenco's eyes were bright and alive, drinking in the details like a condemned man savoring his last meal. In a way, Trish found the comparison very appropriate.

The air was chill with autumn, the sounds of the town somewhat quiet. Aurora was one of those midwestern cities that all but rolled up its sidewalks and went to sleep after business hours. A soft wind rustled the oak trees above. Dumenco looked up, then stared at the sky as the stars seeped into the eastern twilight.

"Thank you," he said. "I will remember this for the rest of my life . . . such as it is." Dumenco seemed to be making a wry joke, and Trish didn't know how to respond. She marveled at the thoughts that must be swirling behind that high forehead.

Long ago, she remembered seeing him in his element, talking to him over in the Ukraine during the days of her post-Chernobyl research. Georg Dumenco had been such a different person then, in control of his life, uncovering the secrets of the universe. Even then, he had been buried in his research for the Soviet government, unwilling to talk about it.

Living in the shadow of Chernobyl, Dumenco had been terrified of radioactive fallout, afraid of its effect on his family. She had not been surprised to learn of his defection to the U.S.

Those experiences in the Ukraine had affected her life, driving her to a deep suspicion at the complacent way many scientists viewed radiation use and exposure. Trish vented her own frustration and alarm through her work in the PR-Cubed. She had also kept in occasional contact with Dumenco himself and followed his work in Fermilab, had even visited him shortly before his accident.

And now she had to attend him as he died from the very thing he feared the most.

Dumenco appeared to be resigned to his fate, interested in what would happen to him from a coldly analytical point of view. "I want to know all the details, my dear lady," he said. Under the light of the sidewalk lamps on the hospital grounds, he looked at the reddening skin of his hands, his swollen joints. He licked his dry and cracked lips, which were already purple from hemorrhages underneath.

"It's not going to be pleasant, Georg," Trish answered, distracting herself by pushing him along. "Maybe it's better if you don't know."

The sidewalk sloped gently downhill, toward the Fox River that curled slowly across the farmlands. Joggers ran by, with steam puffing out of their mouths. A young couple sat on a bench, looking out at the dark river, more absorbed in each other than in the scenery.

"Of course it won't be pleasant," he said. "This is death. It's not supposed to be pleasant. But I'm also a scientist, and I have what you might call a morbid curiosity as to the sequence of events. I am, after all, about to experience them far more intimately than I had ever wanted to know."

Trish swallowed hard, trying to act professional, to look at him as a patient rather than a human being she admired. At least she had dragged him away from his intense scrutiny of the recent accelerator results.

"If this helps you to prepare . . . there's nothing I can do to help you."

"I understand that, my dear lady," Dumenco said. "But knowledge is still more comforting than ignorance."

"You might not say that in a minute," Trish said, but her faint edge of humor became brittle. "Within the first hour or so, you started experiencing what we call the 'prodromal' syndrome, erythema or redness of the skin, fever, nausea, weakness, cramps, and diarrhea. We treated those effects with intravenous fluids to prevent dehydration, antiemetics to control the nausea and vomiting. Fortunately, we haven't had to use vasopressors to constrict blood vessels and keep your blood pressure up to a safe level. So far the IV fluids have been enough."

She continued, focused on the lighted sidewalk ahead, listening to the crackle of dry leaves under her shoes, under the wheels of Dumenco's chair.

"Your bone marrow is also destroyed, your immune system ruined. Your number of white blood cells and platelets are both going down already, and your body won't make any more of them. That means you won't be able to resist infections, and you'll bleed easily—especially inside your body. Although no more red blood cells will be made either, that really doesn't matter. Even the high radiation dose you received didn't much affect the ones you already have, and red blood cells usually live for three or four months. But you won't be around long enough to become anemic. Bone marrow transplants were tried at Chernobyl, but in most cases did not prove to be helpful.''

Dumenco shuddered. ''My family is . . . not available as bone-marrow donors, even if it would help.''

Trish knew that Dumenco's wife and children had not come with him when he fled to this country, and their whereabouts were in question. Trish had been contacted by a member of the PR-Cubed, a Ukrainian in fact, who had been searching for Dumenco's family, citing a study on family effects of Chernobyl survivors. But she had no information to give the man, despite his persistent questions. Dumenco had never spoken to her about what had happened to his family. She expected they had succumbed to something more terrible than radiation, back in Eastern Europe.

She turned back to the problem at hand, as if reciting a report. ''We can do nothing to alleviate the central nervous system damage you received. Your symptoms may include apathy, fatigue, apprehension. You'll be unsteady, your hands will shake, your ears will ring constantly. As you degenerate, you may suffer from convulsions of increasing severity. I anticipate . . . death will follow from respiratory arrest.

''And even if the radiation injury to your brain isn't severe enough to kill you, in a few days the damage you received to your immune system and the lining of your intestines will probably make you go into septic shock. When that happens, treating you with powerful antibiotics might keep you alive maybe a day or so longer— but it would just be delaying the inevitable.''

He swallowed hard. ''At least my hair won't fall out.''

''No, that would take a few weeks.'' She hesitated. ''You won't last nearly that long.''

When she finished, Trish felt ashamed of what she had done. Instead of telling him in gruesome detail, she should have had a better bedside manner. Dumenco could have been made to feel comfortable and at peace.

At times she let herself get carried away, especially with the Physicians for Responsible Radiation Research, thinking more about abstract social solutions instead of *individuals* like Dumenco. Sometimes Trish knew she went too far; she acted without thinking, then had to face the consequences.

"How do you know all this information?" he asked. "From test animals?"

"Treatment of radiation exposure is not an exact science. Every case is drastically different," she said. "We have a lot of general mortality data from Hiroshima and Nagasaki, but many of those victims died from flash burns and infections, lack of proper medical treatment— not directly from the radiation. These are more controlled circumstances." She noticed her voice growing flatter, like a lecturer instead of a compassionate doctor.

"We certainly had enough victims at Chernobyl," he said.

Trish squeezed his bony shoulder. She had been there too. She had seen the horror in Dumenco's eyes, the fear for his wife and children, for himself and his beloved Ukraine.

"You received a *supralethal* exposure, Georg—in the neighborhood of two thousand rads. Orders of magnitude higher than anyone at Chernobyl."

Dumenco turned his head to look at her expectantly. "So what other cases *are* relevant? Or is this entirely guesswork?"

Trish turned down another path, past a line of rose bushes. Squirrels crashed through the fallen leaves, searching for acorns and scampering up the rough bark of the oak trees.

"Our best data comes from two accidents at Los Alamos, part of early nuclear weapons work. The first radiation fatality occurred in 1945, two days after the bomb was dropped on Hiroshima. An experimenter was hand-stacking tungsten-carbide bricks as neutron reflectors around a plutonium sphere, a core for a third atomic bomb just in case Japan didn't surrender after the first two.'' She stared off into the distance. The river seemed so peaceful, the sunset so quiet, the air so fresh.

"He accidentally dropped the last brick on top of the sphere, which made the setup supercritical. He even saw the blue flash of the radiation burst. Even though the man knew he'd been massively exposed, he meticulously unstacked the bricks, put them away, then walked to the hospital and turned himself in, where he died twenty-eight days later. He received about eight hundred rads.''

"Amazing the man could be so calm," Dumenco said. He coughed. "But then . . . you know us scientists.''

Trish walked slowly, pushing the wheelchair. Other patients and their families were enjoying the night air, though many made their way back inside as it grew cooler.

"The other accident occurred nine months later, in May 1946, when a safety trainer was demonstrating how to perform a critical experiment with a beryllium cap over a plutonium sphere. He used a flat-bladed screwdriver to keep the cap from completely covering the plutonium, showing just how close he could come without bringing the core to criticality.

"Unfortunately, the screwdriver slipped, the cap fell closed, and the plutonium went supercritical for an instant before the cap blew off. The safety trainer marked where all the observers had been standing, then calculated everyone's estimated dose. The others received varying exposures, and the safety trainer died nine days later.''

Oddly, Dumenco smiled at her. Trish smiled back, trying not to let the horror show on her face. His exposure was massive enough that he would die long before the more horrendous symptoms manifested themselves, the bleeding gums, loosening teeth, loss of hair, suppurating skin.

Dumenco patted her forearm. "Even with the hazards of nuclear material, that industry still has the best safety record of any, including chemical or electrical. Look on the bright side, my dear lady, you can add my story to your arsenal of horrifying anecdotes. But please put it in correct perspective. And I shall do my best to describe my symptoms to you, to make one last contribution to science. It'll give you a broader benchmark for radiation medicine. Perhaps so people would not be so irrationally afraid."

Trish shook her head, angry at his attitude. "You've already contributed plenty to science, Georg. The Nobel Prize committee doesn't consider just anyone."

Dumenco looked embarrassed. She knew he was an introspective man, trying to unlock the mysteries of the Universe, not for any fame or glory; but he had been immensely proud when his work became recognized, since so much of his earlier research in the Soviet Union had been locked up and classified.

"Have we heard from Bretti?" he asked. "He is on his fishing trip, and I wonder if he even knows about my accident."

"Not a word," Trish said. "I'll do my best to contact him. Maybe Craig can track him down."

"That would be most kind," he said. "My great achievement would have been to win the Nobel Prize . . . I had fantasized about it many times." He looked up at the dark sky, but saw something else, something far away.

"Sweden, in winter. The Nobel Prizes are presented on the anniversary of Alfred Nobel's death. December tenth, I believe, in the Stockholm Concert Hall. His Majesty the King of Sweden hands each Laureate a diploma and a medal, then the Ceremony is followed by a banquet for a thousand people." He smiled wistfully. "I hear it is quite an event."

"I'll bet it is," Trish agreed. She turned his wheelchair and headed back toward the hospital. Many lights had winked on in the windows.

"It would have been nice to be there," Dumenco said with a sigh and a feigned smile, trying to keep a stiff upper lip. "I'll be long dead by the time the ceremonies take place. The Nobel Prize is not given posthumously, but they make an exception if the scientist is already under consideration at the time of his death. I can take consolation in that loophole at least."

"Oh, Georg," Trish said, but didn't know what else to say. She pushed the wheelchair faster. The air had become suddenly colder.

"I've accepted the award many times in my dreams. Luckily I have a vivid imagination . . . as all high-energy physicists must. That will have to be adequate for me."

As Trish looked down at him, she felt anger and helplessness again, frustration boiling beneath the surface. She had already done much work with the PR-Cubed, but they had been ineffective. Trish and the others had been just another organization pointing a finger at the evils of the world. They spoke at dinner clubs and community service organizations, and the audiences briefly agreed with their cause . . . but then a different group came to their next meeting and made a different plea for a different problem. . . .

Radiation accidents didn't have a cute but pathetic poster child around whom the people could rally, like a pretty white harp seal. Maybe, in death, Dumenco could accomplish that for them. But he did have a point—compared to chemical spills, high voltage accidents, and industrial poisonings, the likelihood of anyone receiving a fatal radiation dose was practically zero.

Still . . . Trish had been to Chernobyl herself. She had seen the devastating effects of the fallout. She had treated other victims of radiation exposure, and to her this seemed even more insidious than smallpox or the bubonic plague—because *humans* caused this. Mankind brought the misery upon itself. But was she championing a cause that affected too few people, when her talents might make more of an impact elsewhere?

Georg Dumenco had fallen prey to his own scientific curiosity. Had his work at Fermilab condemned him to death? Had his research made him the target for reprisal by another researcher? Had he come too close to discovering something others wished to keep hidden, one of his former connections in the Soviet Union perhaps?

"Please, let us get back to my room," Dumenco said, preoccupied again. He seemed to heave off the unpleasant thoughts and toss them aside like debris. "I still have a lot of work to do. I should devote my energies to that which is most important?"

She reached the hospital's rear entrance. The glass doors swooped open automatically. "Important, Georg? Is it really that important?"

He looked up at her earnestly. "My antimatter production rate is far lower than expected, at a level close to that observed by Dr. Piter in his CERN work—which cannot be correct." He snorted at the thought of his rival. "That means there is a fundamental flaw somewhere in the experiment. If I can solve this one problem, then I can die happy."

They reached his room, and he began to climb out of the wheelchair even before she had brought it to his bed. He handed her his coat, already distracted, as he reached for the papers on the tray table. "Now, leave me to my data please. There isn't much time."

Trish turned to leave him alone in the room. *No,* she thought, *there isn't much time.*

. . . .

Tuesday, 9:23 P.M.

Fox River Medical Center

Late that evening Paige Mitchell met Craig in the hospital cafeteria. It remained open all night for hospital staff, though visiting hours were long over.

Goldfarb lay in his hospital bed unconscious, on the edge of death. Craig had already spent hours outside the ICU, pacing the floor. He had tried to construct a plan of action, but he kept coming up against a brick wall. The only thing he could do was focus on the Dumenco case, which now included the attempted murder of a federal agent as well.

Craig sat in an orange plastic chair, pulling himself close to one of the Formica-topped tables. While waiting for Paige to join him, he set his briefcase on the tabletop, saw that the surface was of dubious cleanliness, and brushed it off with a spare napkin.

In a moment of stunned respite, Craig sat at the cafeteria table and withdrew his folders of paperwork, skimming notes from his conversations with Dumenco as well as the maps, brochures, and other information he had gathered about Fermilab, the beam-sampling substations, and the Ukrainian scientist's prior work.

The preliminary summary Agent Schultz had given him about the explosion showed no evidence of bomb residue or chemical by-products—nor had the dogs found stashed explosives in any other substation, not even the one where Goldfarb had been shot.

The detonation pattern at the crater did not match any known bomb configuration, shaped charge, or high-energy-density material. The background radiation levels showed an elevated background neutron count, as if from induced radioactivity. And there was that strange power failure at about the same time.

Yet the substation had exploded almost simultaneous with the accident that had exposed Dumenco to two thousand rads. And Goldfarb had been shot in another one of the substations. Foul play was clearly involved, but he couldn't figure out how. Could it be related to Dumenco's current research? The Ukrainian seemed to think so.

Perhaps the dying scientist was right when he had compared his situation with the great mathematician Fermat. If he didn't achieve this breakthrough before he died, it might be many years before someone else could continue his work—even Nels Piter, whose past work in high-energy physics competed with, if not outright contradicted, Dumenco's theories. . . .

Before he could become completely absorbed in the case, Paige set her tray next to his. He had asked for only a cup of hot chocolate, but instead she carried two plates of food she had gotten from the cafeteria grill.

"You haven't eaten yet, Craig," she said. It wasn't a question. "Here, get some nourishment inside you."

His stomach growled, but his expression reflected dismay as he looked down at the plate: a sausage in a bun smothered with onions and sauerkraut and doused with spicy brown mustard. "I can feel my arteries hardening just looking at it," he said.

"It's Chicago cuisine," Paige said. "The world's best bratwursts."

Despite his comment, the food smelled delicious. "If I eat this, you're going to put *me* in one of the hospital rooms—or is that your intent?"

"Nonsense. When in Rome . . ." She smiled slyly. "Just take a bite."

Craig picked up the messy bun and brought it close to his mouth. Then he paused. "How's bratwurst different from any old sausage?"

Paige grinned. "I'm afraid that's classified information."

"A secret recipe?" he asked.

"No—it's just that if you knew what was in it, you'd be sick."

"I can take it," Craig said. "I've seen enough gruesome crime scenes in my day."

Paige picked up her own bratwurst and took a huge, sloppy bite, closing her eyes to savor the taste. She wiped the juices from her mouth. "You know that stuff called 'meat by-products' they put in pet food?"

Craig nodded, already suspicious of her answer.

"Well, the parts of the meat that aren't good enough to be called 'by-products' are set aside for bratwursts." She took another bite to cover her impish smile.

Craig finished his bratwurst quickly, not regretting a moment of it. He licked his fingers and wiped his hands and face with several napkins. "Trish would fall over in a dead faint if she saw me eating this."

Paige studied him, her blue eyes narrowing slightly. "Do you care what Trish thinks about the food you eat?"

Craig sensed a hesitation in her voice. "I used to, although she did have my good health in mind. But not anymore."

"I see," Paige said. "So that's why you dropped everything to fly across the country, just to lend your hand unofficially on a case that wasn't even *yours* until your partner got shot."

Craig's thoughts scrambled as he tried to find a way to salvage the conversation; finally he saw a way out. "Well, it gave me an excuse to come and see you, didn't it?"

Paige laughed. "Good save, Craig."

They fell into an uncomfortable silence, and Craig

finally asked, "So . . . do you like it out here? No regrets about leaving California?"

"Oh, I'll always miss California, but Fermilab has a lot of character, a certain charm . . . if you give it a chance. Of course, I haven't been out here all that long, less than a year. Last winter was pretty rough." She looked over at him. "And this is my first murder case at Fermilab. But I've worked well with the FBI before."

Craig smiled back at her. "You seem to be getting along with your coworkers," he said, then took a sip of his hot chocolate. The sweet richness added a strange counterpoint to the spicy, savory sauerkraut, onions, and mustard. "Rubbing elbows with that Dr. Piter."

Paige flushed. "We're just friends," she said a little too quickly. Craig decided not to press the issue, but Paige felt the need to keep talking. "He's a brilliant scientist, well respected, good-natured, certainly nice enough to spend a little time with. Of course, it seems a bit like dating a walking encyclopedia." Her teeth flashed in a bright smile. "But what girl can resist that suave European charm?"

Craig wadded his napkins, suddenly very much needing to find a place to throw them away. "You didn't have much difficulty resisting the charms of an FBI agent last year."

"Was I resisting?" Paige asked with a raised eyebrow. "And which charms were those, exactly?"

"Oh, you know, the dedication to duty, truth, justice, and the American way. My diligence, my ability to put together the pieces of a puzzle and solve seemingly impossible crimes."

"Oooh, you're giving me a chill." Paige leaned closer to him.

"Speaking of which," Craig said, suddenly self-conscious and wanting to get down to business, "did you find anything else about Dr. Dumenco's background?"

She wrinkled her nose as she thought for a moment.

"Well, he was an eminent scientist in the former Soviet Union, but when the Ukraine broke away from the Russian Federation, he fled to the United States. I know we offered him asylum and a very comfy and prestigious job at Fermilab."

Craig nodded. "The U.S. did that with quite a lot of Soviet scientists. The writing was on the wall—the Berlin Wall, maybe?—when communism fell, Soviet researchers would be up for grabs. Russia was in too much chaos to pay them any more than a custodial wage, which wasn't nearly enough.

"So other countries began to lure the scientists away. We were afraid a lot of the weapons designers, engineers, and physicists were willing to go over to the highest bidder. But as soon as this process started, the United States began to subsidize them, and to a lesser extent, grabbed everyone they could, offering them political asylum and citizenship, a good salary, and a chance to continue their work in a free capitalist society."

"Sounds like a good deal," Paige said, tossing her blond hair over her shoulder.

"For good reason. Less friendly countries were making overtures to get the weapons scientists—Libya, Iraq, North Korea, anybody who wanted their own private little specialist who could take advantage of previous work done in the Soviet Union. One good recruit could leapfrog a threshold country into the ranks of the Big Boys."

"Like what we did with the German rocket scientists," Paige said.

"Right—'Operation Paperclip,' people like Wernher von Braun and his crew from Peenemünde. After the fall of the Third Reich, we grabbed as many German scientists as we could before the Russians got the rest. Those refugees formed the basis of our respective rocketry programs."

"Good analogy," Paige said. She leaned across the table. "Dumenco came here and immediately began doing brilliant work at the Tevatron. He thrived in this place, as if he already had a good head start. You can see by the stack of breakthrough technical papers he published in the last few years, shaking subatomic physics down to the quantum level, you might say.'' She sniffed at her own joke, and Craig allowed himself a smile.

"I couldn't comprehend any of his articles," Craig said, "not even the abstracts, although I'm a reasonably technical person."

"Dumenco's pushing the frontiers of science," Paige said, "moving the borderline between the unfathomable and the simply nonsensical."

"What does that mean?" Craig said.

"Dumenco found answers to some crucial problems in high-energy physics of the so-called 'Standard Model,' leading to a Grand Unified Theory. But because we can only observe indirect interactions of basic particles, even the answers are sometimes so bizarre they're incomprehensible."

"Then maybe I *am* understanding them," said Craig, "because they are certainly incomprehensible."

"The elegance of Dumenco's work gained notice from the Stockholm Nobel committee," Paige continued. "With his initial Fermilab results, he achieved breakthroughs in areas that had stymied people for years."

"Well, what work was Dumenco doing in the Ukraine?" Craig said, flipping to the end of his dossier. "I've got practically every month of his employment here, but nothing about that entire earlier part in his life."

"I couldn't find out much about that either," Paige admitted. "The records weren't transferred over. I've uncovered nothing about his family or his education in the Soviet Union. I think he had a wife, two daughters and a son, but their whereabouts are currently unknown. He may have left them behind when he defected."

"Our government offered this man everything he wished for," Craig said, tapping his pen against the edge of the table. "Sure, he's since proven himself to be a brilliant man—but on what did we base our assumption that he would make so many breakthroughs if we gave him the chance? Yet, we instantly gave him an extraordinary amount of time on the world's largest particle accelerator, granting him all the research assistance and funding he could possibly want? Don't you think that's a little odd?"

"Yes, I do." Paige nodded. "But somebody must have known the work he did in the Ukraine."

"I don't know about you," Craig said, "but knowing that someone tried to murder an eminent physicist currently on the short list for the Nobel Prize makes me very suspicious. Especially when I see that a large portion of his past work has been hidden under wraps."

He tucked his pen back in his pocket. "When something is swept under the rug like that, I see a big suspicious lump. It makes me think that a few of our important answers lie there."

Wednesday, 10:12 A.M.

New Delhi, India

Stepping nervously from the narrow air-conditioned Concord into the New Delhi airport, Nicholas Bretti felt as if he had entered another world. The sleek supersonic jet was a vision of the future, a flying metal island immaculately clean and incredibly well-maintained; but the New Delhi airport was a nightmare that couldn't heave itself out of the past.

A mix of heat, humidity, and overpowering smells slammed into him as he stepped off the plane onto the jetway. He knew he would never be able to forget the smells. Or the people.

Bretti blinked, stumbling ahead, as if all his senses had overloaded. He lit a cigarette to calm himself. Already unsteady on his feet because of the six Grand Marniers he had downed in an attempt to calm himself, he tried to regain his full alertness. This Indian connection was important, his safety net, his only chance at escaping what he had done back at Fermilab. He wouldn't get a second chance to make a first impression on the VIPs coming to meet him.

Swallowing hard, he looked over the jostling bodies just outside the customs area. Gentlemen in immaculate business suits elbowed beggars in torn robes. Women wore yellow and orange cloth wrapped around their bodies; dirty children without shoes or shirts swarmed about. Brownian motion, he thought, *Indian* motion.

People everywhere, all with black hair, brown skin. People. Noise.

The alcohol buzz wore off quickly. He had a headache, and the panic inside him turned to sour, sick despair. Was this the best future he could hope for?

The incredible humidity made his shirt go limp against him, as if he had just been steam blasted. The airport reeked of urine, mold, animal manure, and decaying garbage. Outside, vendors at stalls added their sweet and biting smells of burning incense, spices, and cooking food, perfumes, and curry.

It was a world far removed from Chicago, and even more so from the upscale neighborhood in Fairfax, Virginia, where he had grown up. Now Bretti wished he had gone back home on his supposed fishing trip after all, instead of just faking it for his alibi.

What did he care about the Indian government's desire for antimatter, their intent to use it for medical applications? New isotopes for cancer treatments. If they made breakthroughs in medical technology, their country would make billions on the world market. The Indians weren't really paying him all that much money, after all—and nothing was worth the crap he was going through. Especially not after shooting that FBI agent.

Bretti wanted just to turn around, climb back aboard the Concord, and go back to Chicago. But he was trapped here, maybe for the rest of his life. He didn't know what he was going to do.

He wavered, then swallowed the sour taste of chicken vindaloo from the onboard meal that crawled up his throat. Drawing deeply on his cigarette, he tossed the butt to the floor and ground it out.

"Excuse me, Dr. Bretti?" A man's high-pitched voice startled him, piercing through the drone and clangor of so many people.

Bretti whirled around unsteadily. The man was dressed in white cotton pants and tunic with a matching white hat; brown plastic glasses made his eyes large and goggling. His full mustache curled up nearly to his nose.

"Dr. Bretti? My name is Rohit Ambalal, from the People's Liberty for All party." He carried a blue soft-sided briefcase. "I am here to expedite you through customs. Come this way. Quickly please."

Ambalal motioned Bretti toward a red door to the right of a long line by the customs table. A military guard in a khaki uniform with red-and-black rank insignia stood by the door, eyeing them.

Bretti's mouth felt dry and cottony as his guide started for the red door. *People's Liberty for All party?* he thought. *What the hell is this?* Did it have something to do with his contact, Mr. Chandrawalia?

Perspiration soaked his shirt, as much from anxiety as from the oppressive humidity. The military guard made him very uneasy. Bretti swallowed, but his throat was dry. He tried to think, but could dredge only a little of the background that Chandrawalia had told him some months before. India's leadership tottered back and forth among the dozens of political parties; no ideology held a convincing grip on the nation's government. He hoped he wasn't going to be caught up in some sort of power struggle.

The military guard crushed out his cigarette and stared at Bretti. The bespectacled guide stopped and turned to Bretti. "Dr. Bretti, we must hurry. Your flight to Bangalore leaves soon, and you must clear customs before you board the plane. I will try to expedite matters, but there are people who must ask you some questions."

He had no suitcase, no extra clothes—nothing but what he wore. With a wallet stuffed full of rupees from the embassy, he'd planned to buy clothes in India. With nothing to declare, he should sail through customs.

Except for the Penning trap, still in the diplomatic pouch.

What if one political faction didn't know what the other was doing? Would he wind up in some flea-bitten jail, like that guy in *Midnight Express?* This army guard gave him the creeps. After growing up in the Washington, DC, area, he'd lived around military people all his life—he shouldn't feel threatened. But Bretti had never tried commercial espionage before, never shot a man, never fled the scene of a crime.

What would these people do to him? He certainly couldn't count on his own government to help.

"Dr. Bretti?" Ambalal folded his hands across the soft-sided briefcase, genuinely upset at Bretti's reluctance to follow. "We must process your paperwork, and I must see to the diplomatic pouch. Quickly now."

Behind Bretti, the doors to the Concord sealed shut; in front of him spread the long customs line and the mass of shoving people. He had to trust someone, and he couldn't think straight, thanks to the Grand Marnier and his panic. Chandrawalia had too much at stake not to ensure his safety. He had to count on that.

Bretti forced himself to move toward where the guard held the red door open. Inside the claustrophobic room, two men sat at a long brown table. A large mirror—one-way, no doubt—took up a good part of the wall on his left, next to another red door that led to the open terminal.

Both men at the table wore open-collar short-sleeved shirts and no-nonsense expressions. One man was small, old, and bald; the younger man wore a dark beard. The bearded man nodded for Bretti to take a seat as he spoke in a high, piping voice. "Dr. Bretti, welcome to India. It is a rare occasion that we are blessed with a distinguished visiting scientist. And one sponsored by a consulate, no less."

"It's *mister*," said Bretti, looking down at his hands. "I'm not a Ph.D. yet." Someday soon he'd have that union card so he wouldn't be sniffed at by so-called experts in the scientific fields. He'd worked his butt off for seven years as a grad student, living on slave wages, while Dumenco followed his esoteric goals and treated him like a barely competent manservant.

He suspected that sponsoring professors kept people like him sweating out their servitude to boost their own egos, delaying the awarding of doctorates. Too many people would give anything to get through a program at Fermilab.

But as much as he wanted that title, Bretti also knew it was meaningless unless it was earned. *Truly* earned. He recalled the time he had come home from school in third grade, crying because he had lost a spelling bee. Trying to comfort him, his mother had cut a ribbon from blue construction paper and pinned it on him—declaring him a winner.

Getting the crap beat out of him the next day in school for bragging about the fake award had brought the point home too well.

Maybe after all he had done for them, the Indians would take him on. Bretti could help Chandrawalia's group with their so-called medical applications for the p-bars. After the appalling events of the past couple of days, he needed a fresh start, a fresh home, and a fresh identity . . . somewhere far from FBI investigators and extradition treaties.

The guard took his position by the door, while Ambalal stood like a mother hen at Bretti's side. All the while the bald man sat observing. No one made any introductions.

The bearded man frowned and put down the papers he had been studying. "Ah, *Mister* Bretti, then. It is my understanding you will be conferring with a high-energy research group in Bangalore. This is quite an honor, especially if you are not a real scientist." He knitted his thick eyebrows together. "Tell me, please, why our consulate would sponsor someone such as yourself to speak with this esteemed group?"

Bretti glanced up sharply. "Wait a minute. I didn't say I wasn't a scientist. I'm just not finished with my degree, and I don't believe in calling myself something I haven't earned. It's not right."

The mustachioed party man spoke up behind him. "Dr. Bretti is here on invitation from the Chicago consulate office. He is a personal guest of Mr. Chandrawalia, the deputy head of mission. This gentleman is from America's Fermilab and he has valuable skills to assist India's national researchers." He placed a sinewy brown hand on Bretti's shoulder. "That should be enough for you."

Taking strength from the man's statement, Bretti faced the two men at the table. "That's right. I've coauthored numerous publications in highly respected journals—check them out yourself if you don't believe me."

"Your position in science is not in question, *Mister* Bretti," said the beard, "but rather why such a distinguished diplomat as Mr. Chandrawalia would take such a personal interest in your visit. What precisely do you intend to discuss when you are in Bangalore?"

Bretti shifted his weight in the unsteady chair, listening to the faint groan of metal and plastic. The cold sweat crawled down his back, making his shirt even more clammy. "Why are you interrogating me? I was invited here, by Chandrawalia at your embassy, just as the gentleman said. Isn't that a good enough reason?"

The quiet bald man finally spoke up in a voice too deep for his small size. "We must be sure that the purpose of your visit is purely scientific and not political. You are not here for political purposes, are you?"

Bretti sighed, suddenly relieved. "Is *that* what this is about? I'm not interested in politics, I'm a scientist. I don't give a rat's ass about what your country does, or who influences whom. All I'm doing is, uh, giving a talk and delivering scientific equipment. Nothing more, nothing less. Okay?"

The bearded man scribbled some notes, then glanced over to his bald companion. The small man nodded curtly. "You are not staying in India very long, Mr. Bretti?"

Bretti didn't know how to answer that. What if they

offered him political asylum? He couldn't go back to the United States until the dust settled. "I'm heading back home as soon as I can."

"Enjoy your stay," the bearded man said. "But please watch your company." As he turned, the guard strode over and opened the second red door for him. The bearded man and his bald partner gathered their material and exited, with no words spoken between them.

The military officer once again showed yellow teeth as he motioned for Bretti to leave. Shrugging, but feeling safe for the first time since he had landed, Bretti followed his guide out of the room into a long hallway that led into the main terminal complex.

Bretti turned to Ambalal. "What the hell was that all about?"

"Mr. Chandrawalia is not only a well-respected diplomat, but he is strongly allied with our People's Liberty for All party."

"So?" said Bretti.

"India's political system is an alliance of many parties, none with a clear majority. Any time a minority party such as ours attempts something out of the ordinary, suspicions are raised." They stopped just outside the main terminal area where a mass of people congregated. "Information is power, and if you as a foreigner can supply information to another party, such as People's Liberty for All, then you are a valuable asset."

Bretti's head pounded. It was a crazy country where even *medical research* was a political item. Maybe they were only going to cure cancer for the people in their own party.

Ambalal hustled him along. "They will leave you alone so long as they remain satisfied that you pose no threat to the balance of power." Glancing at his watch, he fumbled inside his soft-sided briefcase and pulled out a ticket. "You have less than an hour before your plane leaves for Bangalore. Please proceed to the gate while I check on the diplomatic pouch. I must make sure your scientific equipment is transferred to the plane."

Wednesday, 6:15 A.M.

Fox River Medical Center,
Intensive Care Ward

Craig slouched in an orange plastic chair, half asleep outside Goldfarb's hospital room.

While the inhabitants of Aurora, Illinois, began to stir for the workday, he sat weary and lost in his thoughts, going over the events that had brought him to this point, sleepless outside Intensive Care where his partner might live or die.

The doctor had finally taken the time to explain Goldfarb's condition and his prognosis. The other agent lay in a coma, shot twice with his own handgun. The first bullet had entered the upper right chest at an oblique angle, fracturing a rib and damaging the right lung. The second shot, more serious, had struck the left chest, contusing and lacerating the lung, causing what the doctor called a "hemopneumothorax." A tube had been inserted into the chest to drain blood and release trapped air. The delay in rushing Goldfarb to the hospital had nearly cost him his life.

The good-natured agent remained sedated to keep him from tearing at the respiratory tubes, and he had grown no stronger through the night. The surgeons refused to bring him around so he could identify his assailant.

Earlier, Craig had driven to the Fermilab blockhouse where Goldfarb had been shot. Agent Schultz took him through the scene, but Craig had been unable to come up with any clues, any insights. Schultz and his own team were stumped as well, and he seemed more than willing to let Craig have his hand on this case. The Chicago agent had plenty of other pending cases back in his main office.

In another part of the medical center, Trish hovered around Georg Dumenco hour after hour, witnessing each step of his degeneration. It would be an ironic twist of fate, Craig thought grimly, if Goldfarb slipped away before the Ukrainian did.

Before the rest of the hospital began its bustle, Trish LeCroix stopped in front of him, crossing her arms over her chest. He looked up, seeing that she had pinned her dark hair back with a pair of coral barrettes. In the open front of her white lab coat she wore a thin gold chain around her neck. Craig dimly recalled that he had given her that chain for their . . . was it their six-month anniversary? He couldn't remember.

Now Trish feigned a smile, her lips were a deep red, a color of lipstick that set off her pale skin and dark hair to good effect. Even during the long night's vigil, she had found time to touch up her appearance. "Let's try not to fill up any more rooms in the ICU, understand?" she said. "Take care of yourself."

"Don't you chew me out, too," he said with a hint of harshness brought on by fatigue. "My boss already did that last night."

She reached forward to squeeze his shoulder, then meticulously brushed wrinkles from his rumpled suit jacket. "I didn't mean it as criticism, Craig, but as concern. I don't want you to end up in one of these hospital beds because of this case."

Without another word, she hurried back toward Dumenco's room. Once again Trish had left before Craig could think of the right thing to say. His mind was too befuddled with weariness and worry. He glanced at his watch. This time yesterday, Goldfarb had been handing him a cup of Starbucks coffee as he got off the red-eye flight from San Francisco.

Down the hall, with a quiet chime of a bell, the elevator opened. Craig lifted his head sluggishly, ashamed at himself for wallowing in guilt. Disbelieving, he saw the tall, dark form of Randall Jackson emerge wearing his dark FBI suit and tie, his expression grave.

Beside him came a much shorter woman with two small girls in tow, each holding one of their mother's hands. Craig recognized Julene Goldfarb, as well as the curly-haired agent's two daughters, Megan and Gwendolyn, ages six and four.

He stood out of respect, once again finding his vocal chords empty of comforting words or phrases. "Julene," he finally whispered, "I'm so sorry."

She hurried forward and let him fold her awkwardly in his arms. Julene had used rubber bands to pull her pale brown hair into long pigtails; she wore no makeup, scrubbing her face clean because she had been crying. He had never seen her look so disheveled. A well-mannered daughter from a large Southern family, Julene maintained her personal appearance as if it were a uniform—now, though, she must have thrown a simple bag together, grabbed the kids, and rushed to the airport.

The two little girls stood concerned by their mother's side. Megan, the older, went to the door of the Intensive Care hallway and peeked through the narrow wire mesh window. "Is Daddy in there?" Her voice trembled.

"He's hurt, Megan. The doctors are trying to make him better," Jackson answered. His face grew stormy.

Julene drew a gulp of air. Her words were muffled in the breast of Craig's jacket. "I always knew he was going to get shot. I knew it! I warned him about every assignment he went on."

"I'm sorry I wasn't with him at the time, Julene," Craig said.

She pulled away and looked up at him, angry. "Why? So you could have been shot too?" Her Southern drawl extended with her stress, blurring her words. She shook her head, flopping the pigtails from side to side.

"Ben is passionate about his job. He loves running out on cases like a cowboy. And he loves working with *you*, Craig. He never shuts up about all the good times you have together, all the excitement." She blinked furiously, refusing to let more tears spill. "If I put my foot down and forced him to a desk job, I know he'd do it for me—" She swallowed another lungful of air. "But if I forced him to make that decision, then I would lose him as sure as by a gunshot. He'd be dead to me, unhappy and bored."

She swallowed hard, then finally forced herself to look through the window and down the hall.

"It'll be all right, Julene," Craig said, grasping her by the elbows and looking into her greenish-blue eyes. "Ben's going to pull through this." He hoped she believed his optimism better than he did.

A doctor walked down the hall and came through the swinging door. Dressed in green scrubs, he had been the ER trauma team leader when Goldfarb was admitted. Craig introduced Julene, and the doctor looked weary as he nodded. "I'll take you on back. But please don't disturb the nurses. Your husband's in critical condition, and we're doing everything we can." Julene and the girls followed him to Goldfarb's room, letting the door swing shut behind him.

Craig remained in the hall with Jackson. The tall agent kept his face set in a grim mask, but his eyes were bright and icy. "So what have you found out so far, Craig? Who's the bastard that did this?"

"No clues yet," Craig answered. "No motive, no evidence. But Ben stumbled upon something—I don't know much else, except that Trish must have been right about foul play in Dumenco's so-called accident. There's too much involved here. Someone intentionally caused his lethal exposure, someone was responsible for that substation explosion, and someone shot Ben."

Craig shook his head, running his fingers through his chestnut hair. "This was supposed to be just a quick little favor for an old girlfriend, to poke around and see if we could uncover something the accident investigators had missed. June chewed me out for it, and now Ben might die."

Jackson crossed his arms over his chest. "But now that it's an official case, we can bring the full resources of a federal investigation to bear. And even better—*I'm* on the case with you." He met Craig's eyes with a hard stare. "You and I aren't going to let anyone get away with doing this to Ben, are we?"

Craig saw Julene and the two girls standing down the hall outside Goldfarb's room. The doctor spoke quietly to them, but no one seemed to be listening.

Craig's heart pounded, the anger pulsing in his own temples. "No Randall," he said. "No, we're not."

Wednesday, 7:21 A.M.

Fox River Medical Center

It was time to work, time to continue the investigation. Jackson's presence was just the incentive Craig needed to dive into the case. The other agent didn't want to waste a moment.

After introductions, Craig and Jackson stood beside Georg Dumenco as he lay back on the bleach-scented white sheets. Jackson retained his composure with a discernible effort. The dying Ukrainian had finally settled in, as if in defeat. Craig wondered if he would ever get up again.

The old scientist's skin had reddened with overall swelling, but also dried in patches in a strange rash, worsening to sores that stood out on his arms and his cheeks. The macerated flesh covering his knuckles and fingers was cracked, oozing blood-tinged fluid. His hands were so swollen and stiff he could barely hold a pencil—and this seemed to frustrate Dumenco more than the pain.

Craig was astonished at how quickly the physicist had begun failing, his body crashing out, everything compounded as one bodily function collapsed, then another, like an avalanche. It had been three days since his massive exposure. Trish had said in a quiet voice that Dumenco probably wouldn't last three more.

Dumenco reluctantly pushed aside the data-output sheets and computer printouts he had been studying and focused his attention on the two FBI agents. He tried to set down his pencil, but it fell awkwardly and rolled off the bedside table to land on the floor.

Jackson bent over to pick it up. Seeing that the lead had broken off, he reached inside his suit jacket and pulled out a silver-plated mechanical pencil. "Here, you can have this," he said. The physicist nodded in gratitude.

"Have you found anything in your experimental data that might help us?" Craig asked. "Any ideas?"

Dumenco didn't mind talking about his work. "Only that something is very wrong with my experiment. The p-bar production rate is nine orders of magnitude lower than I had calculated." He coughed. "Nine orders! This makes no sense. I must talk to Bretti, but he is away on vacation. He hasn't even called."

"Then we should find him on vacation," Jackson said. "Maybe he can give us some leads."

Dumenco shook his head disparagingly. "My grad student works well, but has no initiative. After seven years, he is no closer to completing his doctorate than when he started. I wouldn't expect him to come to any conclusions on his own." He sighed. "Perhaps I can talk to Nels Piter. . . ."

Then Dumenco looked up, suddenly alert. "I understand Agent Goldfarb was shot yesterday. Another 'accident,' I suppose, or do they believe me now?"

Craig nodded. "Oh, they believe you," he said. "I've managed to get this classified as a major case with the Bureau. Things will happen faster, with more resources."

Now that he himself was the agent in charge, the case had grown more extensive, with tangents and connections sprawling ever wider. Agent Schultz was continuing his focused study of the crater explosion, but kept running into dead-ends. No known explosive could have caused the damage pattern exhibited, and no chemical residue had been found. Craig and Jackson would investigate from the other end, trying to determine how Dumenco was the focal point of these events.

Jackson stepped forward, all business. "As part of this investigation, we'd like to go into your apartment, sir. Agent Kreident has already been to the accelerator site, the beam-sampling substation, and your offices, but we need more background. Perhaps something in your personal life might open another door for us. We'll start by having a team of agents check on Bretti."

The Ukrainian toyed with the mechanical pencil Jackson had given him. "By all means, you may search my apartment—but I rarely spend time at home. I have some work there, some files, but nothing important. In fact, if you see anything you like, just let me know. I haven't quite had the time to make out a will." With a wistful look back at his data, he glanced over at Craig. "You'll have to get my keys from Dr. LeCroix. She confiscated them last time I went to my office at Fermilab."

He frowned, then looked up again as a thought occurred to him. "You may have to watch out for news reporters. They came to the hospital yesterday, but dear Dr. LeCroix got rid of them. It seems she is at odds with her partners at the Physicians for Responsible Radiation Research. They want to use me as a martyr to gain attention for their cause." His laugh turned into a phlegmy cough. "I wouldn't want to cross Dr. LeCroix. She's a dynamo when she gets angry."

"You're telling me," Craig muttered. Jackson looked sidelong at him.

Dumenco blinked his red, gummy eyes, trying to focus. "I fear that media reports could put me in . . . extreme danger. When your enemy is aware that your death is fast approaching, he has many things to fear. Someone may still try to kill me before I can reveal anything that should remain a secret."

"And what would that be?" Craig asked. "And who is your enemy?"

Dumenco feigned a smile. "Come now, Agent Kreident, that would be tempting fate. Others may suffer retribution for my indiscretions. Innocents. I would rather die without having to atone for that guilt."

Craig drew a breath, frustrated. Was the man hiding something, and who was he protecting? "Do you want us to solve this case, Dr. Dumenco?"

"Indeed, I do. But I also want to understand why my final experiment seems critically flawed. And I don't wish for anyone else to get hurt. Perhaps these goals are mutually incompatible."

He turned back to his papers, finished with the agents. "I am finding it difficult to think straight. What if the Nobel committee hears about the flaws in these results? It calls into question my previous work."

In frustration he pounded his fist against his forehead and left an astonishingly clear bruise. He seemed to be battling a growing terror and helplessness as moments slipped away from him. "I need every minute remaining, Agent Kreident. Just make sure no one steals any more hours from me. The person who did this may be too impatient to let me die on my own time . . . though I am doing it as fast as I can."

Dumenco spat into a hospital cup. "Let me know what you find in my apartment," he said, "but please, I have to think. So little time . . . so little time."

Batavia was one of numerous suburbs that spread out from Chicago like ripples in a pond. The sprawling suburbs exhibited the Midwestern elbow room so different from the crackerbox California houses with their micro-yards. Even the low-rent districts had grassy yards and long driveways.

With his Fermilab salary, Dumenco could easily have afforded one of the spacious ranch homes complete with a lush green lawn and a brick pedestal around the mail-box out by the road—but for some reason the physicist had chosen to live near the center of town in an apart-ment building four stories high, faced with red brick.

Perhaps, Craig thought, the older structure reminded Dumenco of community barracks housing he had lived in back in Kiev under Soviet rule.

"Repeat after me," Craig said. "No comment. No comment. No comment. Good, now we're ready for any reporters."

"None standing outside at least," Jackson said as they climbed out of the gold rental Taurus. Jackson had driven, pushing the seat back as far as it would go. Goldfarb, much shorter, had been the previous driver.

"By now they must have realized nobody's home," Craig said. "Dumenco lived alone—who would be there to talk to? He was a workaholic, so the neighbors wouldn't know him well." Craig withdrew the key from his pocket. "Third floor," he said. "Apartment 316."

They hadn't been able to find Trish again that morning, but Craig supposed she needed to sleep occasionally, too, especially after her long vigil with Dumenco. He had retrieved the keys himself from the hospital's personal possessions lockers.

They climbed the stairs rather than taking the elevator and emerged onto the landing, looking down a carpeted hall of closed identical doors. As they walked along, Craig heard the reverberations of televisions behind some doors, children crying or playing, mothers yelling.

When they reached 316, Craig was relieved to find no reporters there either, although the business card of someone from the *Chicago Sun Times* lay on the floor as if it had been stuck between the crack but then fallen loose.

Jackson bent down to scrutinize the lock in the door. "Have a look at this," he said, keeping his voice low. Small wiry scratches made a faint starburst around the keyhole. "Looks like not everyone uses a key to get in."

Craig frowned. "That might not be fresh, but watch it." He slid the key into the lock, and the door swung easily inward to a large apartment suite. Craig stepped inside, feeling dust motes stir around him. He could always tell when a place had been sealed and abandoned, as if time had stopped.

Soft sunlight drifted through drawn ivory blinds onto dark green carpeting. Shelves full of knick-knacks, painted Russian eggs, and gilt-edged religious icon paintings adorned the walls next to framed photos of onion-domed Ukrainian cathedrals. A gilded cross stood atop a small old-model color TV set. The extended rabbit-ear antennas were canted at an odd angle.

He drew in a breath and called out, "FBI—don't move." Silence answered him. Nothing stirred inside. Maybe he was being overly cautious.

Craig smelled an odd, exotic, cinnamony smell, cuisine he'd never before tasted. But deeper and sharper, overlying the spices he smelled an acrid tang . . . smoke, smoldering plastic. He looked around, curious and quiet. The dim apartment seemed to be holding its breath.

They walked carefully across the spacious living room, sniffing, searching for the source of the odor. Moving in tandem, they turned right, following the acrid smell down a short hallway, past a bathroom and a musty guest room, then to Dumenco's small bedroom.

His computer had suffered a violent internal meltdown. The plastic slumped in on itself. Curls of brown-orange smoke oozed from the interior. His entire box of diskettes had likewise been slagged. Blackened and bubbly, melted polymers oozed across the desk, steaming on the surface.

Craig ran forward, waving his hands to clear the pungent smell from the air. "That's acid. I remember that stink from chemistry class," he said, covering his nose. It was already too late to prevent further damage. "Whoever sabotaged this wasn't taking any chances." The FBI had ways to find ghost phrasings from even the most carefully erased disk drives; but to Craig, it looked beyond hope.

"This was very recent," Jackson said quietly. He suddenly stood up straight, listening. With his other hand he flapped his fingers together in a gesture for Craig to continue talking.

The tall dark agent crept out of the room, following the noise he had heard. Feigning nonchalance, Craig spoke out loud as if Jackson were still beside him, "I'll check out the dresser. Dumenco could have hidden secret notes in the underwear drawer. Here, you take those over there."

Pulling out his weapon, Jackson remained outside the door, poised and ready to spring.

Craig opened the drawers, ruffling around in the clothes to provide a diversion for Jackson. Someone with very unorthodox methods had been here in the past hour, and they might not have finished their job.

Jackson inched down the hall, past the small bath and guest room. Still buying time for his partner, Craig opened another drawer and looked down into it. Under a spare set of bed sheets he found a framed photograph.

Curious, Craig pulled out a small, old snapshot of a young woman in her late twenties and two young children, both girls. Another photo showed a young man with the aquiline nose and facial features of Dumenco himself but subtly different—a son, perhaps?

Craig pocketed the photos, sure they might give him some lead to Dumenco's mysterious past. Jackson inched further down the hall. Craig slammed another dresser drawer. "Nothing in that one." Without another word, he trailed after Jackson.

Now he also heard a stealthy movement from the kitchen. Reaching into his pancake holster, Craig withdrew his handgun, wishing he still had his smaller caliber Beretta for these close quarters. They moved forward together in silence.

Sliding around the corner, he bumped one of the low pictures of an onion-domed cathedral. The frame smashed to the floor with a loud noise.

Knowing they had blown their ploy, he and Jackson

sprinted for the kitchen. "FBI!" he shouted. "Remain where you are."

Instead, they heard a loud splashing noise, something dumped into a bucket of water, then breaking glass in the kitchen window.

Both agents burst into the room, handguns drawn and looking for targets. "Don't move!" Jackson shouted.

Craig saw a figure duck through the smashed open window and land with a loud clang on the fire escape. "There he goes!" Craig said.

But before he could turn, they encountered a thick, billowing wall of greenish yellow smoke gushing into the small room. Noxious fumes belched from a bucket on the kitchen floor like deadly exhaust.

Without thinking, Craig gasped a deep breath and inhaled the gas. It felt as if someone had exploded firecrackers in his lungs. His eyes were on fire; his nostrils burned. He choked, staggering back. "Jackson, get—" He coughed and spluttered.

Enveloped by the greenish-yellow smoke, Jackson fell to his knees. Craig knew it was homemade chlorine gas, the kind used against American troops in World War I. Any first-year chemistry student knew how to make such a weapon from household chemicals. In the confined kitchen area, the gas was strong enough to overwhelm both men instantly.

Unable to breathe, Craig dropped to the floor himself, seeking cleaner air. Jackson collapsed beside him, wheezing. Like a distant hallucination he heard footsteps clanging down the fire escape and running away.

Desperately, Craig dragged himself toward the broken window and fresh air. He gulped in gasps that still reeked of chlorine but at least caused no further damage to his seared lungs.

The gas clouds clustered at the ceiling, making the paint blister.

Jackson wasn't moving, though, and so Craig turned back, grabbing his partner's collar, dragging him by the arms toward the air. Reaching out with one spasming hand, Craig fumbled with the back door, trying to turn the deadbolt. Finally, he succeeded in cracking open the porch door, which led out onto the wrought-iron balcony.

Craig and Jackson huddled by the door, trying to draw in deep breaths, but each gasp burned. Craig's lungs were ablaze, as if he had breathed in the acid that had been used to destroy Dumenco's computer. Jackson retched and coughed beside him, incapacitated. Craig raised his head to the window, took another huge gulp of fresh air.

On the other side of the building, he heard a car start, then drive off. Their attacker had escaped, but Craig couldn't continue the pursuit. He slumped back, struggling just to remain conscious.

Wednesday, 4:33 P.M.

Bangalore, India

Nicholas Bretti did not loosen his grip on his airline seat until the small plane had landed safely at the Bangalore airport. He wondered if he ever relax again, ever sleep without nightmares, would ever stop jumping and twitching at every little unexpected sound.

It wasn't likely to happen any time soon.

Exactly two hours after leaving Mr. Ambalal and the Liberty for All party in New Delhi—fifteen hours after taking off from O'Hare in Chicago, and less than a day after shooting an FBI agent—Bretti was sober and ready to meet the people who had paid his bills over the past year. He had to make this good, or else they would never help him out of this mess. What other choice did he have?

He worried that his reception in Bangalore would be no different from what he had experienced in New Delhi. Despite the $25,000 he had already pocketed, he was beginning to wonder if Chandrawalia would make good on his promise to come through with the rest of the money.

Twenty-five grand—a year's salary. Was that enough for the hell he had gotten himself into? Shit, no. Now it was up to the Indian government to salvage the situation, but he had no idea if they would be sympathetic.

Exiting the jet ramp into the terminal, Bretti was mobbed by a dozen children. They swarmed around him, plunging their hands into his pockets, searching for coins and jabbering the only English phrases they knew, "Please give, sir! Please give!"

Scents of incense and curry mixed with the pungent odor of unwashed bodies. Unprotected by the buffer of a customs area this time, Bretti fought his way through an ever-shifting mob toward the airport exit.

The terminal building bustled with people, some wearing sarongs, others, like the children around him, in shorts and dirty white T-shirts. He saw men, women, boys . . . but there were no little girls in sight. Maybe the families kept them locked up somewhere.

A cackling chicken flew into the air as a family tried to stuff it back into a cage at the check-in counter. A dark-robed old woman with a small gold stud through her nose and a red mark on her forehead, clutched a baby goat to her breast.

Fifty feet away by the outside door, a man wearing a black-and-yellow splotched shirt held up a sign, BRETTI. Bretti made eye contact with the man, who waved for him to follow. "Here, sir!"

Bretti pushed through a forest of chattering, begging children. They all tried to touch him, all pleaded for his help. Bretti felt one hand slip into his back pocket. Grabbing a slender wrist, Bretti whirled the young pickpocket around, keyed up and angry from his long tension.

With wild black hair and a dirty face, the boy could not have been older than ten. He laughed as Bretti held him up by his arm; the boy dangled in front of the other children and tried to swipe at Bretti with his free hand.

Before Bretti could admonish the pickpocket, another hand clawed at the back of his pants. Bretti threw the boy backward, bowling over two other children behind him. He knocked the prying hands away. "Get out of here, you little bastards!" He shouted, and the kids howled with laughter.

Bretti pushed his way through the crowd, paying no attention to who he ran into or pushed out of the way.

He kept a free hand on his wallet. The crowd parted as he shoved through.

The man with the sign waved out the door. He smiled beneath a scrawny mustache. "This way, please, sir." He disappeared from sight.

Bretti pushed out of the crowded building toward a dark blue sedan with tinted windows. A driver wearing a black British polo cap stood beside the long car. When he saw Bretti, he opened the car door.

The humid air still stank outside the terminal, but at least there were fewer people. Bretti strode toward the car, his skin crawling from the overpowering crowds. The driver opened the door, and Bretti dove into the luxury of the air-conditioned interior. As he relaxed back into the seat, someone pounded at the tinted window. It was the first boy who had tried to lift his wallet. The boy and two of his friends pressed their faces against the tinted window, trying to look in. They hammered with their fists, then pressed their tongues against the window, leaving long, slimy wet spots.

The man with the sign slipped into the car's front seat, and the driver pulled out immediately, oblivious to the children, the crowds, or any other obstacle. The first man turned and grinned. "Welcome to India, Dr. Bretti. How was your flight?"

"*Mr.* Bretti," he said sourly. The car moved slowly through road construction as they left the airport. "I have an important package in a diplomatic pouch—"

"We have made arrangements for it to be delivered, sir. Only the very best for your visit. The Sikander Lodi Research Center is only a short drive from here. You are to meet with the scientific staff before going to the Regency Hotel. Very nice accommodations—four-star."

"Great," muttered Bretti. "Four-star." He dreaded finding out what the Indians meant by that.

Looking through the saliva-streaked window, he spotted a gleaming, arrow-straight building that rose a hundred feet into the air, as modern as anything he would find in Chicago . . . but it was surrounded by dilapidated shacks that swarmed with pigs, chickens, and scrawny dogs. Barefoot men sat on their haunches smoking cigarettes while men in expensive suits hurried past them into the skyscraper. It was a comedy of extremes, an excess of dissonance. Two young men urinated openly against another ultra-modern building.

The limousine eased into a traffic circle behind a cart pulled by a camel. White Brahma bulls munched on grass in the center of the circle. A pair of monkeys scampered across the windshield, then dashed off onto the hood of another vehicle. Bicyclists, sandal-footed pedestrians, women in sarongs paraded in front of him. A dark *raj* wearing a British pith helmet, red jacket, and white gloves nonchalantly directed traffic at the end of the traffic circle.

Bretti shrank back in his seat, overwhelmed by the people, the chaos. "This is like wandering through the movie set of *Jumanji*."

His guide twisted in his seat. "Yes, much to see here, sir." He hesitated, as if worried he might offend Bretti. "If I may make a small suggestion, I noticed that sir was having difficulty with our street urchins. They mean no harm. But if sir would be kind enough to keep his wallet in his front pocket, then he will not have to worry."

Bretti grunted and transferred his wallet to his front pocket, dreading how much he would have to get used to in this crazy, mixed-up place. His stomach felt like lead. What if he had to remain here in exile for the rest of his life? Maybe even prison in the U.S. would be better than that.

The limo turned right and stopped at a gate in a high brick fence that shielded a large, enclosed compound from view. The driver flashed an ID, and the guard waved them through.

Once inside, Bretti felt as if he had been transported to another world. Yellow, red, and blue flowers provided startling color in immaculately groomed gardens arranged in curving lines that drew the eye toward a central white building, four stories tall. Neatly trimmed trees with white lines painted around their bases were widely spaced in radial lines emanating from the main building.

Bretti noticed several cottages and a dormitory beside the central building, with a volleyball net and swing sets in the rear. Three satellite dishes, each thirty feet in diameter, pointed at different azimuths. Aside from the guard that had waved them in, he saw no people or animals. Only blessed peace and quiet.

They drove along a curving path to the front of the building. A big-boned man with a potbelly and a blue turban stepped out from under an awning as the car glided to a stop. He made no attempt to open the passenger door, so Bretti opened it himself and stepped out.

"Dr. Bretti? I am Dr. Punjab, director of the Sikander Lodi Research Institute. Mr. Chandrawalia has told us much about you."

Bretti pressed his lips together. He was too weary and too frazzled to keep correcting these towelheads. How was he ever going to live here, settle down, adjust to this backward, noisy, crowded culture? "I'm glad to be here, finally. I've been told my equipment will be arriving here after me."

Dr. Punjab led him inside the main building. "Actually, your equipment arrived several minutes ago. We had a special courier meet your plane. Would you care to inspect your device in our high bay area?"

"Sure." Bretti followed Punjab inside the air-conditioned building, annoyed that his Penning trap was getting better treatment than he was. But he had gotten himself into this. Chandrawalia had made no promises, other than payment for the delivery of antiprotons stolen from the accelerator.

In the wide lobby, display cases showed scale models of huge capacitor banks, satellites, launch vehicles, and computer-generated images. Explanation cards beneath the models were written in nine different languages, English at the bottom.

A greeting line of eleven scientists and engineers, all but one wearing a turban, bowed and shook his hand. Everyone smiled. Bretti found most of their names impossible to pronounce, and his eyes glazed over.

Before they entered the high bay experimental area, one skinny man stepped up and said, "I am most anxious to learn about how you enhance your beam to increase p-bar production. It is a miraculous breakthrough."

"Uh, thanks." Bretti wondered if they would be very upset when they learned that the enhancement process had all been Dumenco's wild theory, not his own. And that he had brought the antimatter in one of the old, simple magnetic bottles instead of a crystal-lattice trap. But all they really wanted was the antimatter, for their high-tech medical applications and cancer treatment possibilities. They'd get the rest of the p-bars later; that was the important thing.

Dr. Punjab steered him up a long flight of metal stairs to a balcony that overlooked a cavernous high bay. Punjab's staff followed at a polite distance.

Four stories high and half a football field deep, the high bay experimental area sprawled in front of him. A yellow twenty-ton crane hung from the ceiling; white-painted concrete blocks each a yard long and two feet thick were stacked in a maze, creating small storage alcoves against the wall.

At the center of the high bay a tall cylinder stood twenty feet across with six blue rectangular arms, each as big as a boxcar, spread out radially like a six-sided star. Bretti saw the diplomatic pouch container holding the Penning trap near the central cylinder.

Dr. Punjab grasped the railing and spoke, pride evident in his voice. "This is Experiment three hundred twenty two, our one hundred megajoule capacitor bank. It is capable of discharging hundreds of megamperes of current in less than five microseconds to a center load—we can produce over thirty trillion watts of power here. It is the largest fast capacitor bank in the world." He pointed at a long, thin tube on the side of the bay near where Bretti's still-crated Penning trap sat. "Our anti-matter injector will dump your p-bars directly to the center of the load."

Bretti looked out over the experimental area and sniffed. "This looks like a high-current physics experiment. What does this have to do with medical applications? How are you going to treat patients if the machine is half the size of a hospital?"

"Medical applications? Oh, yes." Punjab smiled tightly. "This is a proof-of-principle experiment, Dr. Bretti. We have much larger plans for your antimatter."

Bretti glanced around the bay area. "Well, use it sparingly. I'm not sure when you'll be getting the rest."

Punjab scowled at him. "You are not in a position to dictate terms, Dr. Bretti. Come. You must show us how to extract the antimatter."

Bretti followed the chief scientist back down the metal stairs to the high bay floor. Whirring sounds of a machine shop came from a door at the base of the stairs. He smelled hot metal, lubricants, capacitor oils—refreshing after the nauseating smells of sardine-packed humanity. Technicians dressed in blue lab coats and orange or green pants milled around diagnostic units set in cement-block cubbyholes. Weirdly out of place, two guards with rifles sauntered along a catwalk, high above the floor.

Bretti peered at one of the capacitor boxes for Experiment 322, reading the manufacturer's mark on the side. "Maxwell capacitors? This all seems pretty standard for a high-capacitor lab." He glanced at the guards patrolling overhead. "Mr. Chandrawalia emphasized the need for secrecy. Why?"

Dr. Punjab studied Bretti for a moment. While the rest of his staff remained in the background, he brushed back his beard and spoke in slow, carefully measured tones.

"Mr. Chandrawalia explained to you the, ah, commercial applications of what we intend to do here? Manufacture artificial medical isotopes to sell on the world market?"

"Of course," said Bretti. "It would take years to get permission to do that at Fermilab—if they ever allowed it in the first place. The accelerator is a research tool, and if some congressman ever found out that we were pouring millions of dollars into underwriting India's latest commercial activity, he'd have a fit. But we're in *India* right now, and it seems a little cloak-and-daggerish to keep all this so secret."

"We have our own reasons for operating the way we do, Dr. Bretti. There are other countries, notably Pakistan, who would do anything to ruin things for us. There is intense competition for a niche in this, ah . . . *market*."

Bretti shrugged. India's preoccupation with Pakistan was similar to the U.S. and the ex-Soviet Union during the Cold War. But, whatever motivated a country wasn't his business. As long as he got his money, he didn't care. If they wanted guards around, they could keep them.

Punjab nodded toward Bretti's Penning trap, still in its shipping container. "Please, we are anxious to begin our experiments. Tell us about your increase in p-bar production, how you enhance your beam. This is accomplished by a resonance change in the cross-section, is it not? Where did you get the gamma ray laser to do this? And you need to show us how to extract the antimatter from the salt trap, as well."

Bretti quickly stifled his uneasiness. He had brought only a simple Penning trap, a normal, low-density magnetic bottle. Why did they keep harping on the crystal-lattice trap? It was a fairly standard design, one pioneered by stuffy old Nels Piter—but, boy, did Piter crow about his accomplishment again and again, until the Nobel committee had noticed him this year. But

then, Bretti knew people like Piter rarely produced more
than one important discovery in their lives . . . if that.

Of course, if Bretti himself had to stay on the run all
his life, lying low, he wouldn't have an opportunity to
do much better.

He quickly ran a hand through his dark goatee. "First
off, I'll need a 110-volt line to take over from the batteries." Bretti opened the lid of the shipping container
and rummaged through the packing material to expose
the cylindrical device. A blue-turbaned man brought
over an extension cord, and Bretti connected the trap.
Dr. Punjab's staff stood in a semicircle around him,
some quietly scribbling in black lab notebooks.

Bretti stepped back. Dr. Punjab leaned forward to inspect the device and frowned. "This is not a crystal-
lattice trap!" He looked up, scowling. "Do you take me
for a fool? This magnetic bottle cannot hold nearly
enough antimatter for what we need!"

Baffled, Bretti shrugged. "What difference does it
make? I've got some p-bars, and that's what you want.
Enough for you to get started. This trap holds about ten
to the fifth particles—"

Dr. Punjab bellowed, "We need *trillions* of times
more than that! This is a joke! You bring us a *picogram*
when we need milligrams. What are you trying to do,
Dr. Bretti? Where is the rest of the antimatter you promised?" He breathed heavily through his flared nostrils.
Punjab's staff murmured angrily behind him.

"Calm down, would you?" Bretti glanced around,
and the men seemed to step closer to him, closing in,
threatening. The armed guards on the catwalk above
paused and stared down at him. "Look, we had an explosion. An accident happened at the Tevatron. The
beam fluctuated and my full crystal-lattice trap dumped
its entire load of p-bars. This magnetic bottle holds the
most antimatter I could divert from an unenhanced beam
in a single day. I had to get out of there, fast!"

"We paid you in advance, Dr. Bretti. We expect you to meet your obligations."

Bretti nervously wet his lips. "You gave me a down payment, and I'm giving you a down payment. I have until next month to deliver the p-bars, per our agreement. I had to come to India . . . early. Things happened back at Chicago, and since I had these particles in storage, I thought I could get a jump on things and deliver some of them now, allow you to start your experiments with a little amount, just as you wanted."

"We have no time for this nonsense." Punjab angrily dismissed him with a wave. "Go home, Dr. Bretti. I will ask Mr. Chandrawalia to use another source to get our antimatter, and you can forfeit the rest of your payment."

Bretti's heart pounded with panic. So much for remaining here, for requesting asylum, for going to ground in Bangalore. If he even mentioned his crime, about being on the run, Punjab would probably truss him up and deliver him directly to the authorities.

"No, wait! I can do it. Really, I can. I already have another working crystal-lattice trap installed in one of the substations. The Tevatron is running almost nonstop now, and with Dumenco's beam enhancements I can get you a milligram of p-bars in a few days." He looked wildly from side to side, seeking support from anyone on Dr. Punjab's staff. They all looked at him skeptically.

He continued to jabber. "Look, I've gone through a dry-run this time. The production cross section has increased and I've diverted antimatter from the enhanced beam. I proved I can safely transport p-bars in a diplomatic pouch. It'll be easy to bring you the rest of them. I can be back next week. Two at the most."

Dr. Punjab stared at him, tight-lipped, considering. Bretti knew they had him over a barrel. A squat technician stepped over to Punjab and whispered rapidly in a foreign language. Surprised, Punjab asked a question in the same language. The squat man strode to a telephone by the wall, dialed a number, and waited for a moment before speaking.

Bretti shifted his weight from foot to foot during the exchange, antsy, but he forced himself to keep quiet. Inside, he felt furious with Dumenco. The old scientist was responsible for getting Bretti into this whole mess by botching his work, somehow causing the beam-dump accident that resulted in the power shutdown, and causing the failure of the antimatter-loaded crystal-lattice trap.

Finally, the technician got off the telephone and reported back. Dr. Punjab nodded stiffly, then turned to Bretti. He seemed to force the words, as if having great difficulty keeping his temper in check.

"It is . . . unfortunate that you did not tell us from the beginning that you did not bring all the antimatter. But you are right: You have shown that it is possible to divert the p-bars and transport them here. Now, you will return to Chicago immediately and bring us back what you have promised."

He motioned with his head and two younger staff members stepped forward. "My colleagues will escort you back to the airport. The Concord leaves New Delhi in six hours." He pressed his lips together and stared at Bretti for a moment. "Do not fail us again. Mr. Chandrawalia will go to great lengths to ensure that the money he has already paid you is not wasted. He will meet with you again to make sure you understand."

Bretti swallowed, knowing that he had just been, reluctantly, given a second chance. He tried to look grateful. "I'll be back in a week. I promise."

But as he turned to go, he didn't know what he dreaded more—returning to Chicago and the manhunt arrayed for him, or coming back and being stuck here for the rest of his life.

Wednesday, 12:07 P.M.

Fox River Medical Center

After driving at breakneck speed from the Fermilab Public Affairs Office, Paige hurried down the corridor in the medical center. Her dress shoes clicked along the much-scuffed linoleum floor. She dodged nurses and orderlies with carts, family members taking older relatives out in their wheelchairs for a stroll. No one seemed particularly concerned to see a young woman dashing down the hall, scanning the room numbers. In the hospital it happened all the time.

"I'm spending altogether too much time in this place," she muttered.

Finally, she found the examining room where Craig Kreident sat looking gray and shaken. Even from here she could smell the reek of chlorine bleach.

Without noticing her, he tried to regain his self-composure by retying his tie. Craig coughed again, wiped his reddened eyes, then looked down at his uncooperative fingers. He flexed them and tried once more to knot the necktie.

"I can help with that," Paige said. She was glad to see how his face lit up when he saw her. She stepped behind him, put both hands over his shoulders and pressed close as she untied his abortive attempt at a knot.

Adjusting the ends, she flipped the necktie around until she had knotted it properly. It had been a long time since she'd fixed a man's necktie. It wasn't normally a skill young women needed to learn, especially in these days of increasingly casual attire. But Paige had learned in order to help her father when he had grown weak from the cancer that sapped his strength.

Working in California and Nevada for the nuclear weapons industry, Gordon Mitchell had preferred to wear a bolo tie, if any at all, but occasional design reviews or government inspections required extra formality. Paige had assisted him on those mornings when he fretted over his wardrobe so much he didn't even take time to gulp his usual coffee and orange juice.

Craig looked as though he still felt the terrible effects of his bout with homemade chlorine gas. She felt a pang of sympathy as she finished straightening his tie. Craig stood up and gave her a grateful look as he brushed down his white shirt front. He coughed, still reluctant to draw a deep breath into damaged lungs. He reached for his suit jacket like a knight replacing a battered set of armor after losing a jousting tournament.

"I can't imagine you went through all this just to become a blonde," Paige said with an impish grin as she ruffled her fingers through his chestnut hair. "There are easier ways to bleach your hair."

He looked up at her, as if trying to regain his sense of humor. "And what would *you* know about bleaching, ma'am?"

Paige laughed and stepped back, crossing her arms over her denim blouse. Craig attempted to laugh along with her, but broke into another coughing fit. Sitting down hard, he picked up a blue plastic pitcher on the table and poured himself a cup of water. He swallowed two long gulps and then spat into the sink. "My mouth tastes awful."

"Yes, but your tongue is a very clean shade of white," she said.

He looked in the mirror, sticking his tongue out.

"So, are you really all right?" Paige said with genuine concern.

Craig ran water in the sink and splashed his face. "My eyes burn, my nose burns, my throat burns, my lungs burn—but all in all, it's been a pretty good day. No question in my mind that we've got a real case here . . . as if I had any doubts in the first place."

"Who could it have been?" she asked. "Did you see the person who attacked you? What was he looking for in Dumenco's apartment?"

Craig shook his head. "We interrupted him, but he managed to destroy Dumenco's home computer. All of his disks, maybe just as a precaution. But Dumenco wasn't dumb enough to do any important research on his home computer, with no security."

"His work wasn't classified, so he could have worked at home whenever he wanted."

"Sure, but Dumenco's real 'home' was in his lab anyway. He wouldn't have stayed in his apartment when he could have been at Fermilab. That apartment was just a place where he went to sleep once in a while."

Paige laid a hand on his shoulder. "How's Jackson?"

"Seems to be all right," Craig said. "Trish hasn't come in to check on us yet—apparently she's away from the hospital. But the attending physician says we'll both recover. That chlorine gas knocked us flat, but we got to the window soon enough, managed to crack the door open a bit. No permanent damage." He took another slow, gradual breath, musing. "I wonder what Jackson would look like as a blond?"

"Probably not any better than you," she chuckled.

Craig broke out coughing instead. "I'll be all right. Just need a little rest."

"What you need is a good dinner, the best Chicago cuisine has to offer."

"As long as it's not more bratwursts and sauerkraut." Craig looked over at her. "Are you asking me out on a date, Ms. Mitchell?"

"It *is* the nineties," she said, feeling warm inside. *Yes,* she thought, *it would be good to start seeing him again.* She hadn't realized until just that moment that she really did miss his smile. Not that she didn't enjoy formal dinners with Nels Piter, but Craig had a certain naive honesty she had come to miss, and that was something Piter certainly didn't have.

She grew serious. "I think we should spend some time discussing the case. You know, like old times back in Livermore or out in Las Vegas."

"It's a deal," Craig said, "but I need to change clothes first."

She wrinkled her nose at the lingering chlorine smell. "Yes, Craig, I think that would be a good idea."

When Paige stepped out of the examining room, she saw Trish LeCroix waiting by the door. As Paige exited, Trish looked down at a sheaf of papers, as if pretending she hadn't been eavesdropping or wanting to see Craig herself. "Why, it's Dr. LeCroix," Paige said. "Craig was just looking for you."

"Call me Patrice," she said stiffly. Her words bore little friendliness.

"How is Craig's condition?" Paige asked.

Trish flipped her papers over. "I wouldn't know. I've been busy. Now if you'll excuse me." She turned to walk down the hall, and Paige had to hurry to keep up with her. Craig had described Trish as being somewhat cold and self-centered, and Paige could see how the woman gave that impression.

"Wait," said Paige. "Have you talked with his doctor?"

"I'm sure he'll be all right," Trish said offhandedly. "The fumes only caused a bit of superficial damage. He'll have chest pains for a while, maybe an occasional bloody nose from the damaged soft tissue, but nothing too serious. Agent Jackson's worse off, but he's tough. They'll be back on the case without even taking time for a coffee break. FBI agents, you know—they think they've got to be more macho than anybody else."

Paige wondered why Trish was so cold and impatient. Out of curiosity, she had tracked down some of "P. LeCroix's" impassioned editorials written for the Bulletin of the Physicians for Responsible Radiation Research. Her writings were anything but lukewarm.

"If you'll excuse me," Trish said, "we all have very little time. Craig had a trivial exposure to a mundane hazard that anybody could concoct with a few household chemicals. It's nothing compared to what Georg Dumenco is going through." She pressed her lips together in a frown. "There's only so much sympathy in the world, and every patient can't have all of it."

Paige blinked and stopped in her tracks, letting Trish continue toward the Intensive Care ward. She found the other woman's behavior to be very odd—very odd indeed.

Wednesday, 7:48 P.M.

Batavia, IL

Holding a hand to his mouth as he coughed, Craig paced the lobby of Little Naples, waiting for Paige. The small restaurant had dark wood paneling that had been popular several decades ago. It was adorned with scenes from the Italian Alps, photographs of immigrants, and an old coat of arms. A local hole in the wall, Paige had said, with extremely good Italian food.

Craig wore a maroon tie, white shirt, and a dark blue suit while his other clothes were cleaned to remove the chlorine smell, though he doubted they could be salvaged. At least now that he was on "official travel," the Bureau paid per diem for sundries such as dry cleaning—and for a new suit, since the old one had been damaged in the line of duty.

Paige walked in wearing the same light blouse and blue skirt she had worn at the hospital, but she had added a smart-fitting jacket and a string of pearls. Craig held out both hands to greet her. "You look great."

"Thanks." Paige squeezed his hands, then flipped her blond hair behind her shoulders. "How are you feeling?"

Craig gave a wan smile, then coughed again. "Hanging in there. Trish seems to think I'll recover quickly."

Paige became serious. "Yes. *Patrice* takes your accident pretty lightly, from what I could see. You've got to take care of yourself—otherwise, you'll be sharing a room with Goldfarb.''

Craig blinked. *Did she just not get along with Trish, or was there a hint of jealousy?* He never had a problem reading body language of suspects—he wished he could do the same with Paige . . . and Trish. He forced a smile. ''At least I'm glad we got a chance to be alone. I'd like to go over some details of the case—after all, we've got a good track record of working together so far.''

Paige cleared her throat as she stepped up to the hostess. ''Mitchell, party of three. Reservations at eight.''

As the young lady ran her finger down a list of names, Craig lifted his eyebrows. ''Three?''

Paige stepped quickly after the hostess, as if she didn't want to talk about it. ''Nels is joining us, if that's all right. I thought it would be good to include him in the discussions.''

Craig's face grew warm. He followed Paige as they wound around tables to a private area by the window. Three place settings adorned a red tablecloth, rotated 90 degrees on top of a white tablecloth. Large red wine glasses and smaller white wine glasses sparkled in the flicker of a single candle. A long-stemmed red rose perched in a clear vase. The hostess moved to pull out a chair for Paige, but Craig stepped forward and beat her to it.

After taking his seat, Craig scanned Paige's face. ''So far, you're the only person I've discounted from Dumenco's case. I don't think it's a good idea to talk about the case in front of Dr. Piter. He could be the man responsible.''

''Nels a suspect? Oh, Craig, he's a perfect gentleman and well respected in his field. It would be like Albert Einstein killing someone out of professional jealousy. He may have a big ego—''

''I'll say,'' muttered Craig, unfolding his napkin.

''But he means well,'' continued Paige.

Craig stopped his retort as a busboy silently poured

water for them. After he left, Craig leaned forward and spoke with carefully measured words. "Someone *did* try to kill Dumenco. Someone *did* destroy his home computer and his personal files. That substation exploded, Goldfarb was shot, and Jackson and I were attacked with chlorine gas. All this might have something to do with Dumenco's work, or the Nobel Prize, or Dumenco's past."

Paige frowned. "Just another one of your complicated cases, Craig."

"Dumenco himself is keeping information from me. I'm not sure what it is, but he's hiding something. And on top of that, he's more concerned with his experimental results than in helping me out. Until I learn otherwise, Nels Piter is going to have to remain a suspect."

He paused for a moment, trying not to change the subject too obviously. "So, just how well have you known Dr. Piter the past year?" He studied her face, looking for any clues as to exactly *what* type of relationship Paige had with the research director.

Paige smiled coyly as she reached for her glass of water. "Craig, now what do you mean by that?"

He fumbled with his napkin. "What's your professional relationship with Dr. Piter?"

"Oh, I thought you were concerned about something else."

He raced through several comebacks, and almost told her the truth—that yes, dammit, he did have feelings for her—but then a thin, nasal voice interrupted them. "Paige, sorry I'm late. I was on the phone with a colleague in Stockholm—he had gotten up early to call me, so I had to hear him out." Nels Piter walked briskly up, bent down and kissed Paige on the cheek.

Paige smiled. "Craig and I just got here, Nels."

Piter took notice of Craig for the first time and curtly extended his hand. "Agent Kreident, good evening. Nice of you to invite me along tonight."

"Yes," answered Craig in a monotone. "Glad you could make it."

The cocktail waitress stepped to the side of the table. "Excuse me, would you care for a drink?"

Piter spoke before either of them could respond. "We'll have a bottle of your best Chianti, please." He shooed her away as Craig scowled, since he didn't particularly like wine. Paige didn't complain, though he had expected her to order an imported Italian beer or something.

The Belgian scientist had high color in his cheeks as he told Paige about the phone call. He made no attempt to hold the details quiet, speaking just loudly enough that the nearest tables could hear. "So I have it on authority that the committee has down-selected to a short list of three candidates."

"And you're one of the finalists?" Paige asked.

Piter toyed with his empty wine glass. "Marvelous, isn't it? They're going to announce the winner Friday. And the latest copy of *Phys Rev Letters* hits the stands tomorrow with the latest Fermilab results of my anti-matter trap design." He threw a glance at Craig. "The device I invented while at CERN. The timing of the article couldn't be better."

"What about the other two finalists?" Craig asked. "Do you know who they are?" He coughed.

"No," said Piter curtly, "just that I'm on the short list. But now that the chances are down to one in three, I can win against anyone."

"Even Georg Dumenco?"

Piter looked as if he had swallowed something very sour. "He's probably on the short list as well. Georg is one of those rare individuals who could have won the Nobel at any time—if not this year, then the next, or the one after. He is extremely well known and liked. And as a Ukrainian, he is a favorite of the judges. So he is sure to win one of these years."

"He's not going to have another chance," Craig said,

coughing to the side. "He'll be dead in a few days."

"Pity they can't award it posthumously." Piter hesitated. He looked down at his empty wine glass and spoke with a hint of bitterness, and with a suddenly quiet voice. "But for me . . . this may be my final chance. My work is several years old, and that's why I'm hoping this new paper will generate some excitement." He looked at Paige. "I cannot afford to let chance play a part in the selection."

Craig folded his hands on the tablecloth, speaking calmly as he watched Piter. "So what does the Nobel process involve? I'm not familiar with the details."

Piter raised his chin, taking on the air of a lecturer as the cocktail waitress returned with a bottle of wine. He dismissed her with a wave after she opened the bottle and poured glasses for each of them.

"Each year the physics committee invites thousands of scientists, members of scientific academies, and university professors throughout the world to nominate candidates for the Nobel Prize. As you can imagine, the competition is intense, and I've been subtly campaigning for years. The nominations are then investigated by dozens of experts appointed by the Nobel foundation. The committee then makes a selection among the candidates and submits a short list of three finalists."

Paige looked at him with a bit too much admiration, as far as Craig was concerned. "So that's where you are now," she said.

Craig pushed his wine glass aside without taking a drink. "I always thought the Nobel Prize was awarded years after a big discovery, so the long-term ramifications could be assessed."

Piter took another sip of the deep red wine and forced a smile. "Yes, indeed. Science is about peer review and reproducible results. The work must be held up and inspected for flaws, and it takes *years* to assess its impact on the body of science. Einstein himself won the prize not for his theory of relativity, but for his much earlier work on the photoelectric effect, which eventually led to the founding of the quantum theory.

"I'll be blunt. My original work at CERN was responsible for my appointment as Director of High-Energy Physics at Fermilab. My novel method of storing antimatter is once again summarized in this new paper, which cements all of those assessments with hard data from the Tevatron."

A waiter appeared at their table in a long-sleeved white shirt and charcoal gray tie. He carried three black folders. "May I interest you in a menu?"

Craig wondered if Piter was going to unilaterally order for them as well. The Belgian research director still had a motive to kill Dumenco, but it didn't seem prudent for Piter to talk so much about the competition. Then again, after working on high-tech crimes for several years now, *nothing* would surprise Craig.

He spoke aloud as he accepted his menu. "Well, I wish you the best of luck, sir. But it's too bad Dr. Dumenco won't have another chance to compete for the prize. He may not even have this one."

Thursday, 4:39 A.M.

O'Hare International Airport

The Concord eased down from Mach 2, approaching the continental U.S. from the north at seven hundred miles an hour, faster than any other airliner in the world. Half asleep, groggy and stiff from time changes, jet lag, and cramped quarters, Nicholas Bretti could have calculated the needle-nosed plane's altitude and temperature from the Mach number displayed on the front bulkhead; but his mind was focused elsewhere, seething.

Even when they had sent him packing, the damned Indians couldn't resist pushing him around. Where did they get off? He was the one risking his neck, he had gotten the opportunity for them. So what if he had managed to bring only a portion of the antimatter he had promised? He was still early, and he had the means to get the rest.

However, upon returning to the U.S., he just might find himself the target of an FBI manhunt. Bretti would have to be very careful. He needed to slip in, grab the hidden crystal-lattice trap from the substation, and arrange to drop it off—but not before Chandrawalia made some further guarantees. Bretti couldn't wait to have words with the smug, whip-thin man from the Embassy. After all, if Bretti got caught, he was damned well going to bring the rest of them down with him and expose all their embarrassing commercial plans.

Too bad he wouldn't have time to pay his respects to

old Dumenco. He wondered if the Ukrainian slave master had kicked off yet. In his imagination, Bretti pictured the physicist writhing in a hospital bed with his skin sloughing off, his hair falling out, his gums bleeding. Dangerous stuff, that radiation. The most amazing part, though, was that Dumenco had been exposed while doing his own work for a change, rather than bossing around his pet grad student.

Still a graduate student. After seven years of research, chasing down elusive leads to prove a new theory, spending all-nighters analyzing someone else's data and trying to contribute to the next experiment on the massive accelerator, he was ABD—All But Dissertation.

Anyone else would have received a doctorate by now, donning the long, black robe, the maroon-and-blue head ornament of the Ph.D. Each year Bretti watched the graduation ceremonies at the University of Chicago, but never as a participant; instead, he stood back and let the others have their fifteen minutes in the spotlight. He watched as new lawyers were awarded their JDs after only three years of law school; watching new doctors awarded MDs after only four years of med school.

And these people called themselves *professionals*! All they had to do was memorize esoteric law cases or obtuse medical language and they "earned" their degrees. These people didn't know about spending *years* in research with a perfectionist, domineering advisor who was never satisfied with what had been done before.

Bretti wanted his name *first* on a research paper, not just as one of the coauthors. Everyone in the technical community knew that the real work was done by the first author. After seven years of kissing up to Dumenco, jumping every time the old scientist snapped his fingers, Bretti deserved a little credit of his own.

And some extra cash. He was tired of living in poverty, eking by on a graduate assistantship's salary. Chandrawalia had given him an opportunity to rise above all that—but now it looked as if he would fall on his face.

At the University of Chicago, Bretti had sought out Georg Dumenco, a respected researcher from the Ukraine, fresh off the boat with mind-boggling ideas of using gamma-ray lasers to induce cascades of antimatter in normal particle reactions. Dumenco had obtained an appointment at Fermilab and needed a grad student . . . just as Bretti was finishing his Ph.D. coursework.

It was the dream of a lifetime. And Bretti had worked like a dog for the following seven years, doing *Dumenco's* work instead of his own. He'd had no chance even to think for himself, much less make his own breakthroughs. Seven wasted years.

Now, stepping nervously from the narrow, air-conditioned Concord into the Chicago airport, Bretti felt as if he had entered another world. The sleek supersonic jet had been a vision of the future, a flying metal island kept immaculately clean and incredibly well-maintained; Chicago's O'Hare airport was a nightmare that couldn't heave itself out of the past.

Bretti bristled at the flood of memories the airport gave him. Even so early in the morning, people jostled his elbows, running past without excusing themselves; lingering scents from the previous day—stale beer, burnt bratwurst, airport pizza, and popcorn—rolled over him. Coffee vendors began to open their awnings, preparing for a new day.

Bretti searched the area for a representative from the Indian consulate, someone who would expedite him through customs. But no one waited for him. Typical. He was on his own, and he would have to handle everything himself.

Bretti snorted and fell into line, waiting with the other passengers as they trudged through customs. "Anything to declare?" He moved slowly up the line, wondering if surly Dr. Punjab had already yelled at Chandrawalia for sending him without the promised amount of antimatter.

He saw airport security, saw TV cameras, wondering

if the FBI was already mounting its forces to rush him. What if they had a warrant for his arrest? What if they had seen him step off the Concord? But why would they suspect he had gone to India in the first place? As far as anyone knew, Nicholas Bretti was still down in West Virginia on a fishing trip.

As he stood in line, he flipped through a newspaper he had bought, searching for a notice about the FBI agent he had shot. Maybe it was old news already. Finally, he discovered a small article about Dumenco and his condition, with a mention of the FBI investigator who had been wounded during the investigation and remained in critical condition.

Alive! The man was alive! Bretti swallowed hard. At least he wouldn't be wanted for murder then, and the FBI agent just might recover. Bretti couldn't decide if that was better for him, or worse.

By the time he cleared customs—thankfully without incident—he was fuming at the ineptness of all civil servants, but more miffed at India for not taking care of him. *They just flew me around the friggin' world in three days—you'd think they'd pay a little attention to getting me back here.*

If he'd had better sense, he would have gone right to the Pakistani consulate and offered *them* the new batch of p-bars. That would show the smug Indians, rub their faces in it, just as they had rubbed his face in the fact that he didn't have his Ph.D. He allowed himself a slim grin at the thought of offering hot new medical technology right to India's biggest enemy. Serve them right!

"Hey, open your eyes!" A large woman, all three hundred pounds of her, glared through thick glasses at him, lumbering out of his way. Not that he could have missed her, with hips the size of Greater Chicago.

Bretti clenched his teeth. He'd had it with people— the crowds, the rudeness, the self-centeredness. "Put on a WIDE LOAD sign, lady. You're taking up half the concourse."

"That's tough titty, you little wimp."

Bretti gawked at her huge breasts, each the size of a watermelon. "And I bet they are."

The woman glared at him, but he pushed past her to the escalator before she could react. He had meant to catch a taxi to the Indian consulate downtown where he could pick up his red Saturn, but he was too focused now on accomplishing unfinished business, business he should have taken care of *years* ago.

He didn't have much time . . . the crystal-lattice trap could wait only another few hours. At the end of the week he could ditch the leased car, fly out with the stash of p-bars, and finally start his life all over again.

If the Indians paid him.

Thursday, 6:12 A.M.

Fox River Medical Center

Silence. He stopped just outside the hospital room.

The hallway was deserted. No visitors, no sounds. Nearly six in the morning, too early for the nurses to be making their rounds, yet late enough that the floor nurse would be dozing. He had checked only seconds before. All clear.

The hall lights were dimmed, half the medical center's fluorescent banks shut down. The only sounds from the other rooms were faint snoring, a cough down the hall, and the constant *ping* of an assisted breathing device. Hospitals never entirely shut down, but they certainly became quiet.

Every movement required stealth, any misstep might cause a disaster. Murder was a tricky business, if you didn't want to get caught.

He stepped up to a dark, unguarded room. No plaque gave the patient's name, but this had to be it—a private room, an updated checklist for the radiation-health specialist . . . a small Ukrainian flag taped over the nameplate. The bastard had never officially renounced his citizenship. The gall!

He glanced down the hallway as someone walked past the cross corridor whistling an old Top 40 tune that echoed through the sleeping building. His first instinct was to flee, to dive into the shadows and hide—but he kept moving, untroubled, unnoticed. That was the key. The night worker paid no attention to him.

Perfect disguise, chameleon, blend into even this odd environment. He wore stolen green surgery garb, and the mask and cap gave him anonymity; a stolen ID badge gave him an appropriate name, if such was required.

He pushed open the door to Georg Gregorivich Dumenco's room. The hinges were quiet, the lights out. A dim trickle of dawn gleamed through the slitted blinds, dappling the waxed floor. The old scientist lay on his side snoring gently, a sheet pulled up nearly to his head and the blanket twisted around his feet. An IV line hung from a bottle and snaked into the old man's arm. No one sat vigil with him, waiting to hear deathbed confessions—no family, no friends, no graduate students. Even here, even now, the physicist had isolated himself from his family.

The legendary Ukrainian scientist, all alone. Helpless.

Reaching into a long pocket beneath the baggy surgery pants, he withdrew a tightly folded sterile green cloth. He quickly unwrapped the cloth to expose a thin surgical knife, carbon steel, razor sharp. The blade caught a flicker of light in a crazy pattern dancing against the wall.

Dumenco didn't stir. It would be like slicing the throat of a sleeping bull, a powerful enough animal when awake, but now unprotected and powerless. *How many times had Dumenco been this close, so helpless?* The timing was never right, the circumstances never so crucial. Only recently had things changed enough to demand action.

Dumenco just couldn't leave well enough alone.

Padding silently across the room, he stood beside the dying man's bed. Clear target. He did not want to risk reaching over the old scientist, whose arm could block the slicing motion across the throat. The cut would have to be a quick slash at arm's length to prevent the blood from jetting onto his stolen hospital garb. That would draw attention during his exit. No clues could be left, no path of the Ukrainian's blood. He would wipe the blade on the bedsheet and disappear into the night.

Keeping a firm grip on the delicate surgical knife, he crouched down and slipped the blade under Dumenco's chin—

"Hey, what are you doing in here?" A woman's voice shattered the silence. "This is my patient."

He jerked away, nearly tripping as he stumbled back. The half blinds on the window slapped as he backed into them. Dumenco stirred but didn't wake up.

The room lights blinked on, filling the white-walled suite with a harsh, overpowering glare. A woman in a white lab coat carried a cup of coffee in a cafeteria cup, held a sheaf of papers in the other hand. A stethoscope hung around her neck; delicate glasses highlighted her face. Dr. Patrice LeCroix. He had talked to her before, one of the more outspoken members of the Physicians for Responsible Radiation Research.

Now she was in the wrong place at the wrong time, and she had spoiled everything.

Her mouth hung open, halfway between astonishment and horror. Coffee sloshed on the floor. He twirled, keeping the masked face and eyes away from her. Cursing, he brought down his head and launched himself toward the door. Before she could sound an alarm. Before she could recognize him.

The woman raised her voice, terrified as well as indignant. "What the hell are you doing here?" Her sheaf of papers fell to the floor as he charged past her. She opened her mouth as if to scream, but no sound came out, only a faint gurgling. Her attention was torn between stopping him and checking on her patient.

He briefly considered killing both her and Dumenco, but precious time had already been lost, attention already directed toward the sleepy room. In a moment, the night nurse would run to investigate, police would be called, an intensive search would be initiated.

Dumenco struggled up in bed now, awake but befuddled.

During his flight, he shoved Dr. LeCroix aside. She fell against the visitor's chair by the door. Coffee spilled over her and on his stolen hospital garb. He felt the hot liquid soaking through, burning. *Not blood, but coffee stains on the surgical garb.* He would be easily spotted, identified.

Slamming the door behind him to gain an extra few seconds, he sprinted away as Dr. LeCroix shouted for help. His shoes squeaked as he ran down the hallway, leaving smudges on the freshly waxed floor.

Within minutes in the parking lot, in his car, on the streets, he could elude any pursuit. Dumenco remained alive, still dangerous—and now he would be even more concerned.

All the more reason to do it right the next time.

Thursday, 7:04 A.M.

Fox River Medical Center

After the early morning attempt on Dumenco's life, Craig rushed in from a restless night's sleep. The Ukrainian was only a day or two away from death anyway—but Craig wouldn't stand by while someone tried to hurry him along. He had heard on the radio on the way in that the Nobel Prize in Chemistry had been announced, and Craig felt a tightening in his gut. The countdown was ticking—if the Nobel could not be awarded to a dead man, had an unconfident Nels Piter tried to increase his own odds?

Hospital security had already swarmed around the site, to no effect. Craig had called the Chicago Bureau office, roused Agent Schultz, and asked for him to assign a protection detail to the medical center. The other agent preferred to be in the thick of things himself, rather than snooping around the site of a days-old blast. The attack on both Goldfarb and Dumenco had finally lent a sense of legitimacy to Craig's own investigation. This entire case went far beyond a mysterious explosion at an uninhabited blockhouse.

Craig also started the Chicago office on setting up a news blackout for Dumenco's protection, keeping all reporters off the hospital floor. It infuriated him that the media had also begun pestering Goldfarb's wife about her husband's shooting and his involvement in the case.

Trish LeCroix stood outside the door to Dumenco's

room, bustling in and around the guards, trying to get her duties done. Before she noticed Craig approaching, he took a mental snapshot of her demeanor, assessing her state of mind. Trish's skin was grayish, her expression tight with confusion and self-doubt. He put it down to her being flustered at being caught in the eye of an unexpected storm; she had always hated it when things didn't go her way, according to a rigid plan. She had enough stress tending the dying scientist, but thwarting a would-be killer wasn't her job. Craig was the one who chased after the bad guys.

When Trish saw him, she strode forward quickly, gave him a hug. He squeezed back, but she broke the embrace quickly.

"Is Dumenco all right?" Craig asked. "Are *you* all right?" He coughed to the side; at least his own gas poisoning symptoms were nearly gone.

"We were very lucky," she said. "But Georg is already in a fragile state. He's entering the final stages of systemic collapse from the radiation exposure. He's quite distraught at the moment."

"Well, I would be too if someone had tried to kill me," Craig said. "But maybe Dumenco managed to recognize something about the killer that could give us the breakthrough we need, if it's shaken him enough to get him to talk. I still think Dumenco's been hiding too much from us."

"Yes, but he was asleep at the time. Besides, I expect to see mental effects from central nervous system damage very soon now. I wouldn't consider him to be completely reliable." She glanced down at her clipboard, avoiding his gaze. "Uh, a delusional state is also likely."

Craig reached into his pocket and withdrew the family photos he'd picked up from Dumenco's apartment. "Maybe this will jog his memory."

They placed sterile masks over their faces, then entered the room. It was a useless gesture to protect the scientist from infection in that way. The radiation had critically damaged his immune system, so his injured body couldn't resist infection. And it had destroyed the lining of his intestines, letting the trillions of innocuous bacteria that normally lived there gain easy access to his bloodstream. It was *those* microbes, deep inside him and now made deadly, that would soon make him go into shock—and die.

Dumenco sat up, wild eyed. "Go away—away from me!" he croaked, as if afraid Craig intended to kill him as well.

Craig stood back in shock, his stomach knotting in revulsion to see how much the physicist's condition had degenerated overnight. His skin was scarlet, and his joints were so swollen he could barely move. His eyes were crimson, covered with a thin film of blood from hemorrhaging vessels.

"Georg, it's us," Trish said in an attempt to be soothing, but her voice came out dry and strained. "Dr. LeCroix and Agent Kreident. You're safe. We have extra guards at your room.

The scientist sagged, and recognition seeped into his face. Craig came closer. "We need to talk to you, Dr. Dumenco. Please, who did this? What did you see?"

Overnight, more medical instruments had been hooked up to his disintegrating body, replacing fluids, deadening the spreading pain, suppressing nausea and raising his dwindling blood pressure. Oxygen tanks had been wheeled in beside his bed, with a respirator mask that he had removed; Craig could still see the marks the mask had pressed into the damaged skin of his face. Only apparatus kept his lungs breathing, his heart beating.

Dumenco squirmed away as Craig spoke firmly. "Dr. Dumenco, you must have some idea who this man was. Why did he try to kill you?"

"No!" he said, moaning as he turned from side to side. Part of the skin on his shoulder split open, oozing blood-tinged fluid, like sap from a sliced-open tree. "I have put us all in danger. I brought this upon myself, and I won't make it worse. Better just to let it die, let *me* die!"

Craig seized on the words and leaned forward. "So you do have an idea! Who is it? We have to stop him."

Dumenco shook his head. "If they knew enough about my work at Fermilab, if they were worried about what I would reproduce, if they could get inside and cause my accident . . . they can find *anyone*."

Trish backed away, sickened and deeply concerned. Her professional demeanor dissolved into that of someone emotionally attached to the patient. "They've been looking for a long time, haven't they, Georg?"

Craig turned to her, struck by her reaction. "Do *you* know something? Trish, what aren't you telling me?"

"Nothing," Trish stammered. "I . . . I'm still shaken by the killer."

Dumenco slumped back in his bed. "Perhaps it is best if you ignore the case, Agent Kreident. Call it an accident, and everything will be neatly explained. I never should have brought you here."

Craig crunched his jaws together in an effort to remain calm. Trying a different tack, he removed the photographs from his jacket pocket. "Dr. Dumenco, take a look at these photos, please. Who are these people, and why did you have their photographs hidden in your drawer?"

The dying physicist blinked and stared, trying to focus his eyes—and then he recoiled in shock. Tears began to stream down the old scientist's face. As his body wracked with sobs, a line of blood trickled out of his mouth. But he refused to answer.

Trish saw the pictures and gasped in surprise. Craig glared at her, and she answered immediately. "His family," she said. "I met them on my Chernobyl trip. But I haven't seen them since he defected from the Ukraine. I know he didn't bring them to Chicago."

"Leave the pictures here, so they can be by my side," Dumenco said.

Trish removed the photos from Craig's hands and stared down at the snapshots for a long moment. A strange expression crossed her face before she lovingly stood them up in their small frames on his bedside table.

"Good thing you took them from my apartment," Dumenco said, his voice rattling. "Otherwise he would have gotten them."

"*Who*, Georg?" Trish asked. "Who would have gotten them? The man who tried to kill you?"

Craig took out his notebook. The family members added a new twist. Was Dumenco protecting them? Were they hostages somewhere? Had they already been killed by the assassin?

"Why are you protecting someone who just tried to kill you?" He took a gamble. "Is it something to do with your physics work in the Soviet Union? What research did you do before you came to this country, and why was the U.S. so anxious to get you here?"

"No records," Dumenco said. "Doesn't matter."

"If it has something to do with who's trying to kill you, it does matter! Why were all your papers and results covered up? They're not in your files."

Dumenco sat up in the bed with a Herculean effort, completely lucid now. Now he seemed almost paternal. "You don't understand, Agent Kreident. There are some vows I made, some promises I intend to keep. And I'm not going to change my mind. Not because I'm so close to death I can put my arms around my own tombstone."

Craig shook his head in disgust, and he tossed a last glance at the photos of Dumenco's wife and children. The frames stood on the data printouts from his Fermilab antimatter experiment. Craig couldn't imagine the scientist doing any deep mental calculations in this state of mind.

"If you have anything to tell me, Dr. Dumenco, we'll have other agents standing by. They can get in touch with me," he said with a bitter voice. "Meanwhile, I have a case to solve, with or without your help."

As he turned to leave, Trish followed him out. He faced her. "And what do you have to tell me? I can see that you're hiding something. Did you see something this morning?"

"No, Craig," she said, her face flushing. "I didn't."

He frowned at her. "I know you too well for that, Trish." But she just met his gaze with stony silence. He had seen the same sort of doggedness when she had moved away from California, leaving everything they had and going on her own to Johns Hopkins.

He shook his head in disgust. "Everyone around here is a marvel of cooperation." As he passed the hospital security officers and the FBI man outside the door, he snapped, "I want this guard to be airtight!"

Craig looked at his watch, then back at Trish, giving her the brush-off. "Paige is picking me up to go to Fermilab. I have another meeting with Dr. Piter." At least *Paige* was interested in solving the case.

He glanced back at the closed door to the Ukrainian's room. "Dead men tell no tales," he said to himself, shaking his head. "But dying men aren't much help either."

Thursday, 9:07 A.M.

Fermilab

Hanging up the phone, Randall Jackson couldn't decide whether to be frustrated and angry...or elated at having found a solid lead. Regardless, he couldn't wait to tell Craig. At the least they'd meet that afternoon in Ben Goldfarb's hospital room, as they had agreed.

Dumenco's graduate student and assistant, Nicholas Bretti had been gone on vacation in West Virginia for the past week. He had not called his advisor, had not shown that he even knew about Dumenco's lethal exposure, though the story had been on most of the major news media.

Explainable enough, Jackson thought, if Bretti was out on a family fishing trip, on the deep lakes and icy rivers in the isolated West Virginia mountains, as he had told his colleagues. Jackson himself rarely watched the news when he was on vacation.

But Bretti's family had no idea where their son was. No, they did not know that he was on vacation, and the last time he and his father had gone fishing was when he had been twelve years old.

Jackson had thanked them, hung up. And let his suspicions grow.

Nicholas Bretti was not where he had claimed to be, and perhaps he held other secrets as well.

■   ■   ■

Jackson flipped through a stack of lab notebooks in the cluttered cubicle while Nels Piter's grad student Frank Chang watched by his side. The hardback notebooks had cloth spines and numbered, lined paper inside—not the typical cheap, spiral bound college special Jackson had used as an undergraduate. But each volume had NICHOLAS BRETTI stamped proudly on the front. Other than the notebooks, the cubicle office held nothing but physics texts, journal articles, preprints, and equipment manuals.

Frank Chang seemed a nice enough guy, with a goofy, friendly grin. With his long hair and small metal glasses, he looked like he belonged more at Berkeley than in the Midwest. And at least he was thoroughly impressed, if not intimidated, by the FBI badge.

Frank Chang stifled a yawn. "Sorry—had a wild night last night." He tossed his long hair over his shoulder and pointed to the top notebook. "If Bretti wrote anything worth keeping, it would be in this stack. That's the most important thing we learn in grad school—document the hell out of everything."

Jackson flipped through the pages. Nothing in here made sense—equations, columns of numbers, scratched-out formulas, "diffusion rates" and "annihilation operators." Craig had directed Jackson to Piter, who had in turn assigned Frank Chang to show him around Bretti's office—a cubicle shared with two other grad students. The tiny room looked more like a repository for missing paperwork than an office.

Jackson looked up, frustrated at not being able to decipher Bretti's scratchings. It reminded him of trying to work with those computer jocks at the Lawrence Livermore National Lab—introverted geniuses. "So what's in here? What was Bretti working on?"

Chang grinned. "The same thing every other graduate student has been working on since Nels Piter blew in from CERN—crystal-lattice traps. Antimatter holding devices. Here, I'll show you.'' Chang waved Jackson over to another desk inside the cubicle. He picked up a small white cube the size of a sugar lump encased in some sort of plastic. One side of the plastic had an array of tiny pin points. "This is a salt crystal, an imperfect one, but it's still useful to show how the trap works.''

Jackson turned the feather-light cube in his hand. "This is salt?''

"Yeah, simple table salt. Sodium chloride. We grow them in the lab. But when we get a good one, we can fix it in a plastic mount, like this one. The tiny pock-marks you see in the plastic are actually banks of solid state lasers—there's another array at right angles to this one, fixed on the perpendicular wall. When the lasers are turned on, they create resonances in the salt crystal, and it allows us to store one particle of antimatter at each molecular lattice site. That way, the antimatter won't react with ordinary matter—it would destroy itself if it did. This is a much more efficient way of storing p-bars than using a big old magnetic bottle. And it all comes from Dr. Piter's work at CERN.''

"Antimatter? How dangerous is this?''

Chang shrugged. "Not very. But only because we can't produce very many antiprotons. At least not right now. That's what Bretti was working on with Dr. Dumenco.''

Jackson held the salt crystal up to the light. The whole thing weighed less than his watch. "Then what's the big deal? Can this tiny crystal hold very much? An ounce or two?''

Frank Chang looked shocked. "Agent Jackson, if every available lattice site in that little crystal contained an antiproton, it would hold nearly three kiloton's equivalent of nuclear explosive energy—one sixth the atomic bomb dropped on Hiroshima.''

"Are you all right, Craig?'' Paige asked after she had parked her red MG sportscar beside the concrete towers of Wilson Hall.

Unlike Trish, she had allowed him to drift in his mental world during the drive through the midwest prairie, strip malls, suburbs, and morning truck traffic. Trish, on the other hand, would have insisted he share every thought and force him out of his introspection into an extroverted therapy session.

"Just having trouble understanding people," he said. From his law school days in Stanford, Craig knew that a dying man's deathbed confession held far more weight than a normal statement. If Dumenco would only be straight with him, it would make much more sense in the long run.

The wind swirled red and yellow leaves around their feet as Paige led him behind the administrative building into one of the experimental buildings. Blue and orange walls, linoleum, and plumbing adorned the inside of the industrial laboratory setting. Craig buttoned his suit jacket as they walked in, searching for Dr. Piter.

"Nels is under a lot of pressure too, Craig," Paige said. "The Nobel Prize means a lot to him. It must be sobering to know that you only have one chance to obtain the most important goal in your life."

"Tell that to Dr. Dumenco," Craig said dryly.

They passed down one flight of stairs below ground, to a computer-run control room. Painted cinderblock walls gave way to poured concrete tunnels, heavy technical equipment, and more chain-link fences and gates. Technicians and other grad students manned the consoles, touching the screens of colored flow charts. The air-conditioning was on high to cool the electronic equipment.

Piter waited for them. He wore a disheveled white shirt, a rumpled tan suit, a loosened brown tie—a curiously sloppy appearance for the meticulous Belgian scientist. Craig immediately noticed the shadowed rings around his eyes.

He peremptorily clasped his hands in front of him. "Good morning, Dr. Piter. Thanks for seeing us again."

Piter appeared flustered. "It's been quite a busy day already. I even had to have one of my graduate students show your colleague around."

"Is something wrong?" said Craig.

"We got a long string of spurious results in the middle of the night—I've been here since about three in the morning. And right when we're trying to verify the run, construction activities on the Main Injector caused a fatal fluctuation in the beam and we had to shut the Tevatron down." He sighed. "And we've got more anomalies, probably caused by Dumenco's unfortunate accident."

The graduate students continued to peck on their screens, bypassing safety interlocks to massage their results. They seemed to be functioning well enough after the substation explosion the previous Sunday evening.

"You'll have to excuse me if I seem a little disjointed." Piter sounded embarrassed.

"Was there a serious problem?" Craig asked innocently. "Is this going to affect your own experiment?"

Piter's face twisted. "While we were at dinner last night, the p-bar production rate went up dramatically, then went back down again. Unexpectedly. Actually, the increase was in line with what Dr. Dumenco had projected. But it seems quite curious that it would happen now. All by itself."

Paige said, "Isn't it good news to increase the antimatter production?"

Piter gave her a thin smile. "In a physics sense, of course, because the p-bars give us the opportunity for many high-energy experiments. But unless we find out why the production rate is fluctuating so drastically, it means nothing."

Craig followed an idea that had just occurred to him. "Could antimatter have caused that substation explosion, Dr. Piter? Some sort of buildup that went critical? Wouldn't that explain your missing p-bars from the flow?"

Piter looked sharply at him. "In theory, I suppose—but there's no way for the antimatter to have left the main Tevatron ring and gone into the beam-sampling substation. It's preposterous."

"Could one of your grad students have tampered with the support equipment?" Craig spoke quietly, looking at the technicians at the control panel.

Piter suppressed a scowl, and didn't even try to keep his voice low. "In an experiment this major, Mr. Kreident, the grad students have little real responsibility. They are just hired help, nothing more."

"Then I see nothing much has changed," said Craig tightly.

"Ah, you have been a graduate student?" Piter looked at him, eyebrows arched as he lifted his chin. "In the FBI?" He moved away from the console and started for the door; Craig and Paige followed.

Craig shook his head. "I majored in physics at Stanford before going on to Law School. I took a course and worked at the Linac—the Linear Accelerator—my senior year. Since I wasn't going on to study physics, I didn't have the pressure on me like the real grad students, but I certainly remember what it was like."

"I see." Piter continued down the huge opening. They walked briskly down another set of stairs to the underground entrance. Their shoes echoed hollowly against the bare cement walls. "We can go inside the Tevatron, now that the beam is shut down. We don't have to worry much about residual radioactivity."

Piter took a right-hand turn and stopped before another control room door. He used a badge-locked key with a magnetic strip and access code, making three attempts before he finally gained access. "Too many disconnections and supposed upgrades," he said. "Nothing works the way it should anymore." Ahead, the underground tunnel curved around, vanishing around a bend in the distance.

Glaring lights shone down on wide conduits mounted to the walls. Banks of superconducting magnets surrounded the beam channels, and substations, and fuse junction boxes; diagnostics stood out in regular intervals.

Technicians moved down the line, a pale young woman with dark hair and a twentysomething man with a goatee and the build of a weight lifter. The woman stopped at each junction box, checking readings as she munched from a bag of fat-free pretzels.

Craig stepped up and spoke quietly. "Dr. Piter, can you verify that you were at the lab early this morning, when you said you were called in?"

Piter looked up with an astonished look on his face. "Of course I can—but what on fool's earth for?"

"Someone attempted to kill Dr. Dumenco in his hospital room this morning. The killer got away, but we have a witness."

"Then why are you bothering me if you have an eyewitness?" Piter drew himself up to his full five feet six inch height. He purposely brushed lint from his suit and straightened his tie. "Surely they don't think it's me?"

"I just want to eliminate as many potential suspects as I can." He paused. "That includes everyone, Dr. Piter."

Piter drew his mouth tight and lifted his chin. "You may confirm my presence here with any one of those technicians. Or one of my grad students, Frank Chang— he's showing your partner around as we speak. We've all been here putting in a lot of hours. I refuse to believe that you would seriously consider me, the Director of High-Energy Research, a possible suspect in any scheme to harm my esteemed colleague, Dr. Dumenco."

"People have plenty of motives to do things out of the ordinary, Dr. Piter. How about the Nobel?"

Piter took a step backward and blinked. "That's just an award, Agent Kreident. It certainly isn't worth killing someone over! In fact, even *coveting* the prize is considered quite unprofessional."

Craig just watched him, knowing that Piter coveted the Nobel a great deal.

He thought he would be going back and forth between the medical center and Fermilab quite a few more times before he had answers to this case.

Thursday, 1:03 P.M.

Fox River Medical Center,
Main Cafeteria

"Have lunch with me," Craig said to Trish, gesturing toward the cafeteria. "It's hospital food, but it's the best I can do right now, considering Jackson is meeting me here at three. And I'm paying. I owe you anyway, because you won our bet."

"Our bet?" she asked with an uncertain smile. She adjusted her delicate glasses, falling into step beside him.

"When you first called me on the phone, you swore that this case would be unlike any of the others I've worked on. You were right." He held open the swinging cafeteria door for her. The food inside smelled as if it had gone through an automatic dishwasher, but his stomach rumbled anyway.

"So I get fine hospital dining," she said, arching her eyebrows. "Good thing I'm not normally a gambling woman."

In the cafeteria line they each took a tray and studied the unappealing selection of foods. Craig refused to take one of the bowls of jiggling, brilliantly colored Jell-O, choosing tapioca pudding instead. He ladled out a serving of mushy spaghetti and meatballs. Trish looked at him sidelong, and Craig decided it might be better if he didn't eat the meatballs after all. Trish chose a dubiously fresh salad, a helping of fruit cocktail, and a carton of skim milk.

They settled down at a table at the far end of the cafeteria. Craig scanned the mix of doctors, nurses, volunteers, and families visiting patients. The noise droned around them, giving them complete anonymity. He still had the nagging suspicion that she knew or suspected something about that morning's attack, and he decided to follow his intuition.

"I've been thinking about you a lot recently," Trish said, self-consciously removing her glasses.

Craig swallowed hard. That was a bold move for opening their first real one-on-one conversation in some time. "Then how come you never called me until a murder case forced you to?"

"Me?" Trish blinked. "How come *you* never called?"

Craig looked away, studying the gelatinous red and white swirls of the alleged spaghetti. He searched for the right words, but Trish had his thoughts in too much of a turmoil. Things had changed. They were two different people from the years they were together at Stanford.

Finally, she answered her own comment. "You're right. We promised not to get into that finger-pointing thing, but I had hoped you would send me a letter . . . or something. I really did want to be friends."

"Well, my caseload has been very full," Craig said with forced enthusiasm. "You know me, devoted to the FBI."

Trish took a bite of her salad. "And I've been intently involved with my own research. Johns Hopkins isn't any more relaxing than your Bureau."

"I don't suppose it is," Craig said.

"Because of my specialty I'm in intermittent demand, whenever a radiation accident happens. But my work with the PR-Cubed keeps me on the go constantly. We're still doing follow-up and tracking of all the studies we did in the aftermath of Chernobyl. Remember when I went over there as a pre-med?''

"How could I forget?'' Craig said. For months she had been wrapped up in her own thoughts, or bombarding him with stories of what she had experienced there. She had merely been a junior member of the team, a relief worker interviewing residents who had lived in the densest fallout plume from the nuclear reactor disaster. It had been her job to keep massive statistics, chronicling the overwhelming tide of medical problems from the Chernobyl survivors.

"The Ukraine is a beautiful country, like our Midwest. It's the breadbasket of what used to be the Soviet Union . . . but that power plant accident was the greatest man-made disaster in history. The fallout spread from the Ukraine into Belarus, even around the world in the jet stream.'' She shook her head, blinking her dark eyes as if to wipe away haunting memories.

Then she leaned forward, fixing him with her gaze. Craig felt a sense of dread as he wondered what she was about to confess.

"I met Georg Dumenco there, in the Ukraine, all those years before. He and his family. He desperately wanted to leave the country, to get his family safe, but there was nothing we could do. Once he emigrated here, I kept tabs on him through the PR-Cubed.'' As she took her dark gaze from him, he felt as if a targeting cross had just slipped away. "So did other people, I think.''

Craig took a deep breath, trying to assess the information. "What do you mean by that? What happened to Dumenco's family, the ones in the snapshots I found?''

Trish shook her head. "Nobody knows. They disappeared during the upheaval, the breakup of the Soviet Union. For years now, somebody . . . somebody at the PR-Cubed . . .'' She trailed off.

Reflexively she drank her milk and ate more salad while Craig waited in silence. "I'm . . . having a hard time with this. It's bringing back too many memories. Dumenco is dying from a radiation exposure, just like those people at Chernobyl. Maybe his family died back in the Ukraine before he came to this country. There's nothing I can do for him, or for them."

"But I'm sure you managed to help," Craig finally said, still trying to get her to open up. "That's what you've always wanted to do, help people."

"But that isn't always the case, is it?" she said testily. "How can you stand it, Craig? This fatalistic inevitability. By the time you're called in to a murder investigation, the crime has already happened. You're always too late . . . and I'm always too late. When I get called to treat a radiation exposure, like Georg's, there's not much I can do. I can't even make him more comfortable as he dies."

She pushed her tray away. "My sole purpose is to collect data on his decline and death. No one in the world could have cured his lethal exposure, but I'm the one they called—so I'm the one who ultimately fails."

"Oh, Trish," Craig said trying to be soothing, but he sounded scolding instead. What other information did she have? What did the PR-Cubed have to do with this? "You help people who receive smaller exposures."

Trish sat back and thought for a moment, then smiled. "You're right. Sometimes I can help. In fact, that's why I've been thinking of you recently."

Craig blinked, unsure of where she was going. *She couldn't be trying to get back together, could she?*

Trish leaned forward. "I treated a friend of yours. They called me in after that Russian General Ursov received his exposure out in Nevada. You were there. The man couldn't stop talking about you."

"*You* treated Ursov?" Craig said in astonishment. But of course, it made sense. Trish LeCroix was one of the few medical radiation experts, and she was well known in her field. When a senior Russian military officer had received the large radiation dose, medical experts would have called someone like Trish. "So you're the one he meant. In a letter he added a postscript saying that our 'mutual friend' sends greetings. I was baffled until now. I couldn't figure out who he was talking about."

Trish smiled. "I guess he played a little trick on you."

"Those Strategic Rocket Forces guys, what a bunch of jokers." He had thought a great deal about Ursov and respected the stoic general for his unwavering devotion . . . and now an idea formed in his mind.

Seemingly eager to be away from the prior conversation, Trish continued offhandedly, "Your friend Paige Mitchell seems a . . . nice enough sort of person. In her own way."

Craig concentrated on his spaghetti. He couldn't tell if Trish was being catty or if she was just trying to gauge his response. "We've worked closely on several cases now," he said, wiping his mouth with a napkin.

She waited, but he refused to give her more details about the cases.

"She's very smart," he finally continued. "Easy to get along with." He left the thought hanging.

He didn't particularly enjoy being caught between two such women. It might be best for him, for the case, and for his own sanity if he spent the next days working with Jackson and trying to steer clear of both Trish and Paige.

Dumenco's accident, the substation explosion, Goldfarb's shooting, the saboteur in Dumenco's apartment, and the mysterious attacker in the hospital—not to mention the Ukrainian's connection with Trish and the PR-Cubed—gave him quite enough to worry about for the time being.

· · · · · · ·

Thursday, 1:17 P.M.

Evergreen Espresso,
Aurora, Illinois

Nicholas Bretti sipped on his double espresso, though he was wired enough, unsettled, edgy. He sat on one of the metal-mesh chairs under a green-and-white sun umbrella, scanning down the sidewalk. Where the hell was Chandrawalia? In downtown redneck Aurora, he shouldn't have trouble finding the whip-thin Indian representative.

At least outside he could have a smoke. The whole damned country was getting to be a nonsmoking zone. Thank goodness India hadn't gone that direction. That was one thing he could look forward to if he went back to Bangalore . . . for the rest of his life.

He swallowed hard, then nervously lit another cigarette with his cheap butane lighter and stuck it back into his pocket. He took a long drag, pulling the thick smoke deep into his lungs. Yes, in India he could smoke wherever he wanted. That was an advantage. He was sure there must be other advantages, at least one or two. There must be.

The too-cute rustic coffee shop was set off the main street, shaded by trees that had just begun to shed their leaves. Inside, Formica-topped tables and red vinyl booths filled most of the floor space. A wooden stage held an old Fender amplifier, two microphones, a stool, and four guitar stands for Friday night festivities. The smell of different coffee beans wafted through the air—

French vanilla, Irish creme, amaretto, mocha, all tumbled together.

Bretti sat alone outside in the clear, cool autumn air. He had never felt so isolated in his life. What was he going to do? He looked at his watch again and groaned. The Indian bastard better show up.

Bretti took another drag, then coughed. Inside the coffee shop, the only other customer—some girl who hadn't even looked his way when he'd entered—kept her nose buried in the *Chicago Sun*. Good. He didn't want to draw any attention to himself.

Chandrawalia had told Bretti to meet him there, in no uncertain terms. Bretti hadn't dared slip into Fermilab yet. He had even cruised past his apartment three times before he finally decided no one was watching the place—but still, he refused to flick on his lights. He had stumbled in the dark to his bed, crashed, and spent most of the night trying to sleep.

Back at the accelerator, his crystal-lattice trap should still be installed down in the beam-shunt tunnel, unnoticed. It had been two days since he had left, two days since he had shot the FBI agent. No doubt teams were crawling over the site, but they would be concentrating on the substations, where the first explosion had occurred and where the shooting had happened. He doubted they would have any reason to scour the experimental target areas.

He had no idea if the FBI was watching for him, if they even suspected. Would they come and arrest him in the middle of the night, have a stakeout inside Fermilab—or would he get away with everything, no one the wiser?

Bretti took another sip of espresso, tasting the burned bitter smell on his tongue as it mixed with tobacco smoke. Then he saw Chandrawalia coming down the street, wearing a blue turban. The tall Indian stood out, even when he was dressed in a short sleeve, open-collar shirt. Chandrawalia gave a perfunctory bow, scraping a heavy chair across the patio concrete to take a seat next to Bretti. He didn't seem to have any intention of ordering coffee for himself.

"You're late," Bretti said.

"Traffic," Chandrawalia said. His dark eyes searched the near-deserted coffee shop. "Your car is still parked at the Consulate garage. When are you going to pick it up?"

Bretti shook his head. "It's too risky. I may just have to ditch it."

Chandrawalia was unimpressed. "I am told that your trip to Bangalore was disappointing to Dr. Punjab. That is very disturbing news to me. I thought we had an agreement."

Bretti tried to look Chandrawalia in the eye, but the man's gaze kept jumping from one spot to another on the street, in the coffee shop. He leaned forward. "I *told* you that I had to get out of the country. And fast. Don't you watch the news? They still might be looking for me after the explosion and after the shooting."

"And why should we help you when you have proven yourself unreliable? And a danger to us as well." Chandrawalia's eyes seemed to click as he swung his entire focus to Bretti. He scowled, showing perfect white teeth against his dark skin. "You did not deliver the quantity of antimatter we had agreed upon. Our work depends on those p-bars. You have caused many difficulties for us."

Bretti fumbled for another cigarette, indignant. "Hey, I brought you more than you ever had before—"

"And now you must do much better. I had to arrange some political favors to get you and your antimatter into India in the first place. Do you think it was easy for me to use a diplomatic pouch to transport your device?"

"I did the best I could," said Bretti defensively.

"No doubt you discovered that other, competing political parties in my government are already highly suspicious of my activities." Chandrawalia leaned forward to emphasize the words. "The next time you enter my country it will not be so easy to get past customs.''

Bretti took another sip of the now-cold espresso, feeling the acid of caffeine roil in his stomach. It was now even clearer just how much the Indians needed him. He started to feel cocky. ''Fine, I've got one crystal-lattice trap hidden in the main experimental target tunnel, and another in one of the substations, collecting stray antimatter. The large one should have collected ten times what I promised you, more antimatter than has ever been stored before. In fact, we may even be nearing the capacity of the device design.'' His eyes glittered—*now* he finally had the man's attention.

''I can go fetch it early tomorrow morning, after midnight, and we can be on our way—but I need something more from you.'' He narrowed his eyes and nervously stroked his goatee.

Chandrawalia stiffened. ''We have already paid you a great deal of money for an incomplete task—''

Bretti pounded his fist on the metal table, rattling his espresso cup. ''And you need to be ready to offer me sanctuary. If things go to hell around here, I may have to run. This isn't like shoplifting a candy bar from a grocery store. The FBI is already on site, and my advisor Dumenco just may be able to figure out what's going on, if he lives that long. He's probably the only one who can unravel what's happening to his enhanced beam, where all the extra antimatter is going. I may have to lie low in your country for a while.''

Bretti swallowed hard, but tried not to let uneasiness show on his face. He wasn't a professional criminal, didn't have any idea how to cover up evidence, keep his alibi straight, avoid suspicion. For all he knew, he could have left telltale, incriminating signs all over the place.

''I'm afraid that is impossible, Dr. Bretti,'' Chandrawalia said coolly.

Fueled by the caffeine-charged espresso, Bretti stood up. ''You don't seem to understand who's calling the shots around here!''

Chandrawalia looked at him with a maddeningly smug expression. "Yes I do, Dr. Bretti. I understand quite well. It is you that does not understand that I do not speak for India—my position is a *concession* of the party now in charge, a position designed so that the People's Liberty for All coalition will support the present government. After our work with your antimatter supply succeeds, perhaps then my political party will be in a position to offer you asylum. For now, we are at as great a risk as you are."

Bretti's cheeks burned. "For doing *medical research*? Give me a break."

Chandrawalia lowered his voice. "Don't be stupid, *Mr.* Bretti." The Indian's words stung. "Even I did not think you to be so dense. If we really wanted the antimatter for commercial applications, we would have gone through your Department of Commerce. These p-bars will be used for weapons applications—*nuclear* weapons, a bold new design."

"That's crazy," said Bretti, confused. "You don't use p-bars in a nuclear chain reaction—" But as he spoke, he realized he wasn't sure. In fact, he had no idea, had never even considered the possibility. *Holy shit,* he thought. *Nuclear weapons? What have I gotten into?*

"Properly harnessed, antimatter injected into an imploding bomb core can dramatically increase the yield. These results have been widely reported by a research group at your own Penn State. In short, with the proper technology, your antimatter will allow us to build far more warheads with far less precious plutonium. It will give India a strategic advantage such as we have never had over Pakistan or China—and the People's Liberation for All party will become heroes."

Chandrawalia's gray beard and mustache surrounded his expression of intense focus. "Tomorrow, you will be ready with your cargo. I will expect you at the airport for the early afternoon flight. You will board the Concord again and return to New Delhi. If you are true to your word, and if you deliver ten times as many p-bars, perhaps we will discuss the matter further.''

He brushed down his jacket, stood, and carefully pushed the metal chair back into place at the table. ''Good day.''

Bretti seethed as he watched the man walk back down the sidewalk. Damned . . . *towelhead!* Then he calmed himself, clenching and unclenching his fists. He would just have to avoid the cops, and the FBI until then. It was only one more day, and they couldn't possibly have had time to check the thousands of employees who might have been working in and around the Tevatron, substations, and admin building during the days in question. Besides, the investigators probably thought he was still on vacation, so maybe they hadn't even considered looking him up.

Nuclear weapons!

He ran a shaking hand through his hair and glanced around the deserted coffee shop, at the traffic rushing past on the street. This changed everything. With every passing moment he felt himself being dragged deeper into a bottomless pit. *Deeper and deeper.* Bretti tried to wet his lips, but his mouth was dry, cottony. The coffee made his mouth taste sour.

He needed another cigarette, but his hands shook so badly he could barely use his lighter.

Thursday, 2:21 P.M.

Aurora, Illinois

Standing at a pay phone outside a gas station near the hospital, Craig flipped open his notebook and found a telephone number he never thought he'd have occasion to use.

His stomach knotted. He couldn't believe he was about to make this call. He kept telling himself it was a bad idea, that he was going against numerous regulations about contacting foreign nationals without prior approval.

But it also might give him answers no one else wanted to talk about.

Thinking of how Goldfarb had been left for dead, how a would-be assassin had come right into the hospital to kill the already-dying Dumenco, and how the Ukrainian continued to avoid answering his questions, Craig decided to make the call—and damn the consequences.

He'd report the contact to the Office of Professional Responsibility and the Oakland security office as soon as he was done. But this was his case now, and he had to pursue it in the manner he deemed best. Besides, it wasn't as if this was the first time he'd done anything June Atwood could scold him for.

He opened the dangling phone book, flipping pages until he found the International Access Code for the Russian Republic.

He had a federal credit card for official calls, but decided in this case it would be better if he paid for it out of his own pocket. Despite the inconvenience, he had bought a handful of prepaid phone cards inside the gas station. He had been on many criminal cases, but this was the deepest Counter Intelligence stuff he had ever tried.

Using the phone cards, Craig punched in the access code and dialed the international number he had written down. He didn't bother to calculate the time difference, because he had to call *now*. Several lives depended on the information he needed.

If General Gregori Ursov was there, he was there.

When the phone rang and was answered by someone in garrulous Russian, Craig spoke clearly and patiently. "English please."

The person on the line said something and ran off. Craig wasn't sure if the person had hung up. The Russian Strategic Rocket Forces probably didn't get many calls from non-Russians.

Finally another voice came on the line, heavily accented. "I speak English. Who is this?"

"I must talk to General Ursov," he said slowly and clearly.

The voice sounded surprised. "Ursov?" He spoke a burst in Russian, yelling at someone behind him, then came back. "No General Ursov here. No Ursov."

Craig knew he had dialed the right number, knew this was a dodging tactic. "Tell General Ursov this is his friend from the United States. This is Special Agent Kreident."

"No Ursov here," the voice said again.

"Tell him it's Craig Kreident," he insisted. "I have an important matter to discuss with him. He owes me his life—he can at least talk to me on the phone."

Another mutter, then the line went silent again except for occasional clicks like gnawing rodents on the wires. He was confident the conversation would be recorded, especially now. He hoped the eavesdroppers enjoyed the change in the pattern of their day.

In the service station next to the pay phone, mechanics used a power wrench to lock on hubcap bolts with such force that no stranded motorist would ever be able to get them free. A dropped wrench clanged on the cement garage floor, while another mechanic drove a blatting car without a muffler around back.

Craig looked at his stack of phone cards, ready to use another one as soon as his time ran out. After all this, he couldn't risk being cut off by a telephone operator.

Finally the Russian general's gruff voice came on the line, blustering loudly. "Agent Kreident! This is most unexpected."

"Hello, General. Thank you for the official citation your government sent me. That was most kind of you, sir. And our mutual friend again says hello. It turns out we're working on another case together, one similar to yours . . . only much worse. A lethal radiation exposure this time."

Ursov suddenly sounded cagey. "I am sorry to hear that, my friend. An accident? And . . . where did this radiation come from?"

"It happened at a high-energy accelerator. Perhaps an accident, or perhaps not," Craig said. "I need some information from you, General."

"Me?" Ursov said, genuinely surprised. "How can I assist you? I am on the other side of the world."

"The victim is an émigré Ukrainian scientist. He defected during the breakup of the USSR—"

"A defector?"

"Encouraged by us. He came to work at Fermilab, our largest particle accelerator, near Chicago."

"I am familiar with CERN in Geneva. It is similar, yes?"

"Yes. From what I can tell, the victim worked for the Soviet Union on some projects—but he has kept extremely quiet about it. However, I believe some of his previous work may have endangered him here. And others. My own partner Ben Goldfarb has been shot. You might remember him.''

"I see why you have such incentive to solve this case. But a defector—''

"The victim has only about two days to live, General. A distinct part of the trail leads back to the physics he performed in the former Soviet Union. I want to know what it was, and why it might have marked him for death.''

Ursov was silent for a moment. "Agent Kreident, I have no knowledge of such matters. You must realize this.''

"But certainly, General Ursov, a man in your position has ways of finding out?'' He pursed his lips, but Ursov didn't rise to the bait. "The scientist's name is Georg Dumenco. He was a highly esteemed physicist. I believe his work must have been ground-breaking, judging from the terms my country offered him when he defected. He's under consideration for this year's Nobel Prize in physics.''

Ursov interrupted him sourly. "Yes, we remember Dr. Dumenco. It is too bad he fled to your country. We would have been proud to have him accept his prize in Stockholm in the name of my country instead of yours.''

"Well he's not going to be accepting it for either country,'' Craig said. "Dumenco is in a hospital bed dying from radiation exposure. I need to know about him, General. Tell me what you can about his work.''

Ursov paused again, as if pondering the implications of answering. "If he conducted his research for Soviet military, those records are classified and sealed. I now merely work for Russian Strategic Rocket Forces.''

"Yes, General,'' Craig said with total skepticism, "and I'm merely an accountant for the FBI.''

Ursov chuckled. More static came on the line.

Craig glanced at his watch. He didn't have a clue how much money was left on his card, but he made ready to slip in another one before the line went dead. "Look, General, I don't need to know the exact nature of what he was doing—I probably wouldn't understand it anyway. But give me a lead, something that'll help me solve this murder."

Ursov sighed. "It will take some time, my friend, and do not expect too many details. I know I owe you my life, but sometimes a life is not worth all that much. At least not to people over here."

"Do what you can, General, and don't take too long."

"Very well—and say hello to the lovely Dr. LeCroix for me. From the way she talks, I believe you still hold a special place in her heart."

"Thanks, General," Craig said, embarrassed, "that's not the information I wanted to hear."

"And say hello to the equally lovely Ms. Mitchell." Ursov sighed. "Ah, to be twenty years younger. You must still work with both of them."

"Yes, sir, I am—but it's much too complicated to go into now." *And boy is that an understatement,* he thought.

Thursday, 3:31 P.M.

Fox River Medical Center, Intensive Care Unit

As they left Ben Goldfarb in his hospital room, Craig and Jackson strode down the hall in their dark suits, making their way past ICU rooms with dying or recovering patients. Their partner's condition was unchanged, still weak and precarious; but the doctors had kept him on a ventilator, sedated and stabilized, with the endotracheal tube in his throat, which prevented him from speaking even if he had awakened. Goldfarb's wife and daughters hovered beside him, giving their silent support.

Trish had gone to her temporary office to study lab results and chemical analyses of Dumenco's condition, leaving the orderlies to do their rounds. Until he heard back from General Ursov, *if* he heard back, Craig saw no point in returning to Fermilab.

Seeing the curly-haired agent lying so severely injured, Craig felt his anger rising. Beside him, Jackson was silent and rigid, held erect by his internal fury and his need to find a target against which to release it.

Craig vowed to talk with the Ukrainian scientist one more time. Craig *knew* that Dumenco held a key piece of information, but refused to reveal it. Craig had no further patience, no more desire to play games. Ben Goldfarb had put his life on the line for that man. Dumenco could be a bit more cooperative. . . .

According to Jackson's research, the Ukrainian's grad

student was nowhere to be found, not at home, not on vacation. Maybe he had just changed his plans, not in itself unusual, especially not for someone without a wife or children. Perhaps Bretti had even come back to work—but finding *any* particular individual at Fermilab was a daunting task, since the scientists and technicians didn't usually bother to make their whereabouts known. Of course, if Bretti had returned, he would certainly have found out about Dumenco.

As he and Jackson strode down the hall toward the dying scientist's room, they saw a blond-haired orderly flash his ID and hospital badge to the guards stationed outside. The two hospital security men glanced at the orderly's ID and let him pass. The white-uniformed orderly slipped inside with his cart of medications and his clipboard.

Agent Schultz from the Chicago Bureau office saw them coming and stepped around from a bank of pay phones he had been using. He greeted Craig and Jackson. "Nothing much happening," Schultz said. "That old guy is going to be dead tomorrow or the day after. What's the use anybody trying to kill him now?"

Craig checked his watch, trying to remember the shift changes. "Makes no sense to me either," he said. "But that doesn't mean I'm not worried." The guards saw them approaching and nodded, alert for any terrorists coming down the hospital corridor.

An intercom called for assistance on the third floor. Pediatrics paged a doctor. Another orderly emerged from a room down the hall carrying a bedpan.

With Schultz tagging along, Craig and Jackson approached Dumenco's room. Creasing his brow, Craig stepped closer, wondering what the orderly was doing inside. Jackson reached for the door, and the nearest security guard moved aside to let the three agents pass.

"Hey!" Jackson snapped, turning on them. "Are you going to just let us barge in there?" The first guard looked flustered, glancing over at his counterpart.

Craig glanced through the wire-reinforced window in Dumenco's door. Oxygen from a wall-mounted valve system ran through hoses to the bed. A thick plastic privacy curtain surrounded the dying scientist, blurring details. Through a crack in the curtain, Craig saw the orderly hunched over the bed, blocking the view. He seemed to be adjusting Dumenco's pillow, his head rest. In front of the curtain, a teenage candystriper unloaded towels from a cart.

"You should at least check our badges." Jackson continued his reprimand, his voice harsh. "I don't care if you recognize us or not. Don't you guys understand what *high security* means? Ever vigilant."

"Sorry, sir," both guards said in unison. Agent Schultz stifled a smile.

Then Craig noticed Dumenco's hand reach up, thrashing in the air, weakly struggling. Battering against the curtain, he struck the back of the orderly's white coat, leaving a reddish stain from his damaged skin. The orderly didn't flinch, but continued to hunch over Dumenco.

Craig shoved the door open and dashed inside. "FBI! Stop right there! What are you doing?" The candystriper looked up, eyes wide. She stood between Craig and the orderly.

The orderly lurched upward, spinning around. His face was stony but flushed, his hair so pale that it looked recently bleached. The orderly's eyebrows had been shaved off as well, leaving only smooth skin on his face. A simple but very effective disguise. He would look entirely different from the dark-haired man Trish had seen during the previous attack.

Dumenco's free hand reached over to claw at the small, wet pillow that had been shoved against his face so hard his skin had bruised. He gasped in a lungful of air. Blood trickled from his crushed nose.

The orderly moved like a cobra. With his left hand he whipped out a long razor-edged surgical knife.

"Don't move!" Craig shouted, whipping his hand back to his pancake holster and pulling out his handgun. "FBI!"

More intent on killing his victim than in escaping, the blond-haired man slashed downward toward the body on the bed. But Dumenco somehow had enough presence of mind to yank the wet pillow across his chest. The blade plunged into the pillow.

The assassin twisted the knife free. Craig leveled his gun, as did Jackson and Schultz, who also charged into the room. The candystriper screamed and backed into the curtain, uncertain where to move in the confusion.

Jackson's eyes narrowed, and he held up his pistol. The assassin slashed sideways with the knife, this time severing some of the tubes and cables connecting Dumenco to the oxygen, IV fluids and life-monitoring apparatus.

Alarms squealed from the disconnected apparatus. A louder, more insistent alarm sounded at the ICU's central monitoring station.

Jackson yelled, "Put down your weapon, sir! Now!" and tightened his finger on the trigger.

From the other side of the hospital bed the murderous orderly grabbed his cart and shoved it forward, moving in front of Dumenco. Jackson pulled his gun back, not willing to risk hitting the Ukrainian or the candystriper.

"Block him off," Craig said, moving toward the door. The impostor orderly ran with surprising power, using the sharp-edged cart like a battering ram. He smashed into Schultz, and Craig heard the sound of cracking bone. The young candystriper scrambled out of the way, gasping.

With deadly precision the orderly threw his knife at the nearest hospital guard, who also stood in his way out in the hall. The blade dug into his right breast, and he staggered back, gasping and coughing blood. Jackson ran after the impostor, but Schultz went down in front of him.

More alarms sounded out in the halls. Doctors came rushing from their emergency stations, while hospital aides stood at the doors, perplexed and astonished.

As the orderly plunged through the door, Craig dove at his legs, but the man kicked him in the chin. His teeth clicked together with a noise that vibrated through his skull. In his spinning vision, he saw black static.

Jackson leaped over a moaning Agent Schultz and passed Craig in hot pursuit after the orderly. "Everybody, out of the way!" he yelled. "FBI!"

Craig struggled to his feet as the first emergency doctor arrived in response to the automatic alarms. "Help them!" he said, shaking his head to clear it as he gestured to where the stabbed guard writhed in pain. Dumenco lay disconnected from the oxygen, IV fluid, and life-monitoring equipment, wheezing, and Agent Schultz nursed what appeared to be broken ribs and a broken arm. "Get help for all of them."

Craig raced down the hall after his partner. The would-be assassin ran for the stairwell with Jackson close behind him. Grabbing a metal cart, the orderly flung it behind him like a carnival ride. Jackson crashed headlong into it. The cart toppled over with a loud clatter, spraying medication cups, syringes, and supplies across the floor.

Jackson didn't slow, hopping over the obstacle and staggering to regain his balance. He held his handgun out, but didn't fire as he charged ahead. People in the hall squealed and scattered out of the way.

The assassin hit the stairwell, ripped the metal fire door open, and bounded down the stairs. On pneumatic hinges, the door began to shut behind him. Jackson, running at full speed, grabbed for the door.

Craig saw the potential trap and shouted, "Jackson— on your guard!"

The tall, dark agent passed the threshold at full speed into the dimmer light of the stairwell. He posed a perfect target—but Craig shouted his warning at just the right instant, and Jackson apparently realized his peril. He threw himself sideways just as bullets smashed into the stairwell's metal door, making large puckered craters.

Jackson wasted no time and swung down his own gun with practiced ease. He didn't bother identifying himself—and FBI agents were trained not to fire warning shots. Jackson pulled the trigger three times, clustering the shots around the impostor orderly's chest. Aim for the center of mass. Remove the threat.

The orderly flew backward into the concrete wall, his chest ripped open. With the impact, he bounced like a rubber ball down the remaining half-flight of stairs, leaving a series of red stains until he crashed against the corner landing. Jackson froze in position, his gun still aimed, waiting to see if the blond man made a further move. But the attacker lay sprawled, his eyes wide but unseeing. Speckles of blood and cooling perspiration dotted his smooth forehead.

It had happened in only a few seconds. Craig finally caught up with his partner, who stood panting and shaking in the instantaneous after-rush of the ordeal.

"Where's his weapon?" said Craig, scanning the floor.

Jackson nodded down the stairwell. "Secure it—I kicked it away."

Furtively, Jackson glanced over at the bullet holes in the metal door only inches from where his chest and head had been. His skin took on a pasty appearance, tinting the rich brown of his face with a grayish cast.

One of the doctors on duty rushed up and knelt over the assassin. It only took a moment to check the man over and determine that nothing could be done to save him. The doctor stepped away.

After retrieving the dead man's weapon, Craig felt cold. He had known there was no other option, but still he shook his head. "Is that our killer?" he asked. "You think that's the guy who triggered the accident at Fermilab?"

Jackson panted, then sank to his knees. "He sure didn't want Dumenco to live through the day."

Then the other implications struck home for Craig. "Just what we needed, a Board of Inquiry in the midst of this. We're already short on time." Jackson seemed too wrung out to do more than just stand motionless. Craig squeezed his shoulder. "I'll back you up all the way, Randall."

He went down the stairs to search the body. His fingers sticky with blood, he patted down the man's clothes, pawing in his pockets.

Naturally, he discovered no identification. With the disguised appearance it would be difficult to tell who this man was, unless the FBI fingerprint database could help out. In the shirt pocket beneath his white orderly coat, however, Craig found two pieces of paper, one bearing a list of names with corresponding cities, and another a small business card. *Physicians for Responsible Radiation Research*, with a stylized logo that showed *PR-Cubed*. Craig's stomach twisted in knots.

What did Trish have to do with this?

Back in Dumenco's room doctors scrambled to put everything back in order. Schultz and the injured guard had been taken off to be treated, but they weren't in any danger.

In his bed the Ukrainian lay devastated. His already horrifying condition had grown noticeably worse, as if he had been through some mangling industrial machine. His face was ravaged, his eyes wild and scarlet.

Trish tended him, trying to soothe him. Her face was flushed, her expression pinched with concern. She'd succeeded in replacing the IV drip tubes and reattaching the electrodes to his medical monitoring equipment. Trish looked up at Craig with concern and questions in her sepia eyes.

He took a deep breath and clasped his hands, still sticky and stained with blood from the dead assassin, behind his back. Other Chicago Bureau agents, local law-enforcement, and the remainder of the hospital security staff, had converged on where the body had fallen in the stairwell.

Soon it would be time for all the paperwork, all the reports. Craig nodded at Trish. "You don't have to worry about that man anymore. Whoever he was. He doesn't have any identification."

Trish looked relieved.

Craig narrowed his eyes and spoke sharply. "So do you want to save us a lot of time and trouble and tell me who he is?"

Trish blinked, apparently baffled. Craig held up the business card, and it seemed to burn in his fingers. "He had this in his pocket. *PR-Cubed*, Trish. Your organization! I thought you were hiding something from me this morning, not telling me everything you thought. Now who is he?"

"He could have gotten that card anywhere—our convention was in town last weekend, and—"

Craig raised his voice, but was still under control. "Who is he, Trish?"

She paled and rested against the metal support bar of Dumenco's bed. "I . . . I thought he might have looked familiar. Someone from the PR-Cubed who was—who said he was tracking down Chernobyl information. He wanted to know where I could find Georg's family members, since I'd had some contact with them in the Ukraine. But I didn't know anything. He asked me several times, and he was very insistent—but I didn't know!" Her voice became thin and watery with her own anxiety.

"Then why didn't you tell me this morning, dammit?"

"Because I wasn't sure. He was wearing a surgical mask, it was dark. I thought I was imagining things."

Dumenco spoke weakly from his bed. "Not . . . imagining things."

Craig marched toward Dumenco, holding out the list, unfolding the sheet of paper. "Dr. Dumenco, I need you to look at these names. Do you recognize them? The man who attacked you carried them."

The dying scientist seemed to have trouble focusing on the names. Craig pushed the list closer, and Dumenco stared at the words. Then tears gushed out of his hemorrhaged eyes. He trembled on the bed, glancing at the names, then over at the framed snapshots Craig had taken from the dresser drawer in his apartment.

"One name, then a city written down. Who are they, Dr. Dumenco?" he said. Trish looked over his shoulder, wide-eyed.

"My . . . my family," the scientist said. "My family's new names . . . all of them." He drew a deep, shuddering breath. "They have been in hiding. They were supposed to be—" He shook his head. "They were supposed to safe, safe from people like him."

He slumped into the bedsheets and continued weeping. "My family."

Thursday, 5:01 P.M.

Fox River Medical Center

In the aftermath of the shooting in the hospital, the FBI's Office of Professional Responsibility swarmed to the Fox River Medical Center, armed with interview questions and forms to be filled out.

Though he hated to have cameras shoved in front of his face, Craig had made the appropriate statements to the reporters, explaining about the ongoing investigation into the soon-to-be-fatal radiation exposure of Nobel Prize contender, Georg Dumenco. An as-yet-unidentified assailant had twice attempted to kill the physicist in the hospital before being killed himself. The assailant was now the prime suspect for having caused the original radiation accident, as well as the devastating substation explosion, and the shooting of Agent Ben Goldfarb.

With forced patience, Craig spoke to the reporters because he wanted to protect Jackson. He took the hard way out with the toughest questions, just answering "no comment," knowing that the press would speculate like crazy—but even if he had wanted to answer in full, Craig still didn't know how the pieces fit together, what the assassin had been after, why the man had carried the aliases of Dumenco's family hidden by the State Department.

Craig went to see Goldfarb again, trying to escape from the insanity, but the curly-haired agent just lay motionless. Julene had fallen asleep in a chair at his bedside, while the two little girls kept themselves quietly occupied with a game of Trouble they had found in the hospital's game cabinet.

While Jackson met with representatives from the Office of Professional Responsibility, giving his detailed statement, Craig paced the halls. Should he go back to Fermilab? Did Paige have anything else for him, any new statement from Nels Piter?

He passed by a waiting-room lounge, pausing long enough to watch a few seconds of *Headline News*. The Nobel Prize Committee in Stockholm had announced their selection for the Prize in Literature, an Eskimo whose poetry had described the plight of the vanishing harp seal. The newscaster speculated on when the few remaining Prizes would be announced; Craig hoped Dumenco lived long enough to learn of their decision.

After the second assassination attempt, Trish remained terribly shaken and refused to leave Dumenco's side. Surrounded by guards and doctors, the physicist seemed distressed and claustrophobic. Craig wondered if the PR-Cubed people had any greater involvement, if Trish still knew more information she kept hidden from him.

Why was it everyone wanted him to solve this case, but no one would give him all the data he needed? None of it made any sense. Craig pressed his fingers against his temples, rubbing the skin there to make his headache crawl slowly away. He knew he was still missing a key piece of the puzzle.

And then his cell phone rang.

Craig fumbled with the tiny receiver as he flipped it open; one of the nurses glared at him, ready to scold him for using the cell phone inside the hospital, but he moved quickly toward the door to a smokers' courtyard. "Hello?" There was static on the line.

"Special Agent Kreident? This is General Ursov speaking. How are you today, my friend?"

■   ■   ■

Craig stood at Dumenco's bedside, livid with anger. "You're not being honest with me!" he said, trying to keep his voice down from an outright shout. He shooed the doctors and orderlies out of the way, while the guards stood at the door.

Trish stepped toward Craig. "What are you doing?" He held up a finger and Trish pulled herself upright, flustered at his harshness.

The Ukrainian scientist squirmed in pain on the hospital bed, somewhat delirious. His crimson eyes took a long time to focus on Craig.

"I just learned of your black-program research for the Soviet military," Craig said. "Why didn't you tell me about it before?"

General Ursov had been coy, giving few specific details but confirming that Dumenco had indeed been a key physicist developing directed-energy weapons for the Soviet military. But he and his family had defected to the West during the breakup of the USSR. While he himself had retained a relatively high profile, Dumenco's family had never been seen again.

"Has someone tried to kill you because of your weapons research?" Craig demanded. "The classified work you left behind in the Soviet Union? Is that what they're after? Is that why someone exposed you to radiation in the Fermilab accelerator?"

"Perhaps," Dumenco croaked. "Probably not." His eyes rolled, leaking fluid that might have been tears or just mucous from damaged membranes. "They didn't want me to talk about the things I had discovered. I had sworn to keep that work secret. But after my accident, they were afraid, afraid I would talk on my deathbed." He shook his head. "But I had promised not to reveal what I know, and I am a man of my word."

"And you haven't revealed anything. But I'm not asking for classified results, Professor. I'm asking for help."

Dumenco was quiet for a long time. He looked to Craig, but could find no empathy.

Dumenco's lip trembled. "When I came here I had to . . . leave my family. Your State Department changed their names to keep them safe. I thought if I remained silent about my research, then the secret police might leave me alone, might leave . . . them alone."

Craig held up the folded sheet of paper found in the assassin's pocket. "Then why do you think he had this list? To mail them Christmas cards? I don't think so."

Dumenco looked devastated at the revelation. "Even I didn't know where they were located. I haven't seen them in a year. Names changed, they moved to different places, an odd stepchild of your U.S. Marshal witness protection program."

Craig stiffened as the appalling truth hit him. June Atwood hadn't told him any of this. Dumenco had kept quiet all these years, and his family had been in hiding, with new lives set up by the Bureau itself!

Trish hurried around to check on Dumenco's IV drip, monitoring his vital signs with the apparatus, but she just wanted to get closer to the old man, trying to offer comfort by her presence.

"So why did this man try to kill you? How did he get into Fermilab, and how do you think he triggered your radiation exposure? Was he a hired-gun from the former Soviet Union, someone leftover from the KGB?"

"My work at Fermilab was beginning . . . to reproduce some of my efforts in the Soviet Union. I should have known it would draw their attention." Dumenco swallowed hard. "But this man could not have operated the Tevatron—it is much too technical for him. He couldn't have caused the accident."

Craig stood back crossing his arms over his chest angrily, but knowing that while the scientist was stubborn, he did at least seem sincere. This entire situation in the hospital might be irrelevant, or at least merely tangential to the original radiation accident.

But if *that* were true, then who had actually triggered the experimental failure that had caused the beam dump in the first place? What was the explanation for the vaporized blockhouse? Did it have something to do with antimatter storage, or the Nobel Prize? Who had shot Goldfarb, and why? And how was *that* connected with all this?

Trish injected Demerol and sedative into the IV. Dumenco watched her with faint suspicion, glancing around the entire room as if a play of light, a dance of shadow might hide another killer. Trish turned to Craig, anger apparent on her face. "That's enough, Craig. He needs to rest."

"No," Dumenco said, the panic rising on his face. "No rest. I have to understand . . . these test results." He clawed over for the well-thumbed data printouts from his p-bar experiment. "They're wrong, and I don't know why." He looked at her with a martyred expression. "If I'm going to die for this, at least I want to be right."

"You have to sleep, Georg," Trish soothed. "You can do it in the morning."

If there's going to be another morning for him, thought Craig. He looked down at the list of names of Dumenco's hidden family members. He would leave Dumenco for now. He had other questions to ask—and SSA June Atwood was damned well going to answer them.

Thursday, 5:32 P.M.

Fox River Medical Center

After much practice Craig had learned how to keep his frustration in check when he talked to the Boss Herself, June Atwood. Usually. After the stress of the past few days, though, with time running out for Dumenco, with the chlorine gas attack on himself and Jackson, and with Goldfarb barely clinging to life, Craig had had enough of tact.

He strode swiftly down the hall, already arguing in his mind. If Dumenco had been involved with the State Department for many years, the Bureau must have a file on him a mile long.

So why hadn't Craig been given a heads up? Of course, he had horned in on this case, coming in through the back door, screwing up the bureaucracy. But that was no excuse.

Craig went to a bank of pay phone booths. The land line would be safer than his cell phone, and he wasn't supposed to use his cell phone in the medical center anyway.

A lone blond nurse with her hair pulled back in a French braid glanced at Craig as he fidgeted at the phone, waiting for June to answer. A woman with a high-pitched voice squawked at the adjacent booth while an old gentleman dressed in a blue bathrobe waited behind her.

June answered breathlessly. ''Craig! I just heard about

Jackson and the shooting. Is everything all right—"

"June," he interrupted, "I need background on Dumenco. All of it."

Hesitation. "You have his file. I've given you—"

"I don't mean the dossier Fermilab uses for its brochures. I want the real details: where he came from, who he worked for, and why he defected."

"Craig, I don't have any idea what you're talking about—"

"June, no PR bull! I want it *straight*. Dumenco himself just confessed that he worked on Soviet black-program research. I know about his family, how they were hidden—"

"Craig!" June's voice came like a shot over the phone. "Can you get to a STU-3?"

Craig answered slowly. "I can get down to the Chicago office, but that'll take nearly an hour. I need to know *now*, June. I've got a murder, attempted murder, and sabotage to solve here—not to mention a victim who's only going to last another day at most. I'm getting more information from the bad guys than from my own office! How do you think that affects my confidence in the FBI?"

The nurses paid him no attention, indifferent to the usual patients' conversations. The man in the bathrobe tapped his wife's shoulder for attention, but the woman just put a finger to her ear and kept talking away on the phone.

"Are you calling from your cell phone?"

"I'm on a land line—it's the best I've got."

June waited a moment before speaking. "All right . . . but this is close hold." She hesitated, then said, "The Bureau had known about Dumenco for years. Our government desperately wanted him over here because of all his former work in the Soviet Union. Fundamental stuff, ground-breaking research he could never publish openly over in Russia. We wanted him to reproduce it here."

"In exchange for protecting his family, and getting them—and him—out of a country that was falling apart, after Chernobyl, after the end of the Cold War."

"That's right. Soviet weapon scientists weren't even known until lately, and they certainly weren't allowed to travel outside the Iron Curtain. But when you've attained Dumenco's stature, you can make a few demands. He went to European physics conferences—complete with KGB escorts.

"But they couldn't watch him every second, prevent him from passing a note to another scientist. That's when he made his break, and he was granted asylum in the U.S." She paused. "We set up a coordinated effort to grab his wife, his daughters, his son. Everything was in such chaos over there at the time, it was easy to do a bait-and-switch."

Craig pressed the heavy black phone close to his ear. "But Dumenco hasn't exactly been hiding. He's one of Fermilab's pet physicists, working and publishing for seven years. The Nobel committee even has his number."

"Dumenco knew he would always be in the limelight somewhere," she said. "But his *family* was the bargaining chip, not him. Unless they were hidden, they could become pawns for the KGB, blackmail to keep him in line. We couldn't have that, so we put them all in a modified witness protection program. Not even Dumenco knew where they were living. Under tight security, the U.S. Marshal's office arranged for him to see his family once a year in a safe house, at a classified location."

Craig swallowed in a dry throat. "So in order to pursue his one love in life—physics—Dumenco had to protect his other love, his family. That's why the assassin kept trying to track down the names and aliases, why he tried to kill Dumenco before he could make any death-bed confessions."

June kept her voice carefully neutral. "That about sums it up."

Craig knew what he had to do. "June, you've got to give me detailed contact information for his family."

"Impossible," she was quick to say. "Absolutely classified."

"Look, June," he said into the phone, his voice hard, "you *owe* it to me, and to Dumenco. You kept information from me once in this investigation, and I'm running up against the clock. Dumenco probably won't last through tomorrow. Give me those names and addresses. We need to get those people out here, preferably with an FBI escort, before it's too late."

June tried to sound soothing. "But those family members are protected and hidden, Craig. For their own safety."

"I don't *care*, June! You can do it. The family was only hidden as a safeguard for Georg Dumenco—and that doesn't matter anymore. In another day the entire reason for isolating them is going to be in a drawer in the hospital morgue. They deserve to see him one more time—he's their father and husband. I'm sure they'd be willing to risk it, if only to say goodbye."

In the waiting room several people sat nervously pretending to read the old magazines scattered about on the tables. Others looked at the ancient television set; the off-kilter hue adjustment made the people on CNN look yellow-skinned and jaundiced.

A candystriper walked by with a cart bearing plastic-wrapped gifts, flowers, chocolates, and stuffed animals. The intercom broke in repeatedly, calling the names of doctors or stating nonsensical phrases; to Craig, it sounded like a conversation during the old CB radio craze in the 1970s.

He continued to wait, but June remained quiet on the other end of the line. He had experienced her cold, silent treatment before when she didn't have a counter-argument for him but still didn't want to surrender the issue. Apparently, she thought that if she remained quiet long enough, the bothersome agent would give up.

But not this time. Craig could dish out the silent treatment as well as June could. In fact, many of his relationship problems with Trish LeCroix had stemmed from his not talking to her often enough. In this circumstance, he could use that character flaw to his advantage.

"All right, dammit," June finally said. "You win. Give me the hospital's fax number. I'll transmit the list to you as soon as I get it. I can't just look them up in a Rolodex, you know. I'm going to have to call in a lot of favors."

"They'll be favors well spent, June," he assured her. After giving her the med center's fax number, he hung up.

But as he turned away from the phones, another thought occurred to him. If Dumenco had walked a real razor's edge, doing work but trying not to reveal too much, the secret police would have watched him—but they would never have tried to kill him in the first place. And certainly not in a slow, lingering death like radiation exposure. It gave him too much chance to talk.

The assassin Jackson had shot couldn't be the one who had engineered the fatal accident. As Dumenco had pointed out, the Fermilab incident was caused by someone extremely knowledgeable about the inner workings of the accelerator, how to cause a fluctuation in the Tevatron, which would lead to an emergency beam dump.

Craig let out a quiet groan. He was exactly back where he had started in the first place.

Thursday, 6:10 P.M.

Fox River Medical Center

Leaning against the door frame of Dumenco's room, Trish looked up at Craig as he returned from his phone call. Her sepia eyes were surrounded by a corona of red. "I haven't felt this hopeless since Chernobyl."

"Is he going to make it through the night?" Craig asked.

"Maybe, maybe not. Human endurance is not a predictable quantity. It's just everything else on top of that—two assassination attempts, the attack on you and Jackson, your friend Goldfarb shot." She shook her head. "I know I'm the one who asked you to look into this suspicious accident, but sometimes I wonder if I should have left things well enough alone, let Georg die peacefully rather than introducing all this chaos."

"But doesn't your PR-Cubed want to use him as a poignant example, a poster boy against the hazards of radiation?" Craig couldn't keep the edge of sarcasm out of his voice. Trish had a penchant for tilting at windmills, and he knew that she had certainly found her birds of a feather in the Physicians for Responsible Radiation Research.

She adjusted her glasses. "Sure, they want to talk *about* him, but nobody else has bothered to come in and talk *to* him. The PR-Cubed is more interested in their ideals than in the real people—I see a lot of that now."

Craig folded his arms while she spoke. She *did* look

worn out. It reminded him very much of the way she had looked right before she packed all her belongings and drove cross-country to Johns Hopkins. Devastated from working the summer near Chernobyl, Trish had decided to specialize in treating radiation injuries. And she couldn't do it in California.

That was when she had left him, calling herself Patrice instead of Trish . . . though Craig never could remember to call her by the right name. She didn't seem to notice much.

Craig reached out to squeeze her shoulder. Trish sighed again, exhausted. "Why don't you get some rest?" he said.

"How can you stand to live this way, Craig? Is this how things are for you now? Always unresolved, always another clue to chase?"

Craig shrugged. "Pretty much. You get used to it."

Trish walked away toward a doctor's lounge where she could rest.

As soon as she rounded a corner, Craig slipped through Dumenco's door. He heard a cough and saw a feeble hand wave him inside.

The Ukrainian lay on his side, his back to the door. A light in the corner burned low, and outside the window a gibbous moon dominated the night sky. His technical papers lay in a disheveled stack, within reach, near the photos of his family. Two intravenous lines ran into Dumenco's arm. His eyes were hollow, his limbs pale and looking like they could snap in two if he tried to lift any weight. He appeared to have aged greatly in only the last hour.

"Agent Kreident," Dumenco said, with a forced smile that showed bleeding gums. "I would offer you another game of chess . . . but there isn't enough time." His face suddenly looked even more stricken. "I'm not going to have enough time, am I?"

Craig pulled up a chair and scooted close to the bed. "You have enough time to help me solve this case."

Dumenco breathed in shallow gasps, as if he had great difficulty merely forcing air into his lungs. He didn't answer.

"I need to know what you've been holding back. What you tell me will stay with me. I promise."

"There . . . is nothing more."

Craig waited. Moments passed, and Dumenco's eyes flicked away, unable to hold his gaze. Craig didn't move, didn't say a word.

"There is no reason for you to stay," Dumenco whispered.

Still, Craig remained silent. He shifted his weight from one foot to the other, determined to wait the man out. Finally, he said, "I know about your family. I know what they mean to you, and I know the terms of your defection. I can find them for you. Bring them here."

Dumenco closed his eyes. "My poor, sweet Luba. I cannot forgive myself for putting her through all this. But if I had left her and the children in the Ukraine . . ." His voice trailed off as he slowly shook his head. Tears welled in his hemorrhaged eyes as he opened them. "You do not know what it is like, to be so close to your family, yet be allowed to see them only once a year. The girls . . . they need a father, someone to tell them how beautiful they have become. And my son—" He paused.

"I understand why you had to do this, Dr. Dumenco."

Dumenco struggled to an elbow. His expression, vacant only moments before, now held a new life. He reached out a bony hand to grasp Craig's suit jacket. "Promise to let me see them one more time. Now that my pursuer is dead, you must bring my family here. Let me see Luba and my children."

"I am already trying," said Craig. "I'll get your family here." In fact, he expected a response from June Atwood any time now.

Dumenco searched Craig's eyes for any hint of betrayal; seemingly satisfied, he relaxed back on his pillow. His cracked lips moved in a wistful smile as though he were reminiscing about a time special to him. "For years I worked at Armazas 16. . . ." he paused, as if unsure if he should go on.

Craig nodded, encouraging him. "The Soviet Union did not even acknowledge the existence of that facility until a few years ago."

Dumenco threw him a glance, then his eyes softened. "Yes, you of all people would know. Armazas 16 was our premier nuclear weapons design laboratory. It was an exciting place, and an exciting time. We were lavishly funded, held in high esteem. Without its massive nuclear arsenal, the Soviet Union would have been no different from any other Third World country. Only bigger, and poorer."

Craig thought fleetingly of General Ursov and his pride in the Russian Strategic Rocket Forces.

"Back then, Mr. Kreident, weapons physicists like myself were the sorcerers—court magicians who transformed a collection of diverse and backward republics into one of the strongest nations on Earth."

"So you designed nuclear weapons? How does that relate to your antimatter work at Fermilab?"

Dumenco shook his head, rustling the pillow. "Not nuclear warheads, Mr. Kreident. *Directed-energy weapons*, particle beams, and lasers—but these required massive but compact amounts of energy. We studied the use of nuclear detonations as power sources, which would of course destroy a weapon each time it was used. The United States itself advocated fielding a nuclear-powered x-ray laser in space. But I set my sights on another, more elegant solution.

"Matter-antimatter reactions could power the directed-energy weapons my nation desperately needed to counter President Reagan's Strategic Defense Initiative, the so-called Star Wars program. It was the only way the Soviet Union could stay in this new arms race. Of course, then the key question was how to produce sufficient amounts of antimatter to make such a scheme practical.''

His brow creased with concern. ''If the Soviet Union had had access to the powerful particle accelerators here or at CERN, we could have gone forward with my antimatter enhancement technique. We would have been successful. We would have been able to counter your SDI, and we would have had true directed-energy weapons.'' He opened his eyes as he whispered, ''But perhaps it is the best for all of us in this world that we did not succeed.''

Craig put down his small notebook as everything fell in place. ''So you pioneered antimatter work in the Soviet Union and brought it with you when you defected. That's why the U.S. wanted you so badly.''

Dumenco nodded. ''At Aramazas 16 I discovered the mechanism for increasing the production of antimatter, for enhancing the p-bar beam, which I am 'rediscovering' here. And it was at Aramazas 16 that I also built the first crystal-lattice storage device, *years* before the esteemed Dr. Nels Piter. But because my work was classified, I could tell no one about it.''

Craig drew a quick breath. ''Does Piter know this?'' The Belgian scientist was banking on his CERN development to win him a Nobel Prize. But if Dumenco had already done the work years before . . .

''Dr. Piter knows very little, if the truth is told. He is a talker, not a researcher. I gave up my efforts with the crystal-lattice trap—I suspect that with the present level of technology, it is too unreliable. Unstable. Unfortunately, we have not had sufficient antimatter available to test the upper limits of crystal-lattice containment. Until now. My own concepts for dramatically increasing p-bar production in the accelerator beam should have changed all this.''

With a gesture more vehement than Craig expected, Dumenco struck the papers on his bedside table. ''But it doesn't work! The Tevatron *should* be creating orders of magnitude more antiprotons, but they just aren't showing up! I have checked and rechecked the experiment. It works, I know it does—but the results aren't there!''

Craig placed a hand on the old man's shoulder, struck to be in the presence of someone so pivotal in the course of political changes, all behind the scenes. The actions of individual people at critical times determined the flow of world events.

"I'll let you get back to your work," he said, cowed. Someday, perhaps, Dumenco's discoveries would be recognized for their importance. Someday.

Craig just hoped the Ukrainian was still alive when the Nobel committee announced their choice. Georg Dumenco had earned the prize, whether or not anybody knew it.

Thursday, 8:49 P.M.

Fox River Medical Center

After he received the fax from the Oakland Bureau office, Craig knew the next part was a job for Paige Mitchell and no one else. He found her in the hospital halls. She had been looking for him.

"Paige, you're the people person, the Protocol Officer," he said, gripping the curling fax in his hand. "You talk well to strangers. You know how to make people feel at ease even in difficult situations."

She smiled and crossed her arms over her cream cable-knit sweater. The loose sweater hung long over her hips, complimenting dark brown slacks. "Keep on like that, Craig, and you're going to make my head swell."

Craig didn't joke with her as he held out the list of names and addresses. "I need you to do some calling for me. Time to break the bad news and bring in the cavalry, for what it's worth."

Paige squinted down at the names, then looked up at him with her blue eyes. "What is this?"

"Georg Dumenco's family. Their names were changed, everything kept classified. He wants to see them one last time."

Paige studied the addresses. "They're right here in the Midwest," she said. "And Dumenco kept them secret?"

Craig shook his head. "The *U.S. Marshal* kept them secret. Dumenco didn't know where they lived—he's only seen them once a year since he fled to this country. Dumenco wanted it that way, for their own protection.''

Paige's eyes widened. ''You mean they've all been here within a day's drive of Fermilab, and they never saw him, never got in touch?''

''Only once a year, under U.S. Marshal supervision, on carefully prearranged visits.''

''But putting the family up so close to him and yet blocked away, *they* must have known everything he was doing. Dumenco was in the paper often enough, at least in the technical journals. His wife could have tracked him down without much trouble.''

''Unless she was afraid. Unless he had told them not to.''

Paige shook her head. ''I can't decide if that was a kindness or a cruelty on Dumenco's part.''

Craig sighed. ''I won't debate the matter with you, but it's time for one last kindness. I've insisted on it.'' He nudged the paper in Paige's hand. ''I want you to get in touch with them and bring them here. Now. Tonight. The FBI will provide the transportation, Code Red.'' He looked down the long halls of hospital rooms. ''Time for a final family reunion.''

At the nurse's station several women and one man looked at computer screens, drank coffee, and gossiped with each other. Overhead, Craig saw one of the fluorescent light bulbs flickering, trying to throw out just a few more photons before it finally gave up the ghost . . . like Dumenco would, sometime soon.

Craig watched Paige's expression grow serious. She swallowed hard and then nodded. Her eyes were misty. ''Of course, Craig, I'll do it. It's the least I can do.''

She went immediately over to a pay phone by the waiting room, picked up the receiver, and began dialing.

CHAPTER THIRTY

Friday, 4:47 A.M.

Fermilab

Nicholas Bretti knew that this early in the morning, the Fermilab grad students would be groggy, fueling themselves with stale coffee and paying no attention to anything but the largest disaster, such as the accelerator going down. It was too late for faculty or staff members to be around, and too early for the cleaning crew.

But it was the perfect time to slip in, move around without being hindered. He could retrieve his crystallattice trap and head back to O'Hare.

After Dumenco's clumsy accident had wrecked his previous stash of antimatter, and after the emergency repairs to get the Tevatron up and running again, the accelerator had provided a good beam almost continuously for days. By now, the sophisticated antimatter trap would be filled nearly to capacity with p-bars.

It was more than enough to set him up for the rest of his life, if that bastard Chandrawalia remained true to his word. Bretti didn't know if he trusted the towelhead after the threats Chandrawalia had made, and after having been deceived all along regarding the intended use for the antiprotons. Why should Bretti keep working with a cretin like that man?

But then what other choice did he have?

Outside, in the pre-dawn darkness, prairie grasses whispered quietly, and the electrical wires hummed overhead. Bright lights shone over the Fermilab site, but few employees or vehicles moved around. The only people here would be Director Nels Piter's paid slaves, working away on someone else's experiment. Bretti thought it was just a bunch of wasted time, as Dr. Piter was good at meetings, good at presentations, good at politicking . . . only his *science* was old hat, not cutting edge anymore.

Signs on fenceposts announced the coming weekend's "Prairie Harvest" community activity, when Fermilab volunteers and their families would go across the grasslands, plucking seeds from weeds so they could scatter them again the next spring in an effort to restore the long-lost primordial tallgrass prairie. After the weekend's activities, the fire marshal would direct controlled burns to raze some of the grass. For now, the captive herd of domesticated buffalo stood around placidly, dim shadows in the night.

Bretti still had a small crystal-lattice trap rigged in the beam-sampling substation where he had shot the FBI agent, but the main treasure was the larger trap down in the experimental target area. He hoped he could retrieve both, to increase his reward. Now that he knew the Indians planned to use the p-bars for weapons work, maybe Bretti could get them to up the price.

He scowled. Fat chance! For all he knew, they would take the antimatter and throw him to the wolves. He had to make sure he was paid up front, before he finally delivered the merchandise.

Snuffing out his cigarette in the ashtray, Bretti pulled his dark blue rental car into the shadows next to the concrete building, glad he had turned down Chandrawalia's offer to get his own car back. He couldn't afford to draw attention to himself. He could slip in and out, and be gone forever. Bretti shivered and pulled his jacket around him.

To the south, in the broad, cleared area of mangled earth, the construction machinery for the Main Injector sat like silent behemoths, ready for another day of hard work. Big plans, big new projects—Bretti thought of the weapons work the Indians were conducting with their huge capacitor banks and physics machinery at Bangalore. They would never be able to compete with Fermilab.

He used his key to gain access through the side entrance into the experimental target areas, where a quick walk brought him to a series of doors and chain-link gates. After opening two other locks with slightly different combinations, he was down the hall from the main accelerator control. Warning lights glowed red, cautioning that the Tevatron beam was up and running, but nobody would be down here in the target areas. Dumenco's accident would have done a good job of spooking all of them.

The floors were tiled with an orange and blue checkerboard of linoleum, worn but still garish; the ceilings hung with suspended acoustic tiles, water-stained in places from leaky plumbing. The piping on the walls was painted a deep blue.

Years ago, the halls would have been filled around the clock with students and staff alike, everyone eagerly anticipating the latest results of an accelerator run. Grad students would pull large photographic plates that had been exposed in a bubble chamber, and then they would painstakingly measure each swirl, each line and corkscrew of high-energy charged particles, shrapnel from nuclear collisions spiraling in magnetic fields.

The tracks on the film corresponded to fundamental types of matter, most of them known and well-characterized from years of research. But everyone searched for an unknown track, spirals with the wrong curvature, the wrong direction—a new elementary particle.

But that task was now automated. Every second, millions of collisions took place in the counter-rotating beams, and the tracks were scanned, catalogued, and scrutinized by an immense farm of Cray supercomputers in the Feynman Supercomputing Center. Individuals no longer played such a pivotal role in the big science of accelerator physics, replaced by the cold efficiency of automated machinery.

All of which allowed Bretti to move with confidence through the deserted complex, knowing that no one would be around to confront him. He couldn't afford another disastrous situation like when he had unexpectedly encountered the FBI agent.

Bretti opened one more locked door to where a bank of computer terminals showed displays of each of the experimental target areas. Here, he'd have access to the main lattice trap he'd planted.

A thick bundle of fiberoptic cables ran into the room, taped to the floor before running up to banks of diagnostic equipment. Thick concrete walls enclosed the room, shielded by fine wire mesh to prevent electromagnetic interference.

Bretti checked the status of the Main Ring and the Tevatron. Dumenco's gamma-ray laser had been up and running, operating in the small-signal regime, exciting the nuclear resonances so that an elevated, steady supply of p-bars would be injected into the main racetrack.

Bretti allowed a smile to form at the edges of his mouth. No one had discovered that he was bleeding off p-bars, and old Dumenco wasn't in any condition to point the finger at him.

He debated leaving another collector in place, perhaps coming back in several months—by which time he might even have a *gram* of antimatter available! But that would be far too risky—he shouldn't be loitering here even now. No, the Indians didn't deserve any more, and he wanted to be long gone. Cut his losses, eliminate further risks.

Gaining entrance, he quickly typed in a command sequence. He raced past the menu of options and posted warnings that scrolled up on the screen, then waited until the computer confirmed that the crystal-lattice trap had been pulled from the beam.

Now, with nothing to capture the surplus antimatter, the Fermilab researchers would suddenly find a dramatic increase in "events." He expected they would find it quite baffling, and no doubt work to concoct a harebrained theory of physics to explain it all.

Bretti glanced at the clock set above the row of computer screens. It was just after 5 A.M. Time to grab the device and get moving. He had a plane to catch that afternoon.

A few moments later he pushed a lab stool under the joint in the main beam channel that ran to the experimental target area. The thick pipe that made up the channel ran down the upper part of the concrete tunnel. Diagnostic wires, vacuum piping, and metal struts extended from the conduit, accompanied by a faint chugging of the pumps that maintained vacuum. Dim light, thrown out from bulbs screwed into protective cans, illuminated the tunnel with yellow light.

Bretti grunted as he reached up to disengage the antimatter trap from the experimental canister, which had been designed for quick and easy access by the researchers. Hundreds of such canisters hung in the main beam path, and so Bretti's addition had drawn no special attention.

He carefully pulled the crystal-lattice trap away from the interlocking mechanism and held the device by two bulky protrusions, the base for the solid-state diode lasers that trapped the p-bars in potential wells between the sodium and chloride atoms.

The crystal-lattice trap was much more efficient than the crude Penning trap he had transported to India earlier in the week. He was aware of the danger of carrying such a large quantity of antimatter—the glassy crater from the substation explosion provided clear proof of that—but the diode lasers seemed stable.

He stepped down from the stool while holding the

trap, careful not to bump it against anything. The device was designed to be rugged, but he couldn't afford to be sloppy. If he knocked the lasers out of alignment, this cache of antimatter would be enough to wipe out several city blocks.

Bretti eased the small, cube-like container onto its side, then stepped back up on the stool to close the experimental container above. The whole apparatus weighed no more than a few pounds. Electrical wires ran from the container down to the antimatter trap. He would attach the battery and clean up the area.

In less than ten hours he'd be out of the country. And a million dollars richer.

Friday, 6:17 A.M.

Aurora, Illinois

Jackson snatched up his cellular phone on the car seat after the first shrill ring. The traffic in small, residential Batavia was almost nonexistent at this hour. It beat the hell out of putting up with the idiots driving in downtown Chicago, and for an assignment away from the Oakland area, it wasn't bad—except for the fact that Ben Goldfarb was lying in Intensive Care.

"Jackson here," he said, keeping one hand on the steering wheel as he drove toward the medical center. Time was running out, not only for Goldfarb, but for Dumenco as well.

"This is Craig. Where are you right now?"

"Ten minutes from the hospital. I volunteered to watch Dumenco this morning, since the Board will still be investigating yesterday's shooting. Agent Schultz is banged up and won't be back on duty for a while, so I offered to help out the troops from the main Chicago office."

"I'll take that duty," Craig said. "I'm trying to make some . . . *arrangements* for Dumenco in downtown Chicago, and then I have to go to a gift shop Paige told me about."

"A gift shop?" Jackson said.

"Don't ask," Craig said. "It's important. But I was planning to go through the experimental area early this morning, *without* Dr. Piter present, to get a fresh view on Dumenco's accident. Can you cover that for me instead? You might see something I missed the first time.''

"That'll be the day! Okay, I'll grab Frank Chang, the grad student who showed me around Bretti's cubicle." Jackson signaled with his right blinker as Craig spoke, looking for a place to turn around. "Anything special I should be looking for?"

"Get him to take you along Dr. Dumenco's path the day he received his lethal exposure. See if you can figure out what it would take for someone to disengage the safety interlocks. Could our hospital assassin have done it, or did it have to be an inside job, as Dumenco insists? I'm still not convinced that just anybody could work the beam controls."

Jackson pulled onto the shoulder and slowed to a stop, preparing to turn toward the Fermilab site. A single cow stood by a barbed-wire fence, watching Jackson's car. "Craig," he said, "just check up on Ben for me this morning, would you?"

"Mr. Chang, I want to go over the safety interlocks in addition to seeing the experimental target area where Dumenco's accident occurred."

Chang tossed his long hair over his shoulder, grinning with self-importance to be the FBI agent's chosen escort. "You're in luck, since we just brought the accelerator down. P-bar production suddenly shot off the scale at about five this morning, which is pretty incredible. The increase is exactly what Dr. Dumenco predicted. Something screwy is happening in the accelerator, and until the theorists come up with a good explanation, we'll play it safe."

Chang gestured for Jackson to follow him, lowering his voice conspiratorially. "Dr. Piter's going to have a fit when he finds out the accelerator is down again, especially because of increased p-bar production. Sometimes it seems he doesn't *want* to see anything that would verify Dumenco's work. Piter's a . . . sore loser,

I guess you'd say. He's got his heart set on that Nobel."

"What about all the construction work on this extension ring—the Main Injector. Doesn't that interfere with your work? Lots of shutdowns?"

Chang shrugged. "Some of their heavy machinery screws up our delicate beam balance, but we just have to deal with it."

Jackson followed the young man down the tunnels. He smelled ozone, lubricants, cool concrete, metal shavings. "So what's it like working for a person up for the Nobel Prize?" he asked in a forced conversational tone. "Must be exciting."

Chang squinted up at him. "You mean Dr. Piter? I don't really work directly for him, he just holds the purse strings. But the man's a slave driver, a real nanomanager, looking at administrative details down to the billionth part." The grad student shook his head, flashing his goofy grin again. "He's lucky to keep any grad students around."

"So why don't you leave, go somewhere else?" Jackson towered over the young graduate student.

Chang looked appalled. "Hey, I've got a chance to be in on the discovery of the century. If this p bar enhancement really works, then we'll be in an energy range close enough to go for the Higgs boson." He looked at Jackson as if he expected the lean agent to share the excitement, but Jackson didn't even know what he was talking about. "When the Main Injector comes on line next year, the whole accelerator will work in this new energy range, and we just might have a chance to detect it. Wouldn't that be something?" Jackson blinked, but Chang's enthusiasm was infectious.

They passed through a chain-link gate to the main beam tunnel and walked briskly down concrete steps into the long experimental target area. Their footsteps echoed against the bare walls. Industrial lights burned at intervals down the tunnel.

"Dr. Dumenco was down here during the emergency

beam dump," Chang said. "He never should have been in the area, not with the beam on. It's a safety hazard."

"Yes, he sure proved that." As they walked, Jackson continued asking questions. "So what exactly happened to the guy? Some sort of an accident dumped the beam in here?"

"It does that automatically," Chang said. "If the beam fluctuates too much, or if it's contaminated, the system shuts down and the beam crashes down here. Dr. Dumenco happened to be in the wrong place at the wrong time."

Jackson craned his neck. The tunnel was deserted and silent, except for a low, throbbing hum.

Chang nodded to the left. "I can unlock the systems from the control room just around the corner." He pushed away black hair that had fallen into his eyes. "Then you can look around wherever you want. There's nothing dangerous down here anyway." He hurried down the tunnel, disappearing into the shadows.

Alone now, Jackson looked around the huge underground facility, built to re-create conditions that had existed during the earliest seconds of the universe. But with all the concern now about social ills and poverty, Jackson seriously doubted the public would ever go for building anything so massive again—unless the benefits could somehow be more clearly explained . . . and scientists weren't terribly good at things like that. He thought of the expensive Superconducting Supercollider that was supposed to have been constructed in Texas.

For now, though, the big science didn't matter at all to Jackson—he was more interested in finding Ben Goldfarb's assailant. Damn, he hoped his friend would come through all this.

The sound of someone shuffling across the concrete floor drew his attention, coming from farther down the curved tunnel, labored breaths, heavy footsteps, as if someone was carrying a heavy load. It was early in the morning, and few people were around. Frank Chang had gone in the other direction.

"Mr. Chang?" Jackson called out. He looked around. Nothing. He saw only the series of lights that disappeared in the distance, darkness and a cold silence like a held breath. He took a step forward, his brow furrowed. "Who's there?" He felt his weapon in its pancake holster at his hip. "This is the FBI—stop and identify yourself."

Without warning he heard the sound of feet slapping against the concrete floor—someone turning around and running away through the darkness.

Jackson set off after the footsteps. "Stop!" Why would someone be skulking around in the tunnels where Dumenco had been zapped, so long before work hours?

As he ran, the tunnel gently curved ahead of him, and Jackson never quite seemed to reach a place where he could see his fugitive. He heard panting breaths over the background hum of the machinery. "Hey!"

Somewhere ahead the shadowy figure stopped. He heard a key scraping against metal followed by the unmistakable creaking of a heavy door swinging out. He saw a young, disheveled man with flushed skin, sweat-plastered dark hair, and a scruffy goatee—and he recognized the face of Dumenco's grad student Nicholas Bretti, the man who was supposedly on a vacation fishing trip, but who had been impossible to locate. Bretti was here—at Fermilab, in hiding! The young man vanished ahead, running in full panic.

"Nicholas Bretti! FBI—I know you! Stop right now!" Jackson sprinted into the uneven light. He still couldn't see Bretti. He almost ran past a dark shadow at the side of the tunnel until he recognized an opening.

Breathing hard, Jackson cautiously placed a hand on the metal door to a diagnostics alcove and tried to peer through the darkness into the side chamber. Nothing. No sound, no light. *Where's the light switch?*

He tightened his fingers and wondered if he should draw his weapon—but other than the sound of someone running away, there had been no indication that this situation threatened his life.

Ever since Ruby Ridge, FBI guidelines had been crystal clear about the use of deadly force, and this instance certainly didn't qualify. Especially after shooting Dumenco's would-be assassin yesterday, Jackson couldn't take any chances.

But then somebody—maybe even more than one person—had tried to kill Georg Dumenco. And someone had shot Goldfarb, someone had attacked him and Craig with poison gas. Perhaps it had been Bretti.

Jackson took a cautious step into the darkened room. "This is the FBI. Special Agent Jackson—come out and identify yourself." He heard breathing, skittered footsteps—and his own heart pounding.

Jackson felt cold sweat form at his brow. *Man, I wish I had a backup right now.* In his mind's eye he saw Goldfarb being shot all over again . . . except this time it was *him.*

He cautiously reached out with his right hand to pat the alcove wall for a light switch. Again, nothing. He swept his arm in a half circle against the wall and finally found a control box. Fumbling, he switched it on, at the same time drawing his weapon and crouching, ready for the worst.

A row of overhead fluorescent lights flicked on, dim at first, but throwing enough light to show equipment jumbled across the floor. A dozen gray metal carts held oscilloscopes, computers, users' manuals, and instruments. A large-diameter pipe ran through the room about ten feet off the floor, one of the conduits for the high-energy beam from the giant accelerator. He heard a low-frequency throbbing, seemingly from the large conduit. *The beam channel?* Was the accelerator running again?

"Identify yourself." Remaining in a low crouch, Jackson swept his outstretched gun hand around in a semicircle. Inside the room he heard no sound of movement. He had been tricked, somehow. Bretti wasn't there.

Jackson purposely tried to slow his breathing—but his body was kicking into high gear, dumping adrenaline into his system. His heart pounded as he inched into the alcove. The place looked like a high-tech junkyard, a cross between a futuristic lab and a storage facility for computer nerds. Red and green lights glowed from every panel—taking data?

Jackson spotted an emergency phone on the wall to his right. He edged over, keeping his eyes on the equipment in the alcove, wondering where Bretti could have gone. He wouldn't allow himself to get in the same situation as Goldfarb without a backup.

He glanced at the digits while punching in the numbers for Craig's cellular phone. He looked up but could see no movement. Three cheerful tones played, then a metallic voice: "I'm sorry, the number you have dialed is not valid. Please dial eight to access numbers outside the laboratory."

Jackson swung his attention back to the phone—

The lights clicked off, plunging the alcove into darkness. He heard someone moving, gasping deep breaths, then the heavy metal door slammed, sealing Jackson inside.

Stumbling forward, holding his handgun in front of him, Jackson made his way toward the door. He tried to keep low, not sure if anyone remained in the room. He couldn't be more than ten feet from the door, but it seemed a mile away.

His knee struck something hard—one of the metal carts. A sharp edge cut his leg. Finally, he crashed into the door, found the handle. Pushed—

Nothing. Some kind of locking mechanism had fallen into place, and he was trapped.

Then he heard the low frequency thrumming grow louder in the conduit running across the room. Had the accelerator powered up again? Icy sweat bristled on his brow as he pounded on the sealed door.

His situation must be just like Dumenco's, just before he had received his lethal exposure.

Friday, 8:43 A.M.

Fox River Medical Center,
Intensive Care Unit

Despite intensive searching, the FBI computer files had no match for the fingerprints found on the bleached-blond assassin Jackson had shot in the hospital. Craig looked down at the faxed notice he had just received from FBI Headquarters in Washington, DC, and frowned.

He hoped June Atwood wasn't holding out on him again this time.

He crumpled the fax and turned to Trish who stood next to him in Dumenco's room. From her mannerisms, her extreme attentiveness, she seemed more like a grieving friend than a concerned doctor. Even after all of her ministrations, the dying man had entered his final stages and she could do little to help him.

Less than a week ago he had been a driven, intelligent physicist on the verge of winning a Nobel Prize. Day by day, he had disintegrated.

Trish looked at Craig for support, but he found it hard to credit her grief for what it was. Once, she'd been the most intimate friend Craig had ever had. Even before their breakup, though, Trish had spent so much time with her impassioned causes, her intense medical studies, her outspoken work with the victims of Chernobyl . . . he wasn't even sure he knew who she was anymore.

Dumenco tried to sit up, coughing. Fluids had leaked into his lungs, and each breath was labored. Trish had

muttered something about him developing ARDS—
adult respiratory distress syndrome—secondary to his
sepsis. His words were now heavily accented and difficult to understand.

"I feel . . . *detached*, Dr. LeCroix," he said. "My
body is fighting off a thousand infections, as if I'm re-
jecting my own internal organs."

Trish bent closer to him. "That's a good way of describing it."

"Having trouble thinking, too. Connections aren't fit-
ting together right in my thoughts, leading to nonsense."
He coughed out a small laugh. "Maybe *now* I'll be able
to understand quantization. . . ."

It seemed important for Dumenco to give Trish all the
data he could, describing his symptoms in excruciating
detail day by day as he degenerated. He meant to leave
one last legacy to science. Looking pained, Trish wrote
down the notes he dictated.

Craig could hardly bear to watch. Awkwardly, he
reached inside his jacket and pulled out the gift he had
bought at a strip mall. He stepped forward, placing the
flat, squarish box on the table beside the hospital bed,
weighing down the sheafs of experimental papers.

"I brought you something, Dr. Dumenco," he said.
As the scientist turned his attention, Craig opened the
ends of the deceptively heavy cardboard box. Moving
gingerly, he slid out a small but beautifully polished
chessboard made of alternating squares of onyx and
jade; two smaller boxes in his jacket pockets held the
tissue-wrapped chessmen.

"I remember our first conversation, Doctor. You're
right, you should have a chance to play one last game
on a fine chess set. My gift to you."

The Ukrainian's eyes, hideously damaged and barely
able to see, filled again with tears. He reached a swollen
hand toward the polished chess king. His fingers looked
like pieces of meat that had begun to rot.

Dumenco spoke, having trouble forming each word,

as if the thoughts kept eluding him before he could manage to get them out. "I'm afraid . . . I would not be a worthy opponent for you, Agent Kreident. A good investigator like you, sharp-witted . . . more than a match for me."

"On the contrary"—Craig smiled—"judging from our previous game, I think the stakes now are a bit more even."

Working diligently to distract himself, Craig set up the pieces on the slick stone board, though he didn't know if Dumenco had sufficient dexterity to move them.

Trish watched him curiously. Behind her delicate glasses, her rich brown eyes held a warm and grateful expression.

The door opened and Paige Mitchell entered, escorting a shaken-looking Nels Piter. The Belgian scientist's suave dress and cultured appearance looked disheveled, as if too much had been weighing him down for a few days.

Recognizing them, Dumenco grew indignant. "Come to see me off, Nels?"

Paige stepped forward. "Dr. Piter wanted to see you. He has something I think you'd want to hear."

Craig wondered if the Nobel Prize committee had announced their decision. But the administrator scientist had something else in mind. "Professor . . . we've gathered some strange data at the Tevatron. Of course you wouldn't find them surprising." He stopped, at a loss for words.

When Piter paused, Dumenco closed his eyes and whispered, "My results. The p-bar production rate . . . far too low. Should be higher. Has to be higher. Something is wrong with the data, not the experiment."

He glanced at where his papers lay stacked under the chessboard. Craig didn't think Dumenco had touched them in the previous day, but he wouldn't be surprised if the scientist had memorized enough data to work out the difficulties with no other tool but his own degenerating mind.

"I've been tracking the data myself," Piter said with an effort. "Until recently, they seemed to fit within the parameters I had predicted, proving that your gamma-laser enhancement technique was ineffective." Piter swallowed. "Until this morning."

Dumenco jerked his hand sideways in a spasm that knocked the papers and the chessboard off the table and onto the floor. Paige and Trish bent over quickly to pick up the mess, but Dumenco only had eyes for the other scientist.

Craig watched the confrontation between the two titans of science. Even on his deathbed, Dumenco doggedly defended his work. "Your predictions were incorrect," he muttered. *"Wrong."* His swollen hand clenched into a fist, and the skin cracked. He didn't even feel the pain.

Trish stood up, her hands full of scattered papers. "Calm down, Georg. Don't overexert yourself."

Piter shook his head. "You had no data to back up your predictions, and yet you still insisted. I thought you were irrational, self-centered, and blind to the self-evident data—a disappointment to science."

"The data was wrong," Dumenco said, somewhat petulant.

Now Piter looked upset, and he stepped closer. "But how could you *know*? This morning the p-bar production rate went up dramatically, reaching the levels you had predicted all along. I shut down the beam until we could understand the mechanism, discover what is happening. But with this result you've at least proved your theory viable. How did you know it would happen?"

With a great effort, Dumenco sat up in the bed, leaving stains on the crisp sheets. "You do not understand, Nels—I have already *done* these experiments at Aramazas 16. That was the work that brought me to the attention of the United States government. I already *know* the correct results. . . ." He flopped back against the pillow.

Piter looked at him in stunned horror and dismay as Dumenco continued in a weak whisper. "I could not tell anyone about it, so I had to reproduce all the experiments here, from first principles."

Piter took a step away from the bed, stricken. Paige looked from one scientist to the other, then at Craig. Craig tried to remain unobtrusive, attentively watching as the discussion unfolded, hoping some crucial clue would slip out.

"But how?" stuttered Piter. "The Soviets never had an accelerator large enough to act as a seed for your experiments." Then he stopped himself. "Unless your enhancement technique worked from the start!"

"My work was to produce antiprotons to—" He hesitated, as if unwilling to fully explain to Piter. He struggled up in his bed. "I already knew what I was doing when I came here to Fermilab. I had good results at first, but when I went into full-scale production with the gamma-ray laser increasing the cross-section, a large fraction of my new p-bars . . . disappeared somewhere."

Piter was intent now, his face flushed. His thin lips formed a concerned line, as if his whole world was falling apart. "But why haven't I ever heard of your early work? Why didn't you publish your results?"

"Those experiments were highly classified . . . for other purposes. My work ultimately came to naught because we did not have a way to store the additional p-bars efficiently. We did not have a mature enough technology to overcome a saturation instability."

Dumenco paused, then laying back on the bed, whispered, "And neither do you. Your crystal-lattice trap comes close—but it is still unstable. Dangerously unstable. Your solid-state lasers are an improvement over our old cross-feeding laser system, but you need to have them phased together better. Otherwise, your trap easily saturates and becomes unstable. We learned this long before you invented your design.''

Piter reeled. Craig knew that Dumenco had struck the Belgian scientist to the core—the crystal-lattice trap for holding large quantities of antimatter was the breakthrough on which Piter had staked his reputation, the basis for his Nobel nomination. But the world had—supposedly—never produced enough antimatter to test it fully.

And Dumenco had just claimed Piter's precious device would fail.

Craig drew a quick breath. ''Dr. Dumenco, if you said your new technique was producing a lot of antimatter, but the data didn't show it—is it possible the antimatter was diverted somehow, taken away before it could interact with the data-collection diagnostics?'' Both Piter and Dumenco looked at him skeptically. He continued, ''Could it have been collected in one of your crystal-lattice traps, skimmed out of the accelerator beam downstream somehow? And if the crystal-lattice trap is so unstable, could that have caused the explosion in the beam-sampling substation?''

''Preposterous!'' Piter sniffed.

''Yes, it is possible,'' Dumenco said slowly. He looked over at Craig, raising a finger as he stated his theory, letting the thoughts roll off as fast as they came to him. ''If someone is indeed diverting antiprotons from the particle accelerator into a crystal-lattice trap, the best place to store them would be in one of the beam-sampling substations, or in one of the beam-shunt passages. But the trap is unstable. If the lasers ever became misaligned, or experienced a rapid current flux . . .''

Piter swallowed hard, looking defeated. ''You mean, like in an emergency beam dump?''

Dumenco nodded vigorously. ''Yes! Even a microgram of antimatter would have caused such a devastating explosion. It would leave a glassy crater, and the electromagnetic pulse it generated would knock out electrical power systems for kilometers around."

"Just like we saw," Craig said, growing excited. "And Ben Goldfarb got shot in one of those substations."

Dumenco looked over at Piter again. "If your results suddenly showed a dramatic increase in p-bar production this morning, that means another . . . diversion trap has been removed. The beam fluctuations you observed early yesterday morning could have been due to the crystal-lattice trap saturating."

"But why would somebody want to steal p-bars?" Paige asked.

Piter looked down at her, and his voice had a sort of condescension, a withering disappointment because she didn't intuitively know the answer to her own question. "It's *antimatter*, Paige. Extremely rare, extremely difficult to create. It has thousands of high-technology uses."

"I sent Jackson over there earlier to look around," Craig said in alarm. "If somebody is trying to leave with an antimatter trap, we can catch him, see what he intends to do. I need to call for backup."

Craig snatched the sunglasses out of his pocket and pointed to Piter. "Let's go out there, Dr. Piter, now that we know what to look for. Maybe that's what Goldfarb stumbled onto."

Flustered, Nels Piter turned and followed him out of the room.

•
•
•
•
•
•
•

Friday, 9:53 A.M.

Experimental Target Area,
Fermilab Accelerator

Craig and Piter reached Fermilab some time before the backup agents from the FBI's Chicago office. Using his own keys, Nels Piter took him through the access doors and beyond Restricted Area fences down into the underground experimental target channel.

They ran down concrete stairs into the thick-walled underground tunnels. Before them sprawled low ceilings, naked pipes, and garish lights that vanished to a point in the distance, which made the high-energy facility seem to go on forever. The walls were smooth and painted a thick yellowish-white.

Piter nodded to the left. "We haven't used that beam-dump facility since Dumenco's accident. No need to worry about residual radioactivity, though. It dies down quickly . . . well, fairly quickly anyway."

"You really know how to inspire confidence," Craig answered dryly.

In the opposite direction was the main entrance to the underground passages and the Tevatron control rooms. Technicians, graduate students, and contractors for scientific teams set up equipment for international experiments, making the underground corridors bustle like a subway station. In the midmorning rush of activity, they took advantage of the beam's down time. People in lab coats or dark coveralls moved about in the main target areas and diagnostics alcoves, intent on their own work, trying not to get in each other's way.

An announcement came over the scratchy, echoing intercom that everyone was supposed to remain where they were and to offer whatever assistance the Federal agents requested. But Craig didn't think he would find anything in the crowded areas—the Tevatron accelerator was four miles in circumference, and the experimental target tunnel was nearly a mile long.

They briskly set off away from the main entrance. They had a lot of empty area to cover, many places to hide, many places to set a trap. What disturbed Craig most, though, was that he couldn't get in touch with Jackson. The tall agent did not answer his cellular phone.

Piter brushed aside his concern. "Don't worry. With all the copper shielding, high-energy equipment, and thick walls, cell phone transmissions are difficult under the best of circumstances. It's like being in a Faraday cage."

Still, it just didn't feel right to Craig.

Piter hurried along the tunnel at a brisk pace, puffing; sweat glistened at his blond temples. "We should first check the other beam-dump alcoves," Piter said, out of breath. "They're rarely inhabited and would be an ideal place to hide suspicious equipment, such as this alleged antimatter trap. Few workers ever have reason to go inside. Dr. Dumenco shouldn't have been there either—as he's learned too clearly."

Craig jogged easily alongside the dapper scientist. "Unless someone intentionally caused the crash and the exposure." He watched for Piter's reaction out of the corner of his eye.

Piter snorted. "Intentionally killed him? Preposterous. I can believe someone may have wanted an experiment to backfire or be delayed, for whatever reason—but murder is another thing entirely."

"Yes," said Craig in a monotone. "Yes, it is."

They hurried down the long corridor, running so intently that technicians and scientists hustled out of their way. A repeat of the announcement came over the intercom, and Craig knew that other Chicago agents must have arrived, descending into the tunnels of the giant accelerator. Bandaged and on administrative leave, Agent Schultz might even have used a little influence.

Craig listened to the humming of the upper and lower accelerator rings built into the side of the corridor. The superconducting magnets throbbed, barely audible. When the Tevatron operated, the magnets formed a shaped field that curved the beam of high-energy particles in a precise circle. When the beam was on, the protons and antiprotons accelerated around and around, picking up energy with each trip through a booster. The flow was like an atomic fire hose, gushing currents powerful enough to slam a deadly dose of radiation onto anyone who stood in their way.

As they neared the first beam-dump alcove, Craig was surprised to observe that the door had been wedged tightly shut and barricaded from the outside.

Piter frowned. "Those doors are supposed to remain open at all times. It's for general equipment and diagnostics storage." He stopped in front of the barrier, shaking his head. "This makes no sense."

At the sound of their voices, someone pounded against the heavy door from the inside, and Craig heard a muffled yell. Surprised, he and Piter rushed forward to unwedge the lock and pry away the barricade, tugging and grunting to swing the heavy hatch open. They heard more banging, a push—and then Randall Jackson staggered out into the tunnel, blinking in the wash of fluorescent light.

"Craig!" he said, leaning against the smooth wall for support, "I'm always glad to see you—but more so now than usual." He panted heavily.

"What were you doing in there? You were supposed to be looking—"

"I was *trapped*! I caught our man in the act trying to set up something. I thought he ran in here, but he tricked me. It's Bretti—Nicholas Bretti, Dumenco's grad student. The twerp sealed me in, and I've spent the last half hour just waiting here, knowing I was standing right in the high-energy bull's-eye. Not a pleasant feeling, I can tell you!"

"But Dumenco's grad student is on vacation. He left days before the lethal exposure." Piter turned pale. "And the substation explosion."

"I bet he never went on vacation," Craig said. "His parents had no idea where he was. He knew that if he was out of state, we had no reason to suspect him."

"Until now," Jackson growled. "I kept thinking any second the accelerator would crash and send another blast of radiation in here just like the one that hit Dumenco."

Jackson struggled to regain his composure. He brushed himself off and straightened his tie, as if trying to pretend he wasn't bothered anymore. "It was like he was trying to retrieve something he'd hidden. He was carrying something, but I didn't see what."

Craig swallowed hard. "An antimatter trap. It could be one of those unstable crystal-lattice traps." Piter clamped his mouth shut, indignant at that characterization of his invention that had been Nobel Prize worthy.

Jackson said, "If Bretti goes on the run, we'll never catch him—and he's already got half an hour head start, thanks to my stupid clumsiness."

Piter said, "I think he'll be up top. If he's got antimatter traps planted elsewhere, they'll probably be in the beam-sampling substations outside."

"Like the one that vaporized," Craig said.

Jackson nodded. "Yeah—and the one where he shot Goldfarb."

Craig spun around. "Let's get out of this sewer and into the open air. We're too late to do anything down here, but we can stop Bretti at the substation before he gets away.''

Piter huffed at the insult to his giant accelerator, but Craig paid him no attention. He turned to Jackson. ''Get to a phone and have all gates and entrances to Fermilab closed off. We'll converge on the substations around the ring. Nicholas Bretti is our man. I don't want him slipping through our fingers now that he's so close.''

Carefully, feeling a shiver of awe crawl beneath his skin, Nicholas Bretti pulled the small crystal-lattice trap through the access port in the beam-sampling substation. In the garish light of the cramped and chilly blockhouse, he held up the tiny container. It would only take a few minutes to transfer its antimatter to the other crystal-lattice trap, but he would keep a tiny fraction of the p-bars embedded in the salt. They could still be useful— as a diversion. Now, for the last time, he had to cover his tracks.

After today, he wasn't planning on coming back. With the additional p-bars added to the antimatter already inside the main trap, it would keep even Chandrawalia off his back.

Bretti checked the LCD diagnostic panels on the crystal-lattice trap as he started the transfer. The solid-state diode lasers were aligned, confining the antimatter. Each p-bar oscillated in precarious balance within a tiny electropotential trap of crystalline salt molecules.

He knew now that Chandrawalia's pretext of needing the antiprotons for ''medical applications'' was just a sham, a lousy story to cover their nuclear weapon schemes. Maybe now they would be willing to pay him even more—certainly, they wouldn't brush him off . . . not with this much antimatter in hand. He knew what it could do.

Finished with the transfer, he carried the crystal-lattice trap toward the half-open door of the substation as if it were filled with nitroglycerin. He longed for a cigarette, but couldn't take the time. If the antimatter containment grew unstable, he'd be gone in a flash of incandescent energy—himself and most of the prairie inside the Tevatron's ring. Bretti could have calculated the exact amount of energy released from the annihilation of so much antimatter, but his stomach tightened at the thought.

Of course, the survivors and investigators would take years to piece together what exactly had happened, what had turned most of the Fermilab accelerator into a glassy-smooth crater . . . if the bumbling detectives *ever* managed to figure it out.

He had no idea how soon it would be before the trapped FBI agent down in the beam tunnel would be found. But the black agent had recognized him, called him by name—and now Bretti was royally screwed. He had hoped just to slip in, grab the p-bars, and duck out again. Now, he had to keep them off his trail, get the hell out of Dodge, and stay one step ahead until he could board the plane to India and demand asylum or diplomatic immunity, or whatever it was called.

Getting away was worth sacrificing a few precious antiprotons, he decided.

Squinting in the exaggerated shadows of the cramped blockhouse, Bretti carefully inserted the main crystal-lattice trap into a foam-padded suitcase shell, a disguise that would make it appear to be mere carry-on luggage. As far as any inspection would show, he was simply taking a paperweight full of salt. And if Chandrawalia was true to his word, he wouldn't have trouble with any inspections at all.

Bretti would take one last trip on the Concord, and the payoff would be worth more than anything he might have left behind in this crappy, cold, and miserable place. Given the promised reward, Bretti could live like a king, even as a national hero for what he had done.

If he could get out of here.

Sealing the suitcase, Bretti looked at his watch. Time

to move. He carried the other, nearly empty crystal-lattice trap to the door of the substation and connected wires to the wall, and to the door jamb. The next time the door was opened, it would cut power to the cross-feeding lasers—releasing a few hundred nanograms of antimatter.

Enough to blow the hell out of the blockhouse.

Enough to keep the FBI busy for quite some time.

Bretti had to erase his tracks, create an immediate diversion, and keep away from the relentless federal agents. The stakes were high, the time was now, and everything would depend on how he managed to get through the next few hours. He didn't have any other choice.

He already had his ticket for the Concord, a one-way trip to India . . . and safety for the rest of his life, compliments of the Liberty for All party. He had his passport and packed suitcase waiting in the trunk of the rental car.

Lugging the main trap with him, Bretti departed from the blockhouse and carefully closed the metal door behind him, connecting the leads and preparing the booby-trap. Not looking back, he set off across the dry, shoulder-high grasses of the restored prairie. It was the most direct way to his car, with the least chance of him being seen, swallowed by the tall waving grass.

He had just stepped into the shelter of the prairie when he saw a gold rental car racing toward the blockhouse. Kicking up dust, it drove along the narrow access road that followed the curve of the racetrack accelerator. Bretti ducked down in the dry grass, his heart pounding. *Already! Shit!*

He backed slowly away, rustling through the grass as he waited for the fireworks to start.

Minutes earlier, in the first blockhouse around the accelerator ring—where Goldfarb had been shot—Craig, Jackson, and Piter had found nothing, exactly as Craig had expected. Schultz's evidence technicians had scoured the substation for clues. Among the fingerprints found there, Craig was sure they would identify Bretti's—but that proved nothing, since the grad student had been authorized to work in that building, after all.

The site of the second blockhouse held only the glassy crater, which they now guessed had been caused by a failed antimatter trap.

As they approached the third substation, though, Craig felt the hairs tingle on the back of his neck. He wasn't thoroughly familiar with the small and ugly buildings, but something about the trampled grass around the exterior, the mussed gravel around the steel door, the way the padlock hung on the latch, made him think that someone had been here not long before.

Squinting through his sunglasses, he looked over at Jackson. The other agent stood tense, as if he could sense something in the air. The three men cautiously approached the substation door, and Craig nodded to Nels Piter. "Give me the key. Let's open it up and see what we find inside."

The Belgian scientist fumbled with his key ring. Selecting a key and handing it to Craig, Piter stood back and watched. Craig twisted it in the padlock with a click, and hung the lock on the ring, swinging aside the hasp.

Before opening the heavy door, Craig looked around, squinting into the bright autumn morning. The brown grass stretched ahead of him inside the circle of the buried accelerator, rasping together like witches' brooms in the brisk, chill breeze. He sensed someone watching him, but he put it down as nerves. Fermilab's famous buffalo wandered out on the prairie, incongruous among the high-tech substations and high-voltage electrical wires that ran around the lab. An intense silence hung in the air.

Craig pulled on the door. Before he could say anything, though, before the words could even form in his mind, an explosion ripped through the thick-walled blockhouse.

The blast hurled Craig backward like a punch from a giant fist. All he could see were dazzling flames and a bright wall of light.

Friday, 11:36 A.M.

Fermilab Accelerator,
Beam-Sampling Substation

The overpressure wave hurled Craig backward into Nels Piter and slammed the battleship-steel door against the outer wall with a thunderous clang. He covered his head with his arms, sheltering Piter with his body. His ears throbbed from the boom, and heat seared his skin.

The concrete-block walls split and cracked, squirting flames like blood leaking from a cracked scab. A secondary fire crackled with plumes of greasy, noxious smoke, but the blaze found little fuel inside the blockhouse. Broken fragments of cinderblock and metal rebar rained around them like a snowstorm of junkyard objects.

Moments later, Piter groaned and rolled to the side. Craig stood up, shaking his head. His suit jacket was torn, dusty, battered, and he did his best to brush himself off.

Jackson had tumbled to the rough ground, skidding his shoulders across the gravel and into the autumn-dead grass. Now he got to his hands and knees, cradling his skull, disoriented and stunned. "Was that another antimatter release?" he asked. "Did we set one off?"

When Craig shrugged, his head throbbed with the sudden movement. His ears continued ringing. "If so, this one wasn't as powerful."

Piter sat down heavily on the gravel pathway, looking

comical with his dapper appearance now smudged with soot and dust. "We shouldn't go inside the rubble, in case there's residual radiation." He gripped his knees with long, angular hands and blinked his pale blue eyes. "We're lucky the blockhouse walls and the heavy door were thick enough to absorb the prompt radiation—otherwise, we'd be going to the hospital like Dr. Dumenco."

Jackson was silent for a long time. "Bretti set that up deliberately," he said finally, keeping his voice under control. "A boobytrap."

"Just like how he must have boobytrapped Dumenco in the beam-dump alcove," Piter said quickly.

"After he locked me down in the tunnel, he knew we'd come looking for him. So he was waiting for us here. Could have been a diversion, or maybe he's just homicidal." Jackson's voice was a growl. "That guy is really starting to annoy me."

"After this explosion, and after shooting Goldfarb, and after dumping the lethal exposure on Dumenco, it's safe to say he's got a bloodthirsty streak a mile wide." Craig placed his hands on his hips, scanning the silent prairie that stretched around them for miles. "I've got a gut feeling, though, that we missed him by only a few minutes."

He heard sirens swelling in the distance, emergency response crews from Fermilab racing to the site of the explosion. Bretti had grabbed their attention, all right—but by now the grad student could be anywhere.

They would comb the area inch by inch, get all available FBI and law-enforcement personnel to barricade the exits. They had to trap Bretti here before he did anything else.

From his hiding place in the thick grass, Bretti watched the explosion. He had jury-rigged the power to disengage from the crystal-lattice the moment the substation door opened the merest crack; but he didn't think the FBI would be so close behind him. He should have had more time, even just a few more minutes.

He hadn't wanted to kill the agents outright—just incapacitate them, get them out of the way so he could make his last run, escape from this place forever. Of course, he had already shot another FBI agent, the curly-haired one, even though he hadn't meant to. At this point, with everything that had happened, with everything he had already done, Bretti hoped the other agents would make a distinction between *Attempted* Murder and Murder.

But those FBI men looked really pissed off.

All the more reason to get out of the country, politically safe from any possible extradition. He'd gotten in much too deep to talk his way out, and he had to keep plunging forward no matter who else he had to step on. He just wished he had a little more faith in Chandrawalia and the crackpot nuclear weapons schemes of a renegade political party.

Fermilab was already crawling with FBI, and the new explosion would only draw their attention. He had to create another diversion, a major one. Seven thousand acres was one hell of a large area to search. If he could keep them busy with several emergencies, it would dilute their manpower, limit the FBI's ability to watch for a single man who knew his way around.

Luckily, Bretti had parked his car outside the Fermilab perimeter, near the temporary living quarters for visiting scientists. He shouldn't have a difficult time getting there . . . if he played his cards right.

Out in the grass, the wandering herd of buffalo—great shaggy beasts as stupid as they were large—stood aligned like iron filings to a magnet, staring at the site of the blockhouse explosion, as if the loud noise had somehow penetrated their fuzzy awareness. He could get past them without a problem, given a sufficient distraction.

Taking out his disposable cigarette lighter, Bretti bent

over, struck a flame, and ignited the dry grass in front of him. He checked the wind, judged which way it was blowing, and ran the opposite direction.

The flames gnashed at the dry grasses. It was about the time of the year for the community service groups, the ecology-minded volunteers, to come into the prairie restoration areas and set their autumn fires. By simulating a natural lightning strike, they burned the dry grass to promote the growth of the ecosystem they were trying to restore.

Bretti himself would be the lightning today.

He ran along, dipping the cigarette lighter to the dry vegetation, like a graffiti artist with a spray can. The flames spread like acid soaking into filter paper. Bretti crouched to ignite another flashpoint, sprinted ahead, then lit another island of dry grass.

The numerous blazes swelled rapidly. Even against the breeze the flames began to eat their way back toward him, hungrily consuming the dry fuel. Bretti ran at top speed, sweating and panting, in a direct line across the featureless prairie toward the shallow holding ponds, the accelerator ring, and the outer boundary of the site.

If everything worked right he could be home free in less than an hour.

With his head still ringing from the explosion, Craig scanned the waving, crisp brown prairie. He rubbed his nose, finding a trickle of blood from one nostril, but he figured he could survive. The grass blades spread out like a lake of kindling enclosed by the boundary of the particle accelerator. He froze, as dread formed a chip of ice in his chest.

Out in the sea of grass, another column of smoke rose. A brush fire that spread rapidly toward them.

Craig saw the figure running behind the flames. Though the prairie grass was tall, the man's head and shoulders rose above the swaying blades once he stood up to run.

"There he is!" He grabbed Jackson's arm.

"Let me at him."

Craig spun about to face the Belgian scientist. "Stay here, Dr. Piter. Jackson, call for immediate backup. Tell the fire crew to worry about the grass blaze more than the blockhouse."

Jackson yanked out his cellular phone, punched in a number for the local FBI team already responding to the explosion.

Piter smoothed his suit jacket, still trying to regain his dignity. "I'm going back to my office," he said. "This is no game for me."

Ignoring him, Craig ran at full speed into the grass, pumping his legs, heading toward where he had seen the figure run. But the smoke grew rapidly thicker. The flames rushed onward, pushed by a stiff October breeze.

As Craig approached the edge of the flames, he cut left, trying to find a thin patch of smoldering ground he could stomp through. The air smelled of thick pungent smoke, burning vegetation. Birds flew up from their hiding places, but the tearing-paper crackle of the blaze drowned out their squawking cries.

Jackson puffed up beside him. "Didn't anybody ever tell you you're not supposed to run into an oncoming flame front?" he said. "Head over to the pond. We can skirt the fire there and get past it."

Craig saw what the other agent meant and took off, plowing through the grass, stumbling on insidious weeds, old lichen-covered branches, and rocks that protruded from the uneven ground. He swiped blades of grass out of the way like a safari explorer plunging through an uncharted jungle.

Black smoke filled the air. His quarry, Bretti, had fled far on the other side of the fire while he and Jackson struggled to continue their roundabout pursuit.

Soot and ashes and sparks flew around him, and the blaze swept toward them no matter how fast they ran.

Jackson pounded Craig on the shoulder to smother an ember that had settled on his suit jacket.

The downside to the other agent's plan about getting to the holding pond was that the vegetation also grew thickest around the water's edge. The two agents stumbled through the weeds with the flames hot on their heels.

The rippling wall of fire approached with a hissing roar. Craig turned to see they had no choice but to head into the pond itself. Without a pause, Jackson rammed into him, knocking him down the slope toward the muddy water. Craig maintained his balance in greenish-brown pond scum up to his knees, while Jackson, over-exerted, stumbled, and sat down in the water.

Kicked onward by the increasing breeze, the fire struck the obstacle of the pond and curled around it, devouring the grass at the water's edge. Frogs hiding in the shore weeds splashed into the pond, while indigenous birds took flight. Craig ducked and kept his face low to the water.

Finally, once the fire line had passed, Craig helped Jackson splash out of the pond. Dripping, they sprinted across the burned stubble, the ground still smoldering and charred beneath their soggy shoes. Thick with smoke, the air scraped Craig's throat and lungs raw. His eyes burned, stinging from the heat and the soot, but he kept racing toward where he had last seen Bretti.

The grass fire had already consumed an amazing section of ground. Helicopters thrummed overhead, and emergency response teams finally arrived at the newly destroyed substation half a mile behind them. Ground fire crews rushed out across the flat ground to control the blaze, but it would take them a long time to get up to speed and pull their act together.

Craig was in close pursuit now. Bretti had to be near. He staggered into the smoke, unable to see, frequently losing his balance. Once, he barely caught himself from plunging face-first into the hot embers of a burned tree.

Just ahead, though, he spotted a dim figure moving through the murk. He yanked out his handgun and bellowed an ultimatum. "Bretti! Federal agents—give up now, sir!" Craig's smoke-clogged throat made his voice hoarse, and his words came out as a raspy croak. The soot burned his throat and eyes and nose, which were still raw from breathing chlorine gas less than two days earlier.

The fleeing suspect, barely seen, did not respond. Instead, the figure moved closer, threatening. Craig blinked his burning eyes, desperately trying to get a positive ID. "Bretti, this is the FBI!"

"Craig!" Jackson shouted from the side, and then pointed, forcing him to take a closer look. "It's not hunting season yet."

Craig realized that the large form was one of the domesticated male bison, its hide singed. Lost and disoriented, the beast lumbered past, snorting, its huge round eyes red-rimmed. Frightened and aggressive, the bull thundered away from the flames, avoiding their noise.

"You have a lot of faith in your firearm, if you expect a weapon of that caliber to do anything more than piss off a buffalo."

"It's a Sig-Sauer," Craig said, abashed, "a little more powerful than my old Beretta." He continued running after the fleeing grad student. They dashed across the blackened ground until finally—covered with soot and drenched with both perspiration and stagnant pond water—they reached the end of the burn zone.

Craig bent over, placing hands on his shuddering knees as he squinted into the distance beyond the Fermilab boundary, toward the cluster of buildings in Batavia, the streets, parked cars . . . a wealth of places to hide. He removed his sunglasses, blinking in the light, straining to see ahead—but he saw no sign of their suspect.

Craig took a deep breath shaking his head. Sweat dripped into his eyes from his chestnut-brown hair. Once again, Nicholas Bretti had escaped.

Friday, 11:44 A.M.

Fox River Medical Center

On the last day of his life, Georg Dumenco's exiled family members began to arrive—spectators at a premature wake. Paige led them in, hesitant but proud to perform one last service.

On his hospital bed, Dumenco looked hideous with his skin blistered, reddened, and sloughing off in wet flakes; it seemed a mercy for him to remain drugged, but the scientist rallied and fought, insisting on a last few hours of use out of his brilliant mind.

Upon learning that his prediction was correct after all, but that the antimatter was being bled off and thereby ruining the data from the detector apparatus, Dumenco sagged into stunned relief, as if prepared to die now that he had verified his precious theories.

The Ukrainian struggled to wakefulness and squinted at the new visitors in his hospital room, trying to see through the translucent curtain surrounding his bed. Paige thought Dumenco's face bore a dreamlike expression, as if he couldn't believe that his family had finally come to him, that this wasn't just radiation-induced delirium.

Paige stood beside the visitors, trying to remain unobtrusive. This was their moment with their long-lost Georg. She had the flight schedules. The FBI had arranged for their tickets with the greatest expediency, rushing them from their hiding places across the mid-western United States.

Dumenco's wife, Luba, his youngest daughter, Alyx, and his son, Peter, had come from Minneapolis, while his eldest daughter Kathryn ironically had just begun college at the University of Chicago. She lived close to her father, but was discouraged from seeing him . . . until now, when he lay on his deathbed.

Kathryn came forward in new blue jeans with her two hands clutched in front of her. Her straw-colored hair was cropped short, sticking out in a scarecrowish style that made her look like a waif. Her lower lip trembled. Her eyes were huge and shadowed as if she hadn't gotten much sleep.

Paige's heart went out to her, though she said nothing, just watching the tableau. Living in Chicago, young Kathryn had probably learned on the news that her father was dying and had spent days in anguish wondering whether she should break the secrecy, to put her entire family at risk by going to see her father one last time.

Luckily, Craig had taken care of that choice.

The wife also came forward to hold Alyx and Peter tightly, both of them shuddering as they stood beside the bed rails. Luba seemed afraid to approach the radiation-damaged wreck that had once been her husband. Georg Dumenco lay breathing raggedly through an oxygen mask, his eyes darting back and forth, sometimes with recognition, sometimes without.

Peter reached tentatively forward to touch his father's hand, but then drew back, afraid he might cause further injury. The scientist looked so fragile, as if the soap bubble of his life could easily burst. Instead, the young man hunkered down, leaning against the visitor's chair and began to whisper. Kathryn stood next to him, still biting her lower lip like a ghost.

In his bed, Dumenco managed a smile.

Because of his high-profile research, the technical pa-

pers he published, and his consideration for the Nobel
Prize, Georg Dumenco would have been easy to locate.
Paige was sure the family members must have followed
the career of the man who had arranged for them to flee
the Ukraine. But, because of the sharp and secret eyes
of enforcers from the former Soviet Union, Dumenco
had insisted that they never get in touch with him, never
be seen with him.

It seemed a horrible prison sentence to Paige, but the
man who had tried to kill him in the hospital, who had
broken into his apartment, destroyed Dumenco's computer and incapacitated Craig and Jackson with chlorine
gas, had proven such precautions necessary.

Carrying a bag under one arm, Trish LeCroix stepped
into the hospital room like a worried mother hen. Paige
watched her fidget in her clean white doctor's uniform,
her figure petite, her nails done perfectly, her hair short
and no-nonsense, her glasses delicate and stylish. Trish's
every move spoke of carefully planned elegance.

Paige could see why Craig had been attracted to her,
but the woman seemed more like a trophy than a human
being. With her aggressive work for the PR-Cubed, her
time spent studying the fallout and repercussions of
Chernobyl, and her impeccable training and residency
record, Trish LeCroix had many passions and convic-
tions . . . and little flexibility. Craig must have just gone
along with her, distracted by his FBI duties.

Paige smiled, thinking that for being so decisive in
his work as a Federal agent, where he could discern the
faintest connections, Craig was naive and almost passive
in personal relationships. But his slightly-embarrassed
nervousness, which he always tried to hide, was one of
the things Paige found most endearing about him.

She had forgotten how much she'd missed him over
the past year.

Trish crossed her arms over her chest and scrutinized
Dumenco's family, then glanced over at Paige. She wore
a sour but grudgingly tolerant expression.

Trish reached into the bag and removed various items: an ornate gold-plated cross, framed photographs of Ukrainian churches, and colorfully enameled religious icons that looked like collector's plates. Trish set them up on the bedside table and around Dumenco's room, firmly pushing his stacked technical papers aside.

The scientist's wife nodded in gratitude, perhaps recognizing a few of the keepsakes. The younger daughter, Alyx, helped to display a few of the items, thankful for something to keep her busy. Paige stared at Trish, her blue gaze filled with questions.

"I went to Georg's apartment. He gave me his keys," Trish said defensively. "I took a few things from his walls. I thought he'd be glad to have them around him."

Earlier, Paige had set up the polished stone chess pieces Craig had brought for Dumenco, placing them where the dying man could reach them if he wanted. Dumenco had made no move, no suggestion that he wanted to attempt a game of chess, but he seemed to enjoy looking at the pieces nevertheless, hypnotized by the way the light played across their slick curves.

Alyx's blond hair, longer than her sister's, flowed down between her shoulder blades. She picked up one of the small icon paintings and clutched it as she stood beside Kathryn, looking down at her father. Luba stood stoically, gripping the shoulders of her children; she stood in silence as the boy Peter continued to talk aimlessly. Now he was saying something about various baseball teams and pitchers.

Dumenco sat awake, watching them. His eyes were bright and sparkling. He leaned forward, reaching out with one swollen hand, then he winced as his entire body convulsed.

As Dumenco shuddered, Trish hurried forward. She glanced down at a prep tray and selected a filled hypodermic syringe, which she prepared to inject into one of the IV lines taped to Dumenco's arm.

"What are you doing?" Paige asked quietly, touching her elbow.

Trish's dark eyes flashed. "He's in pain—can't you see that? I'm trying to relieve some of it."

"But won't that make him unconscious?" Paige asked. "He's barely awake now."

Trish kept her harsh voice low, as if to prevent the stricken family members from hearing her. "All of his major organ systems have been destroyed or damaged. I don't know how he's managed to last this long, but he's literally falling apart. The pain must be excruciating."

"I know that," Paige said, also keeping her voice low. "But his daughters are here, his wife, his son. You said yourself that he doesn't have much time left, maybe hours, maybe days."

Trish shook her head. "He'll never survive to the end of this day."

"Then leave him awake and conscious for these last few moments with loved ones he hasn't seen in a long time."

"I'm a doctor. I'm supposed to ease suffering and relieve pain," Trish said, holding up the hypodermic as if it were a dagger. "How can I let him lie here and ignore his condition when I know what agony he's going through?"

"What are you afraid he's going to say with his last breath?" Paige said coldly. "Something about you? Something you don't want anybody to hear?"

Trish looked at her in astonishment. Paige knew all about Trish's activist work, the lectures she had given, and how many hard-line stands she had taken . . . but now, all the hypothetical situations had changed, and she was faced with a real patient—and perhaps for the first time, a real man she had known very well.

Trish backed off without answering Paige's question. She returned the hypodermic to its tray. "We'll leave him awake for now," she said. "But I have to watch him very carefully.'' She stood back at an uneasy distance from Paige.

Dumenco's family clung together at his bedside and waited for the scientist to die.

Friday, 11:57 A.M.

Fermilab

Craig stood on the blackened grass, angry and disheveled. Bretti had escaped from right under their noses. And the grad student now had an extraordinarily valuable—and dangerous—cache of antimatter. The sheer rarity of antiprotons made the sample Bretti carried in his crystal-lattice trap worth thousands of times more than any precious metal or gem.

But where would he sell it?

And, if Dumenco's comments were correct, the crystal-lattice trap was also disastrously unstable. Bretti had a bomb large enough to take out dozens of city blocks. Did he even know?

Behind him, fire trucks from the towns of Batavia and Aurora formed a semicircle to contain the grass fire. Crews dressed in metallic-silver suits with full-face mask respirators dangling at their sides pushed aside a firebreak and wetted down the brown prairie as a last line of defense against the spreading flames. Other crews sprayed streams of water high in the air back and forth across the grass fire.

Jackson trudged up, his dark face smudged with smoke and his suit jacket flapping open in the wind. Holding up his cell phone, he wiped his arm across his sweaty brow. "We're lucky this still works. Dr. Piter is getting us Bretti's home address from the head office—our own info on Bretti is back at the temporary command post. I'd like to be the one to catch that little bastard.''

Craig took a deep breath, then straightened his sunglasses. "Get the Chicago office to set up roadblocks while we check out Bretti's place. See if Schultz will send us some backup. And get a search warrant.''

"Got it." A cloud of smoke from the fire swirled around them as Jackson immediately started punching in numbers. The lean FBI agent held the cell phone to his ear. With the prairie fire raging behind him, he looked like a lone survivor from a bombing raid.

Jackson pulled the rental car up to the empty curb in front of a line of duplex ranch houses. Beside him, Craig squinted through his sunglasses at the mailbox numbers out by the road. "Number one hundred twenty two should be right around the corner, on the right.''

"You don't think he could have found an *older* part of town to live in, do you?'' Jackson said as he punched in numbers in his cell phone, checking on their backup. "What a bunch of dumps.''

"He's a grad student, remember?'' Craig said. He remembered his own days of starvation wages, when even a professor's salary seemed like a huge amount of money. A duplex like this was a *nice* place to live, compared with some of the student dives he had seen.

At Stanford, while working part time for the private investigator Elliot Lang, Craig had spent many hours studying for classes, thinking through term papers, fighting boredom outside rows of apartments in San Francisco, keeping a tail on a cheating husband or a supposedly injured worker milking an insurance claim. Back then he only had to wait and watch, maybe take a few pictures.

Now they were walking into a literally explosive situation.

Jackson put down the cell phone. "Schultz says the

backup won't be here from downtown for fifteen minutes.''

Craig thought quickly. They had already obtained a verbal okay for the search warrant from a local magistrate who had worked with Agent Schultz in the past. ''I don't think Bretti's coming back here—not after what just happened out at Fermilab. But he may have left something inside that we need to know.'' He recalled the vital information he had found in the abandoned home of the leader of the Eagle's Claw militia near the Nevada Nuclear Test Site. ''And if Bretti's on the run with an unstable container of antimatter, he can go a long way in fifteen minutes.''

Jackson nodded. ''Okay, let's take a look.'' He sounded anxious to get to the renegade grad student. Almost *too* anxious, to avenge Ben Goldfarb's shooting.

Craig shrugged on his suit jacket, glancing up and down at the other low-rent houses to see if they had been spotted. He straightened his tie, trying to keep from telegraphing his nervousness.

Together, moving like two professionals, they started toward Bretti's duplex, the left-hand side of the building. Weeds and crabgrass covered the small yard. A crumbling concrete driveway dotted with fresh oil spots ran from the street to a one-car garage. A chain-link fence split the yards in two.

They stepped back, out of sight from the front window. Craig pressed his lips together, looked around one last time, and drew in a breath. ''We've got to move.'' He rang the doorbell, ready with one hand on his Sig-Sauer, one hand near his badge and ID wallet.

Jackson's nostrils flared, and Craig looked at him firmly. ''Remember the Rules of Engagement, Randall— this isn't Ruby Ridge. The best way to help Goldfarb is to bring this dirtball in alive.''

Jackson gripped his pistol. ''I understand.'' No one answered the door, and Jackson knocked, pounding hard against the door.

Craig gestured around. "I doubt he's here. You take the back door. Don't wait for me to yell if anything goes down."

"Right. By the book." Jackson briskly jogged around the corner, put a hand on the low chain-link fence and easily vaulted into the backyard.

Craig tried the front door. Locked. He stepped back to kick it in, when he heard a sound just inside the front door. He placed a sweaty hand on his pancake holster, prepared to draw—

Jackson yanked open the door, out of breath. "Back patio door was off its track." He held his pistol with two hands, the barrel pointing up in the air.

"Lucky for us." Craig dropped his hand from his pancake holster.

Jackson shrugged. "I did have to help it a bit."

Craig glanced around the threadbare room as he entered, seventies tract-home vintage. Starving student furniture, plywood-and-cinderblock bookshelves, orange crates covered with sheets for end tables. Empty.

"I didn't go through the house," said Jackson, "but it looks like only two rooms off the main passageway."

They quickly secured the duplex, but Craig knew in his gut that Bretti wasn't home. It didn't look like he had been here for some time.

The single bed was unmade; stacks of computer paper, journal articles, and textbooks were pushed up against the wall. A large cardboard box in one corner held copies of *Physics Today* and *Physical Review Letters*. Three empty cans of Pringle potato chips and a six-pack of Diet Pepsi sat by the nightstand. Dirty underwear was piled in a corner, but too many empty hangers dangled in the closet, some scattered on the floor. Bretti had just cleaned out his clothes.

Craig straightened. "I bet he's not coming back."

Inside the tiny kitchen, Jackson stood over a folding card table, scanning a sheaf of papers. Craig checked the date on the milk in the refrigerator; its freshness had expired a week earlier.

Under the table was what looked like a case of booze. Craig knelt to take a closer look. "Grand Marnier—a couple hundred dollars worth there. He's got an expensive taste for a grad student."

"Or was it a splurge?" Jackson asked. "Maybe he just got a nice payoff."

"Look at this." Jackson handed Craig a preprinted in-flight menu. On the front was printed WELCOME TO THE CONCORD. "What the heck is a grad student doing with a menu from the Concord? Doesn't that thing fly into New York?"

Craig stared at the list of Indian food, written in fancy script: Chicken vindaloo, curry vegetables, Kingfisher beer. "Goldfarb wanted me to go see it in O'Hare when I landed early Tuesday. British Airways was having a special this month, direct from Chicago to New Delhi, India."

"A guy who lives in a dump like this on a grad student's salary doesn't have any business riding on the Concord," Jackson said. "Or drinking a case of Grand Marnier. But what's the connection with India?"

Craig said slowly, tentatively, "Well . . . India's a threshold high-tech country. Maybe Bretti got involved with somebody there."

Jackson scrounged through the papers on the table, looking for a bank statement. "I'll bet if we pull Bretti's finances, we'll find he's made several large deposits. He doesn't seem the type to know how to cover his tracks too well. He's an amateur at this stuff."

"All the more dangerous," Craig cautioned, thinking of Ben Goldfarb. "Dr. Piter said this was only one of two places in the world that could produce p-bars— CERN and Fermilab. And with Dumenco's new method to increase the production of antimatter, Fermilab is the only place that could make enough antimatter for profit."

"Are you saying there's a black market for antimatter?" Jackson was incredulous.

"Yes, and Bretti has a large batch to sell." His mind's eye saw a flash of Dumenco, lying on his deathbed, confessing to being involved in a Soviet black program to power exotic weaponry. "Think about it. He just left Fermilab and he's on the run. Right now he's got nothing to lose. He'll want to get out of the country."

Craig stuffed the Concord menu in his jacket pocket and turned for the door. "Let's get to O'Hare. Whatever Bretti is doing doesn't matter as much as what could happen if that satchel of antimatter goes unstable. He could take out the entire airport in an instant."

Jackson raced behind him, leaving the door swinging on its hinges.

• • • • • • •

Friday, 12:17 P.M.

Fermilab

Back to normal, thought Nels Piter. Would things *ever* get back to normal? It had to be over soon. If Dumenco would just hurry up and die, the whole mess could be forgotten, cleanly and efficiently. And with the FBI agents rushing off after Nicholas Bretti, they would be satisfied with the conclusion of their case and just let the Fermilab researchers return to their experiments.

With the imminent publication of Piter's major new paper in *Phys. Rev. Letters*, and the nail-biting wait for the Nobel announcement, and Dumenco's lethal exposure—or even worse, his insistence that Piter's own crystal-lattice trap was flawed, *fundamentally flawed*—Piter felt tense to the point of nausea.

But the Ukrainian had always caused problems for Piter—even on his deathbed.

Waiting for the elevator door to open in the cathedral-like Wilson Hall, Piter straightened his impeccable suit jacket, adjusted his tie. He ran a hand across his hair to smooth down the locks that had been blown out of place.

He felt dirty, sooty from the fire—he should have spent a moment in the rest room making himself presentable. He had an image to maintain in his office. He couldn't stand having things out of place, especially his appearance—because he was very much aware that appearance *was* reality. He tended to avoid public rest rooms, germ-infested places all of them. He would just have to keep his dignity. That would be enough.

The elevator door slid open, and he stepped out onto the third floor, holding his head high as he made for his office, ignoring his administrative assistant Priscilla.

In the front-office hush, it seemed as if the woman's eyes clicked when he walked past, no doubt astonished at her straight-laced boss's unkempt appearance. He heard a chair pushed back as Priscilla stammered, "Dr. Piter. Thank goodness you're back! You've received several calls today from—"

"Please hold all my calls, Priscilla," he said. The last thing he needed was to have reporters pestering him when he really needed to conduct some damage control. A Nobel-nominated scientist dying of radiation exposure; two major substation explosions; FBI agents assaulted, shot, gassed; and a renegade grad student intent on selling antimatter on the black market—and all in less than a week. Piter's mouth twisted.

Striding into his office, he immediately shrugged off his jacket and hung it on a hook behind the door. He tried to brush off some of the grime, but stopped, disgusted that he only rubbed it deeper into the material. He longed for this terrible day to end.

Within a minute, Priscilla knocked at the door. "Dr. Piter, you've received another—"

"I *said* I would accept no calls."

"But, sir—"

"Priscilla, I ask you to honor my request. I simply have too much work to do, and time is extremely short. Our latest press announcement about the *Physical Review* paper takes precedence over everything at this moment."

Her reply was curt and sullen. "Very well, Dr. Piter." But she didn't turn to leave. "Sir, there is a telegram for you. I've left it on your desk. I think you should take a look at it."

Piter closed his eyes. If his administration staff wouldn't leave him a minute of peace, how could he ever prepare for the madness bound to erupt when Bretti's situation hit the press? It *would* make the news, and soon—it was just a matter of time. Worse yet, if the antimatter exploded and annihilated a third of Chicago, then the whole world would see that his precious crystal-lattice trap was fundamentally flawed.

And that turned his stomach and left him sick with fear.

Sighing, Piter turned to his private washroom to clean up before he moved on to decide what he would do about that imbecile Bretti.

How would he explain the discrepancy between his pioneering work at CERN and Dumenco's findings that his crystal-lattice trap was flawed? What had Dumenco said—that his solid-state diode lasers needed to be phase locked? And what would happen when his colleagues discovered that when the p-bar density reached a threshold, the container might become unstable? If it wasn't for that damned Dumenco, the world would never have seen so many p-bars, and the threshold limit would never have been reached, at least not in his lifetime.

He noticed the pale-yellow Western Union envelope sitting square on his desk, as if Priscilla had lovingly placed it there.

He picked it up and tore it open—

Then froze, stunned.

A whirlwind of emotions ran through him. Conflicting, competing for his logical mind to untangle. He felt as if he had been taken to the highest pinnacle on earth, and flung down into the deepest depths.

He reread the message, not believing what he had just seen—uncomprehending.

Fire and ice, he felt torn.

He clutched the message and dully sat down at his desk.

It was over . . . after all these years, finally, finally over.

And life would never be the same again.

Friday, 12:38 P.M.

O'Hare International Airport

Craig gripped the armrest of the rental car as Jackson took the exit to the airport at high speed. A white-haired man in a Jaguar honked and extended his middle finger as Jackson whipped into the far right lane, cutting him off.

Craig pulled his cell phone away from his ear as he struggled to maintain his balance in the car. "Hey, Randall, we need to get there alive if we're going to stop Bretti."

Jackson unblinkingly kept his hands on the steering wheel, precisely at the 10:00 and 2:00 position as proscribed in the Bureau's evasive driving course. "You're starting to sound like Goldfarb, man." Instead, he accelerated.

Craig didn't argue with the lean agent. This was personal for him, deeply personal—and he only hoped Jackson could maintain his professionalism.

Agent Schultz at the Chicago Bureau office spoke over the cell phone, and Craig pictured the man still bandaged up, stuck at his desk and wishing he could be in the middle of the action. "We've diverted the team of agents from Bretti's house, and our SWAT teams have scrambled. We've informed airport security. Did you want any uniformed police officers as backup?"

Craig lurched into the side of the door as Jackson weaved around traffic. "No, keep them away. The last thing we want to do is to spook Bretti. He's got enough explosive power in his briefcase to turn O'Hare into a smoking crater—and I don't think he even knows it. Keep this a federal operation, and let me run it from inside. Special Agent backups only."

"What about equipment?" Schultz pressed. "Do you need any NEST or FEMA support?" The FBI worked closely with the Department of Defense's Nuclear Emergency Search Team as well as the Federal Emergency Management Agency; but this was totally out of the box. The destructive potential Bretti carried in his briefcase was as great as a small fission bomb, but unlike radioactive material, the antimatter was undetectable.

"There's no nuclear signature to help find his antimatter trap. And if it goes unstable, you'll need the Red Cross more than anyone else. Just have additional agents stake out the International terminal, especially the Concord gate. We'll be running surveillance around it. Remember, we don't know Bretti's plans, and were not even sure he's here." He swallowed hard, not wanting to consider the possibility that they might be so far off base. "Were you able to find out if Bretti had applied for a visa to India?"

"We've queried the Consulate office in Chicago, and they're taking their sweet time getting back to us. I think they're giving us the runaround."

"Use what pressure you can. If Bretti is going to India, it's got to be in their records . . . unless the Indians are using some diplomatic Vaseline to slip him through under our noses. Call the State Department if you need help prying that information loose."

"I'll do what I can on this end. Good luck, Kreident."

"Thanks. We're almost there." Craig flipped the phone shut and held on. He spotted the airport Hilton and the arching terminal building ahead.

Craig had worked around scientists during his student days at Stanford, before going into patent law and then law enforcement. Researchers were just like any other focused group of people, but usually more intelligent, more introspective, more introverted—classic Meyers-Briggs "INTP" personality types—motivated by personal competence and attention to detail.

But they were also motivated as much by greed, professional jealousy, profit, fame . . . all the usual temptations other people experienced. Craig had to understand the grad student's motivations to be able to negotiate with him. And he certainly hoped this situation could be resolved through negotiation, rather than firepower.

As a frustrated grad student, who had worked for seven years with a Ukrainian èmigrè, Bretti would have wanted to do something big, something to get attention, money, women. He had worked under the shadow of a world-class high-energy physicist who kept his major black-program work completely secret; and while Dumenco published paper after paper, made "new" breakthrough after breakthrough, poor unremarkable Bretti had not even completed his doctorate. He would have blamed everybody else for his own lack of initiative, his own lackluster success.

And when the opportunity came to make a big splash, to do something exciting, something highly profitable, Bretti had jumped at it . . . and then had fallen down the slippery slope. He was an utter amateur, confused, panicked, and desperate. Goldfarb must have stumbled upon him in the substation, startled him—and Bretti had reacted like a cornered rat. Craig wondered if Dumenco had suspected Bretti's experimental sabotage, so that Bretti rigged an accident to kill his mentor. That would explain most of the loose ends.

The chaos of the Departing Flights area was maddening, an obstacle course of cars parked in all lanes; cabs honked their horns and dropped off passengers wherever they chose, men in business suits ran with briefcases, families hauled enough luggage to set up a new home, traffic directors blew whistles and attempted to keep order while being summarily ignored.

Jackson squealed up to the curb marked International. A red-jacketed steward shuffled toward them with a metal baggage cart. Before the man could touch the bill of his hat, Craig was already out of the car, flashing his FBI wallet. "Federal agents, sir. I'll need your cooperation to watch our vehicle." Jackson joined him, leaving the car running.

The baggage steward gulped and looked around, as if trying to find airport security. Craig and Jackson paid no attention to him as they ran inside the main terminal.

A fifty-foot-high ceiling extended to the left and right. Ticket counters for United, American, Delta, British Airways, and other carriers lined up one next to another, as far as he could see. People milled around in disordered clumps and ordered lines, dressed in jeans, shorts, long flower-print dresses, business suits, jogging outfits, sarongs, casual slacks, military uniforms, robes. Friday afternoon, and it seemed as if the entire city had come down either to fly out or see someone off.

Craig removed his sunglasses, stood on his tiptoes, and saw an advertisement for the Concord. "I'll go straight for the gate. You go cover the British Airways check-in counter. You remember what Bretti looks like?"

Jackson strode into the thick of the crowd. He stood a good half foot higher than most of the others and was able to orient himself. "Unless he had time for major cosmetic surgery since he shut me in that beam alcove this morning, I'm not going to forget a line on that little twerp's face."

As Jackson fought through the line toward the counter like a fish swimming upstream, Craig took out his badge and raced to the security checkpoint. He stepped to the left of the metal detectors and the lines, showing his ID. "FBI. It's an emergency."

The security gate supervisor glanced at his ID and motioned for a police officer. The officer leaned over, unimpressed. "Let me see your tin. I don't want to see no paper."

Craig flashed his gold badge and the policeman immediately straightened, then waved him through. "Need any help, sir?"

"There will be some backup here from the Chicago Bureau office," said Craig. "Give them a call to confirm it." It seemed everyone turned to look at him, and Craig hoped the attention didn't alert Bretti.

Running through the terminal and the customs barriers, he checked the TV monitors to see when the next flight to India was scheduled to depart. Ahead, the gate was just opening the line for today's flight. He pushed his way through the crowd, heart pounding.

Set just in front of the customs area, the Concord check in gate was situated so the passengers could walk directly from checking their luggage to meet with an army of customs officials. The setup was artificial, established solely for Concord's month of "New Delhi Special" flights—a convenience paid by the high price of a ticket on the supersonic transport.

The line of people twisted around the corner, patiently waiting for the perky ticket agents. The passengers were serious-looking gray-haired men in business suits; older, casually-dressed couples riding the Concord for pleasure; and a few thirtysomething executives. Everyone in line looked as though they had an expensive reason for being there—a critical business meeting, a vacation splurge, and each one expected to be treated as a VIP.

Grubby Nicholas Bretti didn't belong in company like that, and he should have stuck out, obviously out of place. Craig continued to scan the crowd, but saw no sign of the harried grad student.

Bretti *had* to fly out today. Too many people were hunting for him, and Bretti had to know it. Could he be going out on a regular jet-liner, and not the Concord? Was the India connection just a red herring? Judging from the evidence found in his duplex, Bretti had done this before, had met with Indian officials, and had already disposed of at least one shipment of stolen antimatter.

Perhaps the grad student was already in the waiting room—but how could he have gotten through the line so fast? The airline officials had just opened the ticket line when Craig arrived, and it was impossible to rush through customs—

Unless Bretti had some sort of diplomatic privilege, and bypassed the various customs and inspection stations. . . .

Then Craig spotted a tall, dark-skinned man with white hair poking out from underneath a light blue turban, a gray beard and a neatly trimmed mustache. He walked briskly out of the customs area, nodding to the customs officials as he passed, carrying himself like a diplomat.

The turbaned man walked purposely, looking from side to side. Glancing at Craig, he quickly looked away—then his eyes darted back before he abruptly angled away from the customs area while increasing his pace.

The Indian official spoke with someone in the crowd. Craig's heart pounded as things clicked in place. Bretti would need an insider—so no wonder the Indian consulate was dragging their feet getting back to them regarding Bretti's visa. If the grad student was *sponsored* by someone in the Consulate, someone who desperately wanted to obtain the black-market antimatter, U.S. customs would never question an official request from the Indian government. Bretti could have walked right through any normal diplomatic stumbling blocks.

Craig pulled out his FBI wallet as he approached the customs officials. The people parted like water receding from a rising mountain as he pushed his way to the counter. A customs officer glanced up, and he spotted her nametag. BELINDA. Dressed in a white, short-sleeved uniform, the woman brushed back strands of long brunette hair.

"Special Agent Kreident, FBI," said Craig quietly. He turned to the mall area of the terminal and nodded toward the man with the turban. "The man with the turban and the gray beard—he just walked past your area. Do you know who he is?"

Belinda stood on her tiptoes and squinted at the man. "He's from the Indian Consulate's office. He escorted someone through here earlier on official Indian business."

Craig's pulse quickened. "Can you tell me what he looked like? Even a general description?

Belinda shrugged. "A ratty-looking guy—dark hair, goatee."

So Bretti *was* heading out to India. That just about nailed it. Craig felt the pressure of time ticking away. He scanned the international waiting lounge beyond the customs table. People milled around the gates, some sipping coffee, others lounging in padded chairs. Farther down the concourse, a string of bars, newsstands, and duty-free shops provided numerous places for Bretti to hide.

The man with the blue turban had melted into the crowd. Craig looked from side to side, but saw only a blur of unfamiliar faces.

Craig tried to act nonchalant, as if he were one of the hundreds of passengers waiting for flights. *One of hundreds who would die if Bretti did something rash and caused the antimatter to explode.* He used his peripheral vision as he strolled down the causeway. Stopping, he put his hands in his pocket and pretended to look up at the CNN monitor, while he urgently scanned the crowd for a glimpse of someone who might be Bretti himself.

Craig ducked into the men's room and waited until the stalls emptied, one by one; still no sign of the elusive graduate student. He decided to walk down the rest of the causeway, to the gates serving other international flights.

A dark-haired man suddenly appeared from a door on the right. The door opened up to a plush, richly decorated interior—high-backed red chairs, a mirror running behind a fully stocked bar, small tables set off to the side where people might have a quiet *tête-à-tête*: a VIP Traveler's Club.

The man had thick black hair, and his scruffy Van Dyke beard hid his chin; his glasses were old, a style popular ten years ago. He carried a briefcase high on his arm and a small, frayed satchel by his side. The man looked completely out of place in the first-class lounge.

The man was Nicholas Bretti.

Craig focused on the brown briefcase. Smudged with dirt and looking as if it had carried Bretti's work for years, the briefcase had artificial gold locks with a simple single cylinder combination. It looked deceptively plain, but Craig knew that case held the equivalent explosive power of three kilotons of TNT—*six million pounds* of deadly high explosive.

And if what Dr. Dumenco had said was true about the device being unstable, the antimatter trap might break down and release its deadly energy at any time.

Did Bretti even know it was unstable?

Craig froze, then backed to the side, wondering how best to handle the situation. Bretti hadn't seen him yet. He had to call for backup, had to get Jackson here.

Before he could move, though, the bearded man in the blue turban reappeared from another entrance and walked briskly toward the grad student. Looking from side to side he strode up to Bretti.

The two men spoke in hushed tones, but Bretti held his briefcase close. The Indian seemed insistent. Bretti shook his head again, the turbaned official spoke sharply, and Bretti finally surrendered the briefcase, but kept his beat-up satchel.

Craig targeted both men, put his hand on his Sig-

Sauer. He had to move, head off the Indian and keep him under control before anything could happen to the briefcase. The man in the blue turban slipped away from the traveler's club, heading off down the promenade at a rapid pace. Craig had to stop this man first. They could arrest Bretti later.

Craig took a deep breath, ready to emerge from his hiding place.

Then Agent Jackson came charging down the concourse. With uncanny reactions, he spotted Bretti immediately and shouted. "Bretti! Nicholas Bretti, this is the FBI—stop and don't move!"

Craig stepped out, "No, Jackson! Wait—"

But the man in the blue turban had heard the shout, the distraction, and bolted into the airport crowds.

Friday, 1:13 P.M.

Fox River Medical Center

When Nels Piter walked hesitantly into Dumenco's hospital room, Paige saw immediately that he carried a great burden. His hands were shaking, his skin was gray, as if all the blood had drained out of him. His eyes, usually confident, now seemed dead, averted from the world around him.

Paige froze, wondering what horrible shock he had received now, what grave news he had to bring—or perhaps he was just coming to see the dying Ukrainian for the last time. He had left with Craig hours earlier, and now the usually dapper scientist looked worn, tired, and grubby. She wondered what had happened to Craig, if he had succeeded in preventing a further disaster.

As he came into the room, the Belgian turned and closed the door behind him. He seemed desperate to avoid the ominous duty he had to perform. He avoided looking at either Paige or Dumenco, or the gathered family members.

Protective of the dying scientist, Trish LeCroix hovered near Dumenco's wife and children. She didn't speak to them, simply waited nearby, showing that she was on *their* team, a surrogate part of the family . . . and on the opposite side of the room from Paige and Nels Piter.

Piter took another step forward, then heaved a deep breath. Paige saw his shoulders shaking. She suddenly noticed that he clutched a scrap of yellow paper in his hand.

"Nels, what's wrong?" she whispered. "You look like you've seen a ghost."

"No . . . not a ghost." He glanced down at the paper in his hand, but he wouldn't let her see what it said.

Dumenco's daughters Alyx and Kathryn looked over at the other scientist, wondering who this man might be. Dumenco's wife had eyes only for the man in the hospital bed. His son Peter continued to babble, tears on his cheeks, his words droning on, making no sense.

Dumenco himself, though, seemed aware of the newcomer. He shifted awkwardly, turning his blood-filled eyes to see the dapper European. "Dr. Piter," he said, the name rasping through his lips.

"Dr. Dumenco," Piter said, his voice leaden, "I just received this message . . . and I wanted to bring you the news before—" He cleared his throat. "It's a telegram from Stockholm." Piter had trouble making his words coherent.

"The Nobel Prize Committee?" Paige asked. Her heart began to pound.

The tendons in Piter's neck stood out as he swallowed hard. "I . . . I am here . . . it is my duty and my honor to inform you—" He looked down at the paper in his hand, then just began to read. "His Majesty the King of Sweden and the Nobel Prize Committee are proud to announce your selection, Dr. Georg Dumenco, as the recipient of this year's Nobel Prize in Physics. This singularly distinctive honor is to recognize your outstanding achievements in furthering the knowledge of mankind and the universe." Piter looked up. His voice was barely audible. "My . . . congratulations, sir."

With a valiant effort, Dumenco sat upright in his bed, astonished at the news. Paige could see it in his face. The dying, near-delirious man had understood. His face lit up with a surge of new strength.

Dumenco's family looked down at him, then over at

Piter in awe and amazement that somehow knifed through their fog of grief.

The Ukrainian reached out with the last of his strength to grasp Piter's wrist. The dapper scientist stiffened, looking awkwardly down at the man in the bed and then helplessly over at Paige.

"There's something else, Dr. Dumenco—"

Trish rushed over to the diagnostic apparatus, alarmed and concerned. "You must leave. He's having a reaction."

"No!" Piter stood his ground. Tears welled at his eyes. "Dr. Dumenco—it was an accident. I didn't know you were in the beam-dump area. Your work was right all along, and I was simply trying to delay your experiment. Since we were both under consideration for the Nobel, a spectacular announcement like your p-bar success would surely have tipped the scales in your favor. This was my only chance—my last chance, because we both know I'm never going to do breakthrough work again."

Paige blinked, feeling like a detached observer. She watched as Trish took a step backwards and shook her head slowly back and forth.

Nels Piter sighed, slumping his shoulders. "I was in the control room on Sunday night. It was unattended, everything running smoothly, automatic. I didn't *plan* to do anything, but when I saw the opportunity, I changed a few minor parameters, caused the beam to fluctuate, which shut down the Tevatron. I just wanted to delay your experiment. That's all. You know the beam crashes all the time—but I didn't know you were in the dump area. I just . . . I just wanted to delay your experiment so the Nobel Prize committee would pick me this year." Piter held up the yellow telegram and whispered, "I didn't know that you were there. I didn't know."

Dumenco tried to sit up. He reached out a shaking arm and spoke with slurred words. "I . . . I knew it couldn't have been Bretti. And I knew it wasn't the other

Soviet killer. I was . . . waiting for you to come and . . . tell me yourself. The results . . . the data . . . didn't have any other explanation.''

Dumenco suddenly drew a deep, heaving gasp—and his body spasmed as if the effort and the unexpected news had caused further hemorrhaging inside him. The heart rate and other readouts went wild and he began to tremble. ''We do . . . what we must—for science.''

Piter staggered away, clearly ashamed of what he had done. Trish elbowed her way forward to the bed. Her hands fluttering like small birds, she checked his breathing and adjusted the wires clipped to electrode patches on his skin. Then she shook her head. ''He's in the final stages now. There's nothing we can do.''

Paige drew in a breath, stunned at what she thought she had heard. She looked at the Belgian scientist, astonished, dazed, angered. Dumenco's family looked at Piter, uncomprehending, but angry. One of the daughters, the scarecrowish Kathryn, turned and mouthed the words ''Thank you for telling him . . . about the Nobel. It was his life's work.''

Dumenco's final decline lasted another seven minutes. Trish officially pronounced him dead at 1:36 P.M.

Friday, 1:10 P.M.

O'Hare International Terminal

Taking out his weapon, Jackson advanced toward the grad student, keeping his eye on Bretti's hands and the frayed satchel he carried. "Don't move, Bretti. FBI!"

Bretti's eyes widened as he recognized Jackson, realized what was happening. "Hey!" Drawing himself up, he sputtered, but no further words came out.

Craig Kreident came from out of nowhere, shouting. "Jackson, take him! I'm after the accomplice!" Then Craig dashed down the concourse.

As his partner ran off in pursuit, Jackson recovered quickly from his surprise and leveled his weapon. He kept a good ten feet away from Bretti. "I said don't move! Put down your satchel—slowly. And turn around, hands behind your back, now!"

Bretti knelt and let the satchel slip from his grip. He slowly turned.

"Hands behind your back, thumbs out. You heard me!"

When Bretti sullenly obeyed, Jackson snapped out a pair of handcuffs that was tucked into his pants. "Put the backs of your hands together!" He quickly holstered his weapon and strode forward to grab Bretti's hands—

Someone in the crowd finally saw what was happening and screamed.

At the noise, Bretti stiffened, then twisted away. He

looked wild-eyed at Jackson, now holding a pair of handcuffs and standing without a weapon.

Jackson didn't flinch as he grabbed for the satchel. At the same time he jerked out his weapon. He had the case—the antimatter container?—but he needed to cuff Bretti before the little twerp could create a scene, or worse, before he would do something rash with the unstable container.

Bretti struggled backward and looked around in a frenzy. He started yelling hoarsely, "Hey, he took my suitcase!"

Not looking behind him, Jackson pulled the satchel tightly against his side.

Bretti's hoarse voice sounded as if it would break with tears, "You slimeball, give me back my case!" He looked from side to side, pleading his case, trying to gain attention. He took a step backwards.

A massive hand at his right elbow suddenly swung Jackson around. The hand dug into his arm. "Where the hell do you think you're going with that man's bag, mister?"

Jackson saw a red, fleshy face, a man as huge as an offensive lineman.

"Give the man his bag!" demanded the bystander.

Jackson quickly assessed the situation. He fanned around. "Back off, sir. FBI."

The man seemed to see Jackson's weapon for the first time. His eyes grew wide and he took a step backwards. "Hey, man, I didn't realize—"

Bretti took another step back, trying to get away. "Look, he stole my bag!"

A murmur ran through the crowd. "Call security!"

"I'm a federal agent." Jackson pulled the satchel close to his left side. "FBI. This container holds hazardous—"

As Bretti tried to turn and run away, Jackson shifted the bag, but it opened up, only to spill hastily packed shirts, underwear, a swimsuit.

No antimatter at all.

■ ■ ■

Leaving Jackson to apprehend Bretti, Craig set out after the diplomat in the blue turban—the grad student's Indian contact, the man who now held the entire container of antiprotons. Craig thought the man must be oblivious of the sheer danger he held.

He didn't know that one slip, one jostle, one impact might disalign the containment lasers and allow the antimatter to come in contact with the sodium chloride crystals, setting up a chain reaction of annihilation, releasing three kilotons of energy. The explosion would be enough to vaporize the O'Hare International Airport.

The man continued to run briskly down the wide hall, elbowing people aside, pushing his way through the crowd until he could get to safety—a diplomatic receiving area? A consulate limousine outside? Craig didn't know; he only cared about stopping the man, confiscating the briefcase, getting it safely back to Fermilab where the physicists could figure out how to get the p-bars back out of the crystal-lattice trap.

Craig ran to the slidewalk people-mover down the center of the long concourse, grabbed the black plastic rail, and vaulted over onto the sliding metal walkway. He was going the wrong way, but he fought his way past, finally drawing his handgun—but he knew he couldn't possibly fire with so many bystanders around. People screamed.

Craig ran against the direction of movement. If the man was an official from the Indian consulate, he would flaunt his diplomatic immunity—in fact, Craig was surprised the man didn't just stop running and smugly shrug off the FBI's attempt at arrest. But with the antimatter parcel, he endangered the lives of every person at the entire airport.

Stop the threat. Craig would have been justified in using force to stop him, even deadly force—but if he fired, he would risk not only hitting other bystanders, but also a stray bullet might strike the case. . . .

A young couple with a wide baby stroller covered most of the width of the walkway, and Craig sidled past, paying more attention to the man with the blue turban than the people around him. He smacked his foot against the stroller wheel, nearly tripped, grabbed onto the moving railing. The baby began to cry.

"Excuse me," he said breathlessly. "Excuse me. FBI."

The Indian diplomat turned down a side concourse, in front of a gate where a large international 777 disgorged a milling mass of hundreds of passengers, also Indians for the most part—a large group of Hindus, some wearing blue turbans. Craig craned his neck, trying to keep track of the man. "Stop him!" he shouted. "Somebody call airport security!"

The diplomat bumped against a man in a business suit, then barely missed caroming the antimatter case into a rolling luggage cart. Craig felt his chest turn to ice. The man pushed his way farther along, ducking and weaving, trying to disappear into the mass of similarly dressed people.

Finally getting to a clear spot on the sliding walkway, Craig jammed his handgun back into its holster and vaulted into the narrow median between the two oppositely moving slidewalks. "Excuse me! Out of the way please!" He tried to keep calm, but he couldn't let the man get away.

He finally got moving in the right direction, then began to run faster.

The man in the blue turban flashed a glance over his shoulder, and Craig spotted him again by the flushed look on his face. The man also spotted Craig, and realizing he couldn't just disappear into the crowd, broke into an outright run.

"Stop that man!" Craig shouted. "FBI!"

With a burst of speed, the man dashed past a Starbucks stand, and customers backed away, desperately trying to keep their cups from dumping hot coffee. He ducked to one side, hit an Emergency Exit door, which unleashed a piercing sonic blast.

Everyone looked at him. Craig kept running. Another airport security guard rushed in, looking around for the source of the alarm. Far back at the Customs table, other men raced forward. Finally, the backup agents. But they wouldn't arrive in time.

Craig followed the man into a maintenance hall, through the squealing Emergency Exit door. The airport security guard followed, bellowing at him. Craig whirled and grabbed at his ID wallet without slowing. He flashed the wallet open, shoving it toward the security officer.

"Sir, I'm a federal agent, and I require your assistance." He panted, pushing through the door and looking down a narrow, concrete-block corridor. "That man is carrying a highly explosive device."

The security man hesitated just a moment in his step, then launched after Craig, looking a bit green. Craig saw the blue turban disappear around a sharp corner. "Stop!" he yelled again, his voice and his footsteps echoing loudly in the enclosed area. The high-pitched alarm continued to squeal.

Two custodians with a cleaning cart scrambled out of the way, still confused from the flight of the strange man in the blue turban. Craig didn't stop to ask them where the fugitive had gone, charging ahead. Behind him, the security man ran onward, his keys jingling.

Finally, Craig rounded the corner to find the diplomat struggling with a security-locked door. He pounded desperately, then spun around like a cornered rat upon hearing Craig approach. He held up the briefcase like a bullet-proof shield. His gray beard protruded, and sweat trickled down his narrow, dark face.

"Sir, I'm placing you under arrest," Craig said, holding out his ID again. He looked beside him to see that the security man had drawn his revolver, and was holding a heavy Smith and Wesson in shaking hands.

The man with the turban scowled. "I am Mr. Chandrawalia from the Indian Consulate. You have no authority to arrest me. I have diplomatic immunity under your law.''

''You have an explosive device with enough power to wipe out this airport. You are endangering the lives of tens of thousands of people—and I don't give a flip about your diplomatic immunity.'' Craig's voice was hard.

The security man looked as if he very much wanted to be elsewhere.

''Nonsense,'' Chandrawalia said. He gripped the briefcase against his chest. ''This merely contains a large salt crystal, a novelty item. A souvenir.'' He directed his attention to the nervous security man, as if for support. ''I am an official from the Indian government, not a common criminal. This is not a bomb. You are committing an illegal act by detaining me. Your actions will have serious international implications.''

Craig wondered if Chandrawalia even had a clue about the danger he was in.

The Indian lowered the briefcase. ''This is a simple misunderstanding. Here, I'll show you. Just a salt crystal, not a bomb.''

His fingers fumbled with the latches. Craig suddenly wondered if opening the case without the proper precautions would destabilize or even kill the power to the solid-state lasers carefully aligned on the crystal lattice. A simple power shutdown had resulted in the annihilation of an entire substation last Sunday night.

Chandrawalia's finger touched the latch.

Craig whipped out his Sig Sauer, dropping his badge wallet on the floor and stretching the handgun forward in a perfect isosceles firing position. *Stop the threat.* ''If you move another hair I am going to put a nine-millimeter bullet through the center of your forehead.''

The Indian gasped at Craig's tone, at his expression. He froze.

Craig said to the security man, "Take the case from him please. Gently."

"Me?"

Craig said nothing, just kept his eyes fixed on the Indian official. The security man came forward, moving with jerky motions, and took the briefcase from Chandrawalia's hands. The man didn't resist.

"I will lodge an official complaint," Chandrawalia said, his voice hard. "This treatment is inexcusable. I will speak directly to your State Department."

Only when Craig held the briefcase tightly in one hand did he lower the handgun. Back at the end of the service corridor he heard other footsteps, the backup agents running toward him.

"Complain all you want," Craig said. "This is enough for multiple felony charges, with this evidence in hand. You can't just buy antimatter at the airport gift shop. And I'm sure it's enough for your government to waive your diplomatic immunity."

Chandrawalia then faltered, looking uncertain as the other teams of FBI agents rushed in. Craig wondered just how much support this guy would receive from the Indian government, or if he was just a freelancer with big plans.

One of the backup agents stopped next to him while two others took covering positions on either side of Chandrawalia. The agent looked down at the briefcase in Craig's hands. "Did you get it?"

"Yeah," Craig said with a sigh, "I got it."

Cornered, Bretti wet his lips and looked from side to side. He glanced at Jackson, as if considering making a run for it. His rapidly packed clothes and personal items lay strewn about the floor in the lounge. He flicked his gaze toward the open door.

"Don't," said Jackson quietly as he leveled his handgun at Bretti. He remained utterly firm in his stance.

The grad student drew himself up and jutted his chin,

poking out the goatee. "You wouldn't shoot me with all these people here." He took a step backward.

"Try me," said Jackson coolly. "You shot my partner, remember?"

From the look in the other agent's eyes, Bretti decided to believe him.

Friday, 5:32 P.M.

Fox River Medical Center

In Dumenco's room, the silence of death felt like a heavy shroud. His family members stood around the bed, stunned and quietly grieving.

Paige felt out of place as she looked at the destroyed man. Yet, she realized that death had come as a relief to him. Through a sheen of tears, she saw the polished stone chess set Craig had given him, the icons and crosses and framed Ukrainian cathedrals Trish had retrieved from his apartment.

She had not felt so confused, or devastated, since her father had died, nearly four years ago. The anger and frustration from feeling helpless—and, now, knowing what Nels Piter had done to Dumenco—nearly overwhelmed her. She'd thought she would have been able to handle Dumenco's death better with his family here—but she was wrong.

Kathryn and Alyx stood close with their mother, holding each other, relieved to have visited their lost father one last time. Young Peter, barely a teenager, looked the most stricken of all those by the bedside. "But I haven't finished telling you, Father," he said. "I had so much more to say. We didn't even thank you for bringing us here to America. . . ."

Ashen-faced, Trish turned away from the scientist's body and picked up her clipboards, jotting down notes, filling out the death certificate, trying anything to avoid concentrating on what had just happened. "It was so senseless," she muttered. "Another one for the books, for the database. But we still don't know how to do anything about such radiation exposures."

Nels Piter looked awkward at the edge of the doorway, and Paige didn't know what to do, how to deal with him. He had just confessed to causing the accident that had resulted in Dumenco's lethal exposure. Murder. Should she call hospital security? She didn't think the Belgian scientist was a particular risk for wild flight—he had admitted what he'd done, after all. She could wait for Craig, she supposed.

No one paid attention to Piter, no one even seemed to notice him. At the doorway he crumpled up the telegram into a hard little ball and threw it into the wastebasket before he stumbled out into the hall.

Paige followed hesitantly, though she could see he didn't want to talk to anyone. He shuffled aimlessly down the hall with his head low, his shoulders slumped. This wasn't the self-confident man she had known for nearly a year, the handsome, sometimes abrasive, always quick-witted professor. A Nobel nominee.

This man looked defeated. A far cry for someone just achieving his lifelong dream.

Paige stopped to retrieve the paper, snatching it out of the trash, thinking it might be an important souvenir. But as she unfolded it and straightened the wrinkles, she glanced down at the text, reading the words there with widening eyes.

The elevator doors by the nurse's station opened. Craig and Jackson tumbled out, headed directly for Dumenco's room. Paige wondered as an afterthought if they had recovered the antimatter—but it all seemed insignificant now with Dumenco's death.

Craig ran past Piter, his chestnut hair flying and his tie flipped over his shoulder. He skidded to a stop on the hospital's old linoleum floor; Jackson pulled up beside him.

"We captured Nicholas Bretti," Craig said. "He's the one who shot Ben Goldfarb and stole the antimatter. It should only be a matter of time before he confesses to having killed Dumenco." Then he recognized the Belgian's stricken expression and looked up to see Paige also standing there stunned. "Are we too late—?" Craig hurried into the Ukrainian's room.

Jackson remained in the hall, silent for a moment, then he turned back for the elevators. He opened and closed a sinewy fist, as if still trying to massage tension out of his muscles. "I'll go check on Ben."

Paige held up the telegram as Piter sat down dully in one of the visitor's chairs. "Nels—you did it."

The physicist didn't respond. He looked down at the floor as if she was flouting the accusation. But she meant the telegram, not the lethal exposure.

"Nels, you let Dumenco think he had won. This telegram from the Stockholm committee congratulates *you* for winning the Nobel Prize. You're a Nobel laureate, not Dumenco. You did that for him." She felt exhausted, drained. "You let Dumenco die thinking it was him, validating all the black-program work he had done for the former Soviet Union."

Piter looked up, stung. His eyes were red, his face drawn in long lines. "I always thought that winning the Nobel Prize would mean everything to me." He shook his head. "But instead it means nothing."

Paige frowned. "You gave a dying man his final wish. He died peacefully because of you—"

"He *died* because of me!" Piter wavered, then seemed to wither. "My research was *shit*. I tried to push the envelope farther than anyone else, and instead I built a crystal-lattice trap that had been invented years before, in a country that was falling apart!" Piter was almost sobbing.

Craig came back out of the hospital room, looking devastated and angry. "I should have shot Bretti when

I had the excuse," he said bitterly. "He never even came to see all the grief he caused."

Paige stood next to Piter, who sat helplessly in a chair. "It wasn't Bretti," she said, looking at the lethargic Belgian, knowing he wasn't up to repeating his confession. She explained everything Piter had said, while Craig listened in amazement.

Piter looked down at the floor and spoke in a whisper. "Who in his right mind would ever have thought it was possible to generate billions of times more p-bars than had ever been produced before? As long as it only needed to hold small amounts of antimatter, my crystal-lattice trap worked perfectly. But as soon as a threshold was reached, it became unstable. Dumenco knew about it all along. *I* should have discovered that flaw, but I was too blind, too confident—and now my life's work was for naught."

Craig stood tall, intimidating. He started to withdraw his handcuffs, prepared to make an arrest.

But Piter hadn't finished talking. He looked up, and his voice took on a desperate edge. "It wasn't my fault Dumenco was in the area! I didn't know he was in there. He knew the beam dump was off-limits, but the new construction allowed people to circumvent the safety interlocks. He wanted to check out his detectors personally, because he *knew* the data were wrong. He knew he should have detected more p-bars."

"Because Bretti stole them," Craig said.

Shaking his head, Piter drew in a deep breath. "Dumenco knew a lot more than any of us."

Craig said, "I'm going to have to arrest you, Dr. Piter."

"I was only trying to delay his results until the Nobel committee made the selection. If Dumenco couldn't show results that verified his underlying theories, the committee would choose me." He looked down at the floor and whispered, "The greatest day of my life. And it doesn't mean a thing."

Paige looked at Craig and crossed her arms over her blouse. She was struck by the difference in the two men. Unlike Nels Piter, Craig was strong under pressure, silent, thoughtful, unassuming . . . yet extremely confident in his abilities.

The year that they had spent apart had validated her impressions of him, and now seeing Craig come through this stressful week unwavering only made her more certain of his character.

And her growing feelings for him.

She placed a hand on Craig's shoulder. "Try to keep his arrest quiet until the Stockholm committee can be informed. If word leaks out that he's won the Nobel, reporters are going to swarm over him like flies."

Craig nodded, looking at her with an unreadable expression. "Okay, Paige. If that'll help you out."

Then he led the handcuffed Nobel laureate toward the side exit.

Friday, 5:47 P.M.

Fox River Medical Center

Craig stood by the hospital room door, waiting as Dumenco's family paid their last respects. A single light on the dresser cast moody shadows throughout the room as the sun set over the oak-shaded Fox River. The medical equipment and diagnostics had been shut down, and for the first time since Craig had been there, the room seemed peaceful.

Dumenco's wife Luba sat by her dead husband, gently stroking his hand. She moved her lips close to his head, silently whispering a prayer. His two daughters stood by the window, quietly comforting each other. Peter stared vacantly at his father, as if he could not fathom that the man was dead.

Craig waited patiently, not wanting to disturb the family in their grief. He would have time later to try and understand the remaining loose ends. He could see why Paige had avoided spending more time in the hospital room, not because she didn't like Trish—he'd seen Paige take care of herself—but because of the memory of her own father's death.

Now, though, with Bretti's capture, Dumenco's death, and Piter's confession, things could finally return to normal for Fermilab.

Craig missed spending time with Paige, and it hadn't struck him until now how much he really missed her. This was the third major case they had worked together, and each time he discovered more about the intelligent, exuberant Protocol officer. And he wondered how she viewed him.

Earlier, after he had taken Nels Piter into custody, she met him in the hospital lobby and ran a hand through her blond hair. "You've been through a lot today."

"So have you." He paused.

Paige gave a small smile. "I'm fine." She hesitated. "How's . . . how's Trish?"

He smiled wryly and placed an uncertain hand on her shoulder. "I need to have a talk with her. In fact, I should have done this when I first got here." Rubbing his hand down her arm, he turned to go, heading back to the Intensive Care ward. That had been an hour earlier.

Now, a movement in the dark corner of Dumenco's room caught his eye. Trish. A glint of light reflected off her glasses. She stood with her arms folded across her breasts, intently watching the family's reactions, as if she were comparing them against some set standard.

Trish slowly looked his way. Her face lacked expression. She stared at him for a moment, and he gestured with his chin to the door. He followed her out into the hall. Trish lounged back against the wall, her head tilted up and her eyes closed. "It's always hard when someone dies," she said.

"You look like you took it pretty well."

"I have to. It's the nature of the game."

"You always could be detached." Craig braced himself.

Trish glanced sideways at him. "What's that supposed to mean?"

Craig chose his words carefully. "When you first called, asking me to come out here, I thought you might have a deeper interest in this than you said. But now your reaction is so clinical. Judging from the passion you put into some of your PR-Cubed opinion pieces, I thought you'd be railing up and down the halls."

An orderly walked past the elevators; nurses' voices came from around the corner.

"Strictly professional," she said. "I see now that a lot of the PR-Cubed soapboxing was just . . . words, nothing more."

"How so?" Craig asked. "What made it change for you?"

Trish spoke in a small voice. "It's so hard, day after day, seeing people die. I do everything I can for them, work myself ragged. I use every known technology trying to save someone, and then they die for no apparent reason. You have to keep it all inside—aloof, not get involved. Otherwise you'd be racked with grief. I *have* to be detached, damn it. Don't fault me for it."

Craig set his mouth as the words struck home. His own career was much the same, seeing people die, many of them innocent victims of circumstance. If he were to get personally involved, he'd never be able to do his job. "I do understand," he whispered.

"I doubt it." Trish setting her mouth in a firm line, dismissing him.

Craig remained quiet, unwilling to fight about it. He'd already had that experience too many times with her. Instead, he leaned over and put an arm awkwardly around her. "But it wasn't your fault. And we never would have caught Bretti—or Dr. Piter for that matter—unless you chose to get involved and called me." He hesitated. "You've always been involved. I realize that now. It's your way, and you won't ever change—not for Dumenco . . . and not for me."

He drew her close, and for the first time in years smelled her hair. He felt Trish nestle into his arms, and he held her tight.

But he felt nothing for her except pity; pity that she had chosen to excel in a field where she would always feel the pain of other people, no matter how far she tried to distance herself from it.

- - - - - - -

Friday, 9:38 P.M.

Fox River Medical Center

Craig stood by Julene Goldfarb's side, a hand on her shoulder as they looked down at her husband's hospital bed. Paige waited directly behind him, and Jackson knelt with one knee on the floor in front of the bed—the tall, lanky black agent looked very uncomfortable in the awkward position. Ben Goldfarb's two girls fidgeted on chairs at the other side of the room, doing their absolute best to be good and stay quiet. Outside, a powdery snow whipped against the windows.

Craig felt a flash of *deja vu*—four hours ago he had stood with another family, two floors away, as they grieved over Georg Dumenco's death. Luckily, this situation wasn't nearly so tragic.

Craig watched his short, curly-haired partner wince as he tried to roll over on his side. Hanging from supports above the bed, two intravenous tubes ran into his arm, while others disappeared under the sheets. The numerous tubes and diagnostics made Goldfarb look like a mannequin supported by thick strings.

Jackson stood up, helped position his partner, then stuffed a pillow behind him to support Goldfarb while lying on his side.

"Thanks," whispered Goldfarb. "I feel like one of those lab rats."

"I'm not sure the doctors want you to be off your back, Ben," said Julene.

Goldfarb snorted, then started coughing as it tickled his throat. "Everybody wants me off their back."

"Sounds like he's in pretty good shape to me." As Paige leaned over to Craig, he caught a hint of White Shoulders perfume; he felt strangely giddy with her face so close to his.

Jackson turned to the dresser and picked up a paper Starbucks cup covered with a white plastic lid. "Brought you something, big guy." Removing the lid, he waved the cup under Goldfarb's nose. "Bet you hadn't tasted this for a while."

Goldfarb's eyes lit up. "That coffee smells heavenly. Bring it over here!"

"Randall Jackson!" Julene leaned over to pluck the coffee cup away. "You know he's not supposed to have any caffeine."

"I was just going to let him smell it, ma'am," protested Jackson, taking the cup back with a swift movement. "Let him inhale."

"Starbucks is potent enough to have a jolt just in the fumes," Goldfarb said wistfully.

"Mom! Mr. Jackson's spilling on me!" Goldfarb's oldest girl pushed back in her chair as Jackson swung the hot cup of coffee over her. Jackson put a hand under the cup to keep the liquid from sloshing out.

Craig started to laugh when his pager beeped. Digging it out of his suit jacket, he checked the number. June Atwood, calling to check in.

Craig dialed the number from Goldfarb's bedside phone. June sounded anxious and curious. "I got your summary of the events regarding the incidents at Fermilab—but you didn't tell me how Ben is doing!"

Craig smiled at the clear concern behind her stern voice. "I told you it was an incomplete report, June." He glanced at the commotion in the room. Jackson alternated between sweeping the coffee under Ben's nose and keeping it at bay from Julene. Julene resorted to folding her arms and staring coldly at him.

"I think Ben's made it over the hump. Remember how much he moaned about breaking his pinky finger in Nevada—he'll probably milk this for a promotion, or at least a bonus."

"He's lucid?" asked June. "Is anything the matter? I can hear some sort of commotion in the background."

Craig smiled. "Uh, it's nothing. Just a difference in opinion on post-traumatic recovery procedures. He'll be fine. Another few days and he'll be able to fly home."

"I really should have come out myself." June sounded guilty.

"Jackson coordinated everything at the hospital. And you wouldn't have been able to do anything out here— Jackson wouldn't have let you. They're quite a team."

"You *all* are. Including that Ms. Mitchell. I'm looking forward to meeting her."

Uh, oh, thought Craig. "Uh, I doubt you'll have a chance to do that, June," he said. "She's working out here in Fermilab."

Paige looked at him curiously. Craig just shrugged.

"For the time being," said June dryly. "But we'll see about that."

Now Craig was really confused. "What do you mean?"

June sighed. "I don't know how you two manage to do it, but the breakthroughs you and Paige Mitchell have made on the last few cases—even though you've been thrown together by circumstances rather than any conscious design—have gained attention as a model for interagency cooperation. Both the Attorney General and the Department of Energy have already spotted an opportunity."

"An opportunity? What are you talking about?" His boss must have been working on this behind the scenes for a long time, completely without his knowledge.

"An opportunity to quickly solve high-tech crimes, just like the ones you've been working on with Ms. Mitchell. We feel that such a cross-disciplinary government team will not only get the job done because of your joint experience base, but it also costs less money than creating a separate agency. In short, you and Mitchell working together—with assistance from special agents such as Jackson and Goldfarb—is a good idea.''

Craig raised an eyebrow at Paige, who stood with her arms crossed looking at him. She tilted her head quizzically; Craig held up a finger as June continued.

''And that brings me to this call. The Director is appointing you as the Bureau representative to an interagency mobile technical investigative task force, effective today.''

''What does that mean?'' asked Craig. Earlier, he had received the Shield of Bravery, had been promoted to Relief Supervisor for Squad 22—high-tech investigations—and had solved several major cases. Maybe he had attracted *too* much attention to himself.

''From now on, you are on-call for these types of highly technical investigations, like the ones you cracked at Livermore, the Nevada Test Site, and now at Fermilab. You'll head up a small interagency group that has the authority to pull in additional experts, as needed. They're going to be more common, and more difficult to solve.''

Craig blinked. The assignment was so unusual he didn't know if he should be happy or wary. It sounded interesting, but there were other considerations, like Paige.

He snapped his attention back to the phone as June Atwood continued. ''. . . you'll still be based out of the Oakland office, with your own case load, and Jackson and Goldfarb will be part of your support team. But any time you get the call, this task force takes precedence over your other duties. We'll discuss details later, but you'll start as soon as you get back.''

''This sounds great, June,'' said Craig. ''But what does Paige have to do with this?'' She hovered beside him, anxious to know what the conversation was about.

"The Department of Energy representative is going to be Ms. Mitchell, if she agrees, of course. The Secretary of Energy will detail her with an IPA assignment to the FBI—Intergovernmental Personnel Act, good for up to four years, effective immediately. With your track record, you two will continue to work together in the future."

The news made Craig feel both warm and uneasy at the same time. It was great knowing they'd be investigative partners, and this time in a planned, official capacity instead of letting chance throw them together. But then again, he wasn't sure if they would have a chance to develop a real, personal relationship; working together on a professional basis might put a damper on that.

Or perhaps the opposite would happen.

Craig nodded into the phone. "I'll head back to San Francisco tomorrow, then. I think Agent Schultz at the Chicago office can do—"

"No," said June immediately. "We don't need you back here until Wednesday, so take some time off—maybe you and Ms. Mitchell can coordinate your long-range plans. You've got to talk her into this position, after all."

"I think I can handle that," said Craig, glancing at Paige.

"And one more thing. A representative from the State Department will escort you to the Indian consulate tomorrow afternoon. India is making a formal apology for Mr. Chandrawalia's behavior and wants to officially distance themselves from his radical Liberty for All party. They're taking the unprecedented step of waiving Chandrawalia's diplomatic immunity, and they intend to cut off the clandestine weapons work going on in Bangalore, so they're pulling out all the stops for you. They're even bringing out a Dr. Punjab, director of the Sikander Lodi Research Institute, to testify that Bretti was involved in smuggling p-bars into India for weapons research.

"And since you were the arresting agent, their Ambassador is flying from D.C. to Chicago tomorrow to give his personal thanks.'' June paused and added dryly. ''I don't know how you do it, Craig, but between the Russians and the Indians, you're making quite the splash internationally. Just be on your best behavior.''

Craig grinned. ''Right. You'll get a full report next week.''

Hanging up the phone, he glanced up at Paige, who looked entirely curious, impatient, but hopeful. He gestured for her to join him out in the hall. As an orderly shuffled by, and an intercom announcement rang from the ceiling, he ran a hand through his hair.

Paige crossed her arms, waiting for him. ''Well?''

Craig drew a deep breath. ''Got any plans for the next few years?'' Then he explained June's offer.

She stepped close, so that her blue, blue eyes were within inches of his face. He could feel her breath lightly on him. She swept strands of her blond hair over her shoulder. As she was bringing back her hand, Paige rested it lightly on his lapel. ''I always thought we should be working together,'' she said, finally breaking the silence. ''Who says the government can't do things right?''

''Given enough time,'' Craig said.

''I saw you saying goodbye to Trish,'' she said, fishing. ''It looked permanent.''

''It was something I had to do.'' Craig's eyes focused on the elevators down the hall. ''She was an important part of my life, but that's over now. It's time to move on.''

Paige pressed her lips together, nodding. ''You know, I think I feel the same way about Fermilab. After what happened last year with Uncle Mike, I couldn't bear to go back to Livermore—there were just too many memories for me to deal with. But after living here in the Midwest for a year, and now after all this with Nels and Dumenco and Bretti, I think I'm ready to go back.'' She ran a hand through her hair and smiled. "But as team-mates with you this time."

Craig nodded and tried to keep his broad grin from making him look like an idiot. "The Bureau is big on partners. June wants me to stick around here for a couple of days to relax before I head back—maybe we can talk about a few . . . details? We're going to be plowing new ground, setting a standard for interagency teams."

Paige looked up at him. She put a hand on his lapel. "Then maybe we should try to set a new way partners work with each other—starting this weekend. What do you think? You've got a lot to see around Chicago, and this may be my last chance to do some of the important sights. They don't dress up as much in the west, either."

Craig flushed, then laughed at his own embarrass-ment. He thought he was *really* going to enjoy this new assignment . . . no matter how things turned out. "Yes, ma'am, whatever you say. And speaking of dressing up, got any plans for tomorrow afternoon? There's an Em-bassy function I'd like you to attend. You might find it interesting."

Paige's eyes grew wide. "Sounds exciting, Special Agent Kreident," she murmured. "I've never been in an Embassy before. You must be an important man."

Craig shrugged, more to shake off the giddiness he felt from her presence than anything else. "It's not that big of a deal. I'll fill you in on the details on the way over tomorrow afternoon."

Paige looked up with her blue eyes. Her voice was so soft Craig had to strain to hear the words. "If you're not busy, why don't we start tonight?"